Originally published as *Drifting In and Out of Sleep* © 2008

Praise for Awakened to Life

Awakened to Life is the first book by Sarah Hanks that I read (I've since read others and have loved them as well!). I was captivated by the characters and storyline from the very beginning. Sarah's style of writing really draws the reader in and brings a quick connection to the characters.
This book opened my eyes in a new way to life and the struggles a mom can face during pregnancy. I found myself identifying with the themes in the book, and I didn't want to put it down. I enjoyed reading Awakened to Life and I highly recommend it! Not only is it an entertaining story, it will also make you think and reflect.

Melissa Jacobs, Bound4Life
St. Louis, author of *Livin' the Dream*

Awakened to Life by Sarah Hanks explores every angle of the lasting impact of abortion. With remarkable empathy, she presents the thoughts, attitudes, and feelings of each person involved—from the couple faced with this decision to the clinic workers who carry out the process. She even brings in related historic elements. Hanks doesn't shy away from exposing the judgmental attitudes of those outside the decision either. If I could choose one word to describe the overall theme of this book, it would be *grace*. I highly recommend it to every adult and teenager.

Susan Pope Sloan,
writer

Awakened to Life bridges guilt and uncertainty with love, joy, and peace. Sarah Hanks tugs at the heartstrings with this beautiful message of hope.

Courtney Grice,
writer, blogger

This "can't-put-down" novel is an easy and profound read. Weaving together the past (e.g. ancient Israel) and contemporary times, with diverse and well-developed characters, this book explores the controversial issue of abortion from different perspectives. Chapter by chapter, it uncovers the heartache of abortion, offering hope and forgiveness in the mercy of God, as well as the redemptive purposes of God in adoption. Through it all, we see the effectiveness of prayer as a change agent and the power of unified prayer in a community. I highly recommend this book for those on both sides of the abortion issue. It will challenge you with the very heart of God on many levels.

Tammera Riddering

When reading this book, I identified time and time again with the main character, Eve, her prayers and her inner dialogue and struggles. Sarah Hanks beautifully shares the heart of Jesus in wanting everyone to find life and mercy (from the babies to the abortion doctors), the heart of intercessors who stand and pray for abortion to end, and the struggles that those on the receiving end of abortion deal with.

This book shows the mercy of God through the main story, juxtaposed with the realities of the siege of Jerusalem in the time of Jeremiah, because of the innocent blood-shed in the land. The kindness and justice of God are paralleled. This book left me with the desire to pray for abortion to end, but hopeful that, "Who knows? The Lord may relent from judgement and leave a blessing behind."

Alyssa Rea

The celebration and raw grief of the characters was just so real and relatable even without ever having been in that situation…… I could not put the book down!

Janet Lange

Awakened to Life, is a wonderful read. Sarah Hanks has a great facility to present the important issues of abortion and adoption from different peoples' points of view. I also appreciate how the book shows that the power of God is still demonstrated in today's world. This is a book for all readers from teenagers up.

Joanne Radin Swoboda

Awakened to Life

By Sarah Hanks

This is a work of fiction. Names, characters, places, and incidents either are the product of the author's imagination or are used fictitiously. Any resemblance to actual persons, living or dead, events, or locales is entirely coincidental.

Edited by Cassie Hamm.

Cover by Samantha Fury of Fury Cover Designs

Dedication

This book is dedicated to all those who have chosen life for their children . . .
And to those who would, if given another chance.

Prologue: Esther

I have two mothers. One gave me life and the other saved it. Contrary to popular opinion, I was not abandoned by one and taken in by another. Both women rescued me.

My life once hung in the balance. My small, rapidly-beating heart was nearly stilled. Silenced. Discounted. But both of my mothers love me deeply. After all, I'm alive today. There are many who could not say the same.

Chapter 1: Lisa

"Let's go, Lisa. Come on. Take a deep breath and get out of the car. You know there's nothing to be afraid of. You've gone through this before." Mitchell's voice walked the balance between comfort and impatience like a skilled trapeze artist. He grabbed her hand and gave it a tight squeeze. Pressure. He began to sigh but stopped himself. "Come on. It'll be okay."

A light breeze tossed Lisa's hair over her shoulder as birds chirped in the maple trees surrounding the clinic. The beautiful summer morning spoke of new beginnings—far from ominous. Still, the sun glinted off the black fence surrounding them like a jail. A chill ran up Lisa's spine as she stared numbly at the building.

She willed herself to move. *It will be okay. Just get it over with.* She believed herself even less than she believed Mitchell.

Oh, it would be okay. For him. And at that moment, that had to be all he cared about. He didn't care about the nightmares, the shame, the guilt. He didn't care about the gnawing emptiness. His convenience, his life, and his dreams were at stake here—not hers.

Lisa squinted to make out the group of figures in the distance that stood outside of the clinic. Protesters. But they had no signs and yelled no chants. Did they hate her? Were they waiting until she got out of the car to shove her mistakes in her face?

Mitchell caught her gaze.

"Don't worry about them, honey. They can't do anything to you." His honey brown curls brushed against his knitted brows. "They can only shout a couple words is all. Judgmental hypocrites. Just get out and walk fast. Don't even look at them."

She nodded and rested her hand on the door.

"That's it, sweetheart. Let's go. Let's get it over with. I'm here for you."

She forced herself to make every movement. As she opened the door and set one foot, then two, onto the pavement, she reminded herself that it would all be over soon. She could go back to her normal life and pretend none of this ever happened. But no matter how many times she repeated that in her mind, it was a lie. She knew better. After all, she *had* been through this before.

Mitchell hurried a few steps ahead of her, head down, gaze averted as he scrambled toward the clinic. For her, however, every step required effort. She looked again at the small group, straining her ears to hear their accusations, but none came. As she drew closer, there were pleading eyes and a few tearstained cheeks. They stood there silently with red tape over their mouths. The word "LIFE" was written across the strip in bold black lettering.

Why did they care? What did they want her to do, anyway? *They don't understand.* By then, Mitchell neared the door, obviously oblivious to the fact that his girlfriend wasn't right behind him.

Suddenly nauseated, she stopped in her tracks and then turned. She walked towards those silent protesters with steps that were no longer labored but purposeful, even fierce. She jogged towards them. As she approached the group, she felt drawn to a woman with a swollen belly standing at the corner and aimed for her. Not only was the tape on the woman's mouth, a strip graced her stomach as well.

Lisa stopped only a few feet in front of her. She opened her mouth to scream, but her words came out as a tearful moan.

"What do you want me to do? I'm just out of high school. I can't afford a baby. I don't even have insurance. What do you expect me to do?"

The woman removed the red LIFE tape and held it on her finger. She locked her eyes onto Lisa's. Without a hint of hesitation, she spoke.

"I'll adopt her."

Wait, what? *Her*. It's a girl? How could she possibly know?

"Turn around," the woman pleaded. "Go back home and have your baby. I promise you, I'll find a way to take her into my home. I can see that in your heart, you don't want to do this. Let her live. Please."

"Lisa, what are you doing? Get in here! Don't listen to them, baby. Come on." Mitchell shaded his eyes from the sun and squinted at her from his place in front of the clinic's doors. Nice. He'd finally noticed she'd stopped. Exasperation bit at his words, and she hated him for it.

The words were easy for him to say. He'd never been pregnant. He hadn't spent his preschool years playing mommy to dozens of dolls. He'd never written a second-grade essay declaring he wanted to be a mommy when he grew up. Her chest went hot with loathing.

"Lisa. Is that your name?" The woman distracted her from Mitchell's impatience. "Lisa, here's my number." She tore off a piece of paper peeking out of her Bible, scribbled on it, and thrust it into Lisa's hand. "May I have yours?"

Looking back to see Mitchell running towards her, Lisa hurriedly whispered her number, and the woman wrote it down. Impulsively, Lisa reached out for the woman's hand. Their fingers tightened, and their gazes met again. Their eyes pleaded with each other. And then Mitchell grabbed Lisa's other hand and yanked.

"What are you doing? We have to go in." He looked back and forth between her and the clinic, as if he could transport her there by the sheer force of his will. She opened her mouth to speak, but all that came out was another moan.

"She's not going to have the abortion. She's going to have this baby and put it up for adoption." The woman's voice was confident and secure. Could Lisa find shelter in it?

"Look, lady, you don't know what you're talking about. I'm sure that sounds like a perfect solution to you. I'm sure you've never set foot in foster care. Well, let me tell you something: I have. Have you heard horror stories about the system? 'Cause I could sure tell you a few."

A pang of compassion twisted inside Lisa. She'd heard his stories, and they weren't pretty.

"There is no way I'm going to put another child—my child—through what I suffered. It would be better for it not to be born." Mitchell stood only a couple of inches from the woman's face, railing at her. Then he began to spew curses.

Compassion fizzled as anger brewed hot within Lisa. How did she ever end up with him anyway? What kind of guy treated women like that?

The woman didn't back down, didn't flinch. Her voice remained steady, unwavering.

"I'm sorry to hear what you've been through. I can't imagine. But this child is not going into foster care. She's going into my home. We will adopt her."

Mitchell stepped back, dumbstruck. When he spoke, the confrontation had vanished from his tone. "Who are you, lady?"

"My name's Eve. My husband and I are expecting our first in late September. We've always known we wanted to adopt. We were only waiting for the right time."

"You'd have two babies. Lisa's probably due in January. Two babies, three months apart," he murmured, almost to himself. Then he looked at Eve, a bewildered survey that dissipated some of the anger Lisa held towards him. "Why would you do that?"

"Your baby has a destiny. How could I not do what I can?" Her eyes welled up with tears then, and Lisa found herself overcome with a desire to know this woman. To be her friend.

"You're not joking? You're not . . . you're not . . . " Mitchell shook his head, mouth agape.

"I promise. I'll do whatever I can to assure that your daughter is raised in our home."

Mitchell paused and looked back towards the front door again, clearly torn. Lisa's voice finally found itself.

"I can't do it, Mitchell. I can't go in there. I want her to live."

And that was that. She'd made the decision.

Mitchell and Lisa hastened back to the car. Lisa clutched Eve's number. It was all going to be okay. Wasn't it? It had to be, because she couldn't change her mind. She was no longer terrified. And for the first time, she asked herself, *What will her name be?*

Chapter 2: Eve

I had spent the morning standing still, crying out, and counting. Always counting. I couldn't help myself. Each woman who walked into that front door carried life within her. And when those women walked out the door later, that life was gone. How overwhelming.

In the blossoming heat of early June, I stood there, my own baby kicking and turning within me. I counted lives lost as women exited their cars and approached the door of death. One by one, they went in. And there was nothing I could do. Nothing but pray. Each time I stood in front of that clinic, I appealed to God to put an end to this heartbreak.

Only today, a shift had taken place. Today I could count backwards.

Thirteen, fourteen, fifteen, sixteen lives lost, I had counted that morning. Then she came towards me. We pleaded with each other, and she returned to her car. And I counted in reverse. *Sixteen, fifteen.*

It all began to make sense then. No need to spend hours before God in prayer, asking Him if He'd like me to save a baby from abortion. Asking if I should bring a child into my life and home. The girl had been desperate, and I'd answered. I knew my King's heart: He treasures life. I knew His desire: that none would perish.

God's voice seemed clear months earlier. I was going to raise two babies, one boy and one girl. I even picked out the names: Zephan and Esther. An elder at church confirmed those were the perfect names for the two babies God was giving me. Two babies! I was so sure, so certain that I'd received a promise from God. And then came the ultrasound that revealed only one child. When I'd asked the nurse to check again, she'd looked at me with brows raised.

"Hoping for twins?" she asked, as if she encountered this situation daily.

I nodded, my throat dry.

"Sorry. There's only one. But he looks as healthy as can be."

As excited as I'd been to see my child on the monitor, confusion swamped me. Had I not heard correctly? Was it not really God, but simply my own desire? Was the elder wrong as well? I was still learning to discern God's voice from my own. Had I had failed yet again? Only I had been so sure, so confident.

And now a rush of relief filled me. I hadn't missed it. I *was* going to raise two babies. I'd heard God's voice, and He was faithful. Yet as quickly as relief flowed, uncertainty followed. Two babies? That would be challenging in and of itself. But two babies, three months apart? One not my natural-born child? How would that work? Could I possibly love this adopted child as much as I already loved my son? Would the adoption process be as long and grueling as I'd heard? Had I lost my mind?

My husband came up behind me then, putting his hand on the small of my back. "Sorry I'm late," Gideon whispered into my ear. "Traffic."

A hot breath of wind whipped a few hairs from my ponytail, flinging them across my face. He tucked them behind my ear and grabbed a strip of red tape. He began to place it over his mouth but stilled, eyeing the tape still on my index finger. Did I look as bewildered as I felt? His dark brow eyebrows raised in an invitation for me to explain.

I pointed to the parking lot, silently asking him if we could talk in the car. He held my hand as we strode away from the clinic. Once inside the car, AC blasting, my confidence withered away to nothing.

"Evie, what is it?" Concern etched lines on his forehead. I traced one with my finger, smoothing it away. He took my hand in his.

"We're going to have a baby," I blurted out.

"Yes?"

"I mean, another one. Zephan is due in September and Esther is due in January." I paused, allowing him the time to ask the one-word question I knew was coming.

"What?"

"There was a young girl. I mean *young*, Gideon. Fresh out of high school. She was dragging her feet in there, and then suddenly she stopped and headed towards me. I told her"—I bit my lip, then took a breath and plunged in—"if she didn't go through with the abortion, I'd adopt her baby." I winced. Surely a rebuke was coming. One does not make such life-altering decisions without consulting one's spouse.

"Eve!" His voice held more awe than anger. He paused. Then the statement that brought my brimming tears to full fruition: "We're saving a baby's life?"

I nodded, all my emotions in a knot. No regret, but how would our future look now? Gideon stared at me wide-eyed, like a young child watching a chick hatch for the first time. He reached across the car to hold me, wiping a stray strand of hair from my forehead. "Eve, your heart is beautiful. I can feel God's smile upon you right now. "

"Then you're not mad?" I asked.

"I'm proud. I'm . . . I'm grateful." He turned my face towards him, kissing tears off my cheeks. The scruff of his five o'clock shadow tickled. "We'll talk more later, hon. Now let's go back out there. Only—perhaps one baby is enough for today." He winked, and my tears eased as my smile broadened.

Opening the car door, I tried to survey the scene from a "patient's" point of view. The walk to the entrance looked ominous, and the couple dozen silent "protesters" was unusual. *They must think we're crazy.*

Ironically, that thought had never occurred to me before. What would a frightened, pregnant woman think when she saw us? Would she think us a cult? Would she fear that any moment we might take the tape off and hurl insults and accusations? Would she—of course she would—tell herself that we couldn't possibly know her circumstance? That we had no right to judge?

Okay, so we *did* look crazy, but praying at abortion clinics was completely logical. While other protesters came and went, with signs and chants, we stood and asked the only One who could truly change hearts to do just that. Yes, it was counter-cultural, but aren't all things of God?

As I returned to my position on the sidewalk, I counted the number of people at this prayer meeting. Fourteen? Only fourteen? One baby dies every twenty seconds and there are fourteen standing in prayer here and now? Discouragement must have shown on my features, because Gideon leaned over and whispered, "Not by might nor power . . . "

I silently finished the verse: *But by My Spirit, says the Lord.* I thought of the Gideon of the Bible and how his small army, pathetically outnumbered, conquered the enemy without using any physical weapons. All I could do in the face of such an overwhelming issue was pray. So, I did. I stopped counting and focused my attention on my pleas to God. And all the while, my heart fought what my husband had said in the car.

Surely one baby was not enough.

Chapter 3: Ashira

Drums rang out, deafening to her, even from the village. The ground shook with each beat. Bile rose in her throat as her chin trembled.

"Come, Ashira. The ceremony has started. We must make our way." Reuben's voice grew harsh, his face taut.

Our way? Our way? This certainly wasn't her way. Not the way she had chosen. Slowly, she tied the sling tightly around her and placed the sleeping bundle inside, next to her chest. The baby yawned then, and Ashira could not help the tears that edged their way into the cruel night.

"Ashira! He is waiting."

"Isn't there another way? There must be another way." Her voice rushed ahead of itself, crossing the boundaries of the way a good wife would talk to her husband.

"Yes, there is! We can starve. We can die. Is that the way you would choose?"

Yes! Her protest nearly leaped out of her swollen throat, but instead, she followed him as he lumbered out the door and onto the path. Each step brought them closer to drumbeats, to the heat of the great fire, to the tearing of her heart. Reuben kept glancing back at her, making sure she was still moving forward, making sure she did not flee into the night. Ashira knew better than that. If she were to flee, she would not save this child. And she would die herself.

Her steps dragged, but then again, she had given birth not many days before and had lost a lot of blood. Surely Reuben could not expect her to make such haste. The stars twinkled down on her, as if shimmering tears from heaven joined in the sorrow of her heart. A pebble lodged in her sandal, and she stumbled.

He glanced back again.

"There will be more babies," he said. "Molech, he desires firstborn. He will open the skies for us. He will heal our land. We will eat again, and then you will have another to keep."

She nodded her assent through tears as she shook out her shoe. *Why do we serve such a cruel god? Why does he want my child? Why would he exchange life for rain?* At that moment, she wanted to worship any other god. She would have rather become a temple prostitute than sacrifice her child. Reuben had warned her not to name this baby, but she had not listened. From the time she felt the first movement within her, she had known her baby's name. Shai. Gift.

They ascended the hill and shifted through the crowd. Shai awoke. Was that a whine? A cry? The infant's mouth moved, but the drums drowned out any other sound. That was the intention.

Molech stood in front of them. The idol's white-hot hands glimmered, and smoke arose from around him. His ox head radiated the steam of evil. She hated him then—hated this god who required so much of her. She stopped in her tracks, unwilling to go further. She held Shai close to her, tears falling onto rocky ground. Reuben threw an indignant glance over his shoulder.

"Ashira, come!" But she shook her head and fell to her knees, clutching the child to her breast. Reuben came against her. He slapped her face and pried the child from her arms.

"No! No!" Only a few standing close could hear Ashira's screams. The drums drowned out her cries. Some of them turned to watch with sympathy in their eyes, others with annoyance. As Reuben held Shai up and proceeded towards Molech, Ashira reached for the strength to run after them, but she couldn't move. Frozen, she watched Shai's mouth open and shut again and again. *Don't look. Don't watch.* But she couldn't pry her eyes off her child. Reuben bowed before the idol. Then he laid Shai into Molech's hands. The baby fell into the fire below.

Her first child, a gift snatched away, burned as a sacrifice so that Molech would have mercy and save their land from drought.

Ashira did not remember the trip back to the village, nor the days following. Reuben would not speak of the sacrifice, so she must not. Her eyes flooded for days, for weeks. Reuben continued to watch the skies for rain, but they did not yield. Their sacrifice did not move Molech.

Chapter 4: Eve

"Table for one, please." The restaurant proved to be more crowded than my womb, waiters and waitresses rumbling about, multitasking to their limit. Surprisingly, all that business did not create a cacophony of sound, only quiet mumblings and an occasional laugh.

"We have a twenty-minute wait. Should I put your name down?" A mint clacked against the hostess' teeth.

My stomach sank. Zephan's elbow poked my rib, as if prompting me to reply. I sighed and nodded, giving the hostess my name, and resigned myself to a small space on the bench at the front of the restaurant. My stomach growled in protest, but none of the nearby restaurants would have a lesser wait. Not that I could stomach anyway. I'd been out shopping for baby clothes and supplies, a job that seemed finished until the surprising change of events in the last few weeks.

Now I needed two of everything. And girls' clothes. My head spun. The adoption process had gone smoothly thus far, though we'd only begun to fill out the mountain of required paperwork. That much daunted me, but the paperwork wasn't my biggest fear. The social worker had warned us that Lisa might change her mind, and *that* made my blood freeze. But what about the promise of two children? This whole crazy scheme of adopting Lisa's baby had to be God. So why did I worry? *Ye of little faith.*

Might as well do more productive things than worrying. Like pray for the people around me. I glanced around. Teens surrounded one table. I couldn't make out their conversation, but they were grinning and chuckling back and forth. *Lord, let them treasure Your Word and Your ways.*

My gaze traveled to a not-so-happy couple engaged in a quiet war of words. *Father, bring healing and restoration to their relationship.* I continued weaving my prayers throughout the booths, tables, and stressed-out waiters until my eyes fell on a man sitting in the next booth.

My heart almost stopped. I sucked in my breath and averted my gaze. He dined alone, head down, shoulders slumped. I recognized him well; I'd often seen him at the clinic. As I'd stood in prayer, he would walk into the clinic to start his day of work. My blood boiled each time I spotted him. How could he consider taking lives to be a valid job choice? *Oh, God! I don't even know how to pray for him. Change his heart, God. Bring truth into His life and heart.*

Go talk to him.

What? God, no! I can barely look at the man, much less go and talk to him. Rationalizations filled my mind. That wasn't God's voice. It was mine. He wouldn't ask me to do such a thing. What if the man recognized me? But how could he? He always walked briskly, head down, into the clinic. He'd never met my gaze.

Go talk to him, Eve.

I sighed a consent, palms sweating. God and I had been through these types of conversations before. He would be persistent. I might as well save Him the trouble of listening to my protests. I waddled over to the man's booth, one hand pressing into the small of my back. I trembled as my mind screamed at me to run away.

"I'm sorry, sir, but may I sit here a moment? I'm waiting for my table, and that bench is so uncomfortable." I managed a slight smile.

He looked up at me, smiled slightly, and nodded. "Sure. No problem."

What had I expected his face to look like? That of a monster? His eyes were soft as he gazed at my belly knowingly.

"So." I clasped my hands in my lap. "What brings you here dining alone?" *God, what do I say? Give me the words.*

"I'm on break right now. Just catching a bite before I go back to work." He dabbed his mouth with a napkin and pushed his salad to the side of the table.

"What do you do?" I blinked innocent eyes. *Say it. You kill babies. Nice conversation for a lunch break.* I bit the inside of my cheek. Where was this anger coming from?

"I'm a doctor." His mouth upturned in . . . What was it? Pride?

"Oh, a doctor!" *God, give me your attitude. Help me see this man as You see him. You love him. You died for him. You desire Him to come to You. Forgive me for my bitterness.* "Did you always want to be a doctor?"

"Since I can remember."

"What drew you to that profession?" The edges of my heart softened a bit. I prayed for it to continue.

"Wanted to help people. You know, the usual. I wanted to do great things with my life. My father was a surgeon, and his father worked as a medic for the military. I never really thought of anything else I wanted to do." His smile widened as he spoke of his lineage.

"What kind of doctor are you?" I prodded.

"I work with women." His reply came out quieter.

"Oh, like an OB-GYN?"

He looked down, studying his silverware. "Yes, something like that."

"Well, that's wonderful. There's nothing better than bringing life into the world. It's a miracle, isn't it? That this little ball of cells grows inside a woman. A real live human being unfolding before your very eyes. Amazing, really."

He nodded and looked around, as if eagerly seeking a diversion.

"Waitress?" he called to her as she was passing by. She shifted her attention to him, a tray in each hand. "Check, please."

"Coming right up."

"Eve, party of one, your table is now ready. Eve." The loudspeaker boomed my name. I stifled a sigh of relief and stood.

"That's me. Nice to meet you. Thanks for letting me sit here . . . " I trailed off, a hint that he should tell me his name.

"I'm Trent." He reached over and shook my hand.

"Trent. Thanks. Have a nice day." I smiled and turned. He sighed as I left. I held back tears as I followed the hostess to my seat, thankful for each step she led me towards the back of the restaurant, away from Trent, away from people in general. I followed her to a little booth nestled in the farthest corner from where I'd been.

"Your server, Amanda, will be right with you."

I nodded numbly, choosing to sit with my back towards the sea of midday munchers. I closed my eyes and willed the tears to stay at bay.

Oh, God! Did I do the right thing? Was that wrong of me? Did I lie? No, I didn't actually lie, but I was deceptive. Lord, I want to have compassion towards that man. I don't want to despise him. Who am I to throw stones? Have I never sinned? Have I never been deceived? Have I never justified wrong actions? Give me Your heart, God. Let me see people as You see them. I don't want to be angry and bitter. I want to be like Jesus.

"Hi, my name is Amanda, and I'll be taking care of you today. Can I start you off with something to drink?"

I blinked a few times and looked up at the woman. My eyes widened. She had a bulge under her shirt as well.

"Water is fine. How far along are you?" I sniffed back the last of my tears and smiled.

"Far enough." Lines of exhaustion marked her face. "I have three more weeks to go, if this baby is more patient than I am."

"I can imagine. Are you going to keep working until the baby is born?" She should take a break and prop up her feet at my booth.

"Got to. I ain't got a husband to take care of me, you know? I don't have much of a choice."

Shoot. Tears stung my eyes again. "Oh, Amanda," I fought to keep my voice steady. "I'm sorry. What a hard thing. But, you *had* a choice. And I promise you, no matter how difficult your circumstances are, you made the right choice."

I grabbed her hand and squeezed it gently. Overstepping boundaries? Possibly, but I shared a kind of kinship with the woman that seemed to make such an action okay. Her misty eyes and trembling smile mirrored my own.

She bent down closer to the table, a movement that lurched the life within her forward. "My boyfriend left me when I told him I was going to go through with it. We were supposed to get married in the fall. Had all my ducks in a row, you know? Everything was gonna be perfect, then poof! I'm pregnant and I'm alone.

"Sometimes I think, if I had gotten rid of this baby, then I could have other ones . . . babies born with a mama and a daddy married and happy. The kind of home a baby should have. But then I feel this little one do a summersault in my belly, and I wonder if I had gotten rid of him, if I'd always remember . . . if I'd think about how old he'd be if he were alive, if I'd wonder what he would have looked like. What kind of choice is that?"

I searched through my purse, never taking my eyes off Amanda, and pulled out a tissue. I handed it to her.

"You're doing the right thing. I will pray for you and your baby. A boy?" I found a tissue for myself.

"Yes. Sam, I think. I might change my mind again since no one else likes that name." She looked behind her. She must have needed to go take care of her other tables. I didn't want to hold her up any longer, but I had to ask.

"As in Samuel?"

"Yeah. Samuel. Sam. Sammy." She rubbed her stomach gently.

"I think Samuel is a perfect name. Absolutely perfect. And I'll save you a trip; I'll have a water with my order. I assume you have a BLT?" I hadn't even cracked open my menu.

"Sure. Anything else?"

"Yes. Your phone number . . . a way I can get a hold of you to see how you're doing. If you don't mind, that is." I was growing bolder by the minute.

She nodded, backing away from the table. "I'll be back with your order."

Maybe I offended her. Did I go too far? I nibbled on my cuticle. But when I received my check, there was a phone number scribbled at the bottom. *Productive lunch,* I mused while walking out to my car. *I found three names to add to my prayer list. Trent, Amanda, and Samuel.* I spent the rest of the afternoon weaving though isles of baby furniture and supplies, hoping and praying that I'd planted seeds and that God would do the watering.

Chapter 5: Trent

"Check, please," Trent repeated loudly as the waitress buzzed by him yet again. Had she heard him? He twisted the napkin in front of him and looked around again to make sure that Eve woman was nowhere in sight. *"There's nothing better than bringing life into the world*"? Who was she?

The waitress slid past him without a word. Fine. With gritted teeth, he pulled out a twenty from his wallet and threw it on the table.

He hated leaving such a big tip for a waitress who seemed to forget that he existed. It wasn't like he was hurting for money. It was the principal of the thing. His father taught him that hard work and diligence were what got you places in the world. Rewarding laziness contradicted his value system. But he had to get out of there.

He sped to his car, studying the cracks in the old sidewalk. He'd gotten into the habit of keeping his head down in public after a religious extremist had come up to him in the grocery store parking lot and spat in his face. She'd said God's judgments were going to come upon him and he'd rot in hell like a murderer should. Funny how those religious conservatives tried to portray themselves as loving, sweet, and innocent like that Jesus they worshiped.

He'd received enough threats from those people to understand what a hoax it all was. If their savior was like that, give him a good reason to convert. Trent wasn't an atheist.

Sure, there was a God, a creator of some sort. But why did people have to take an abstract idea and make it personal? If God was anything like the people who railed at decent doctors on a regular basis, why would anyone want to be close to Him?

Slipping into his car, he nudged the volume up on his radio. As a teen, he'd relished loud music. There was nothing better than feeling the car shake with every drumbeat. But he'd had to give up loud music when it became necessary not to draw attention to himself. Sometimes, when his wife gardened outside, he still blasted the radio in the den. It kept him young. But when he was driving, especially to work, he couldn't risk it.

He settled back in his seat for the commute back to the clinic. He had a good half-hour drive ahead of him. He could never risk going out to lunch in the general vicinity of the clinic, so a drive to the next town was worth the guarantee that he could eat in peace, without anyone laying a guilt trip on him—

There's nothing better than bringing life into the world.

—without anyone, except for that woman. Her voice continued to echo through his mind.

To be fair, the lady wasn't trying to make him feel guilty. She was only excited about her own pregnancy. No doubt her circumstances differed from the women he helped on a daily basis. She most likely had a financially stable husband. And though she looked young, she wasn't nearly as young as the girls who came to him for help. Why wouldn't she be brimming with joy? That was the way it should be—a secure, happy child born to two excited parents.

Unfortunately, many women weren't as prepared as this Eve seemed to be. For many of the women Trent had seen come through the clinic, a child would only devastate any chance they had of making something of themselves—of bringing themselves out of poverty, of achieving the American dream. Would have been so happy if she were in their position?

The drive went quicker than expected. All too soon, he pulled into his "reserved for doctors" parking spot. He took his customary deep breath before opening the car door and striding into the clinic. He glanced up at the shouts of a few picketers. He rarely did that. Their signs and enraged looks loomed at him from the corner of his eye. They stood on the other side of the parking lot, too far to be a threat.

Then there was the line of silent protesters. He never could make himself look them in the eye. What did they think they were doing? Who did they think they were saving?

In actuality, thanks to this strange spectacle, they had lost three clients this week alone. One girl's mother had called to say her daughter had been so intimidated by a group of silent protesters that she hadn't even been able to make it to the door. The other two had changed their minds in the waiting room, muttering about "choosing life." Three women were conned into guilt at their choice to take control of their own lives.

What would happen to these women? And what about their children? There was a reason these women made appointments in the first place. Chances were, the only thing that had changed in their lives was the unnecessary burden of guilt.

Ducking through the employee entrance at the side of the building, he viewed the schedule for the rest of the day. He frowned as his eyes swept over a familiar name. That girl had been in before. Twice. Such was the nature of the business.

Second timers, third timers, and beyond were normally his easiest clients. They had been through it all before and asked few questions. They were prepared for the small amount of pain that resulted from the procedure and normally didn't complain. It was the first timers, those nervous, shaking girls who probably had never even had a Pap smear, who made the job difficult.

Chapter 5: Trent

Three first timers and only one third timer scheduled for that afternoon. Good thing he'd been able to take a longer lunch.

It wasn't as bad as he was dreading. Two girls had their mothers by their sides, assuring them all would be okay. Thank God for supportive parents. Even if they hadn't had enough sense to talk to their kids about birth control, at least they'd wised up and realized their duty as parents.

The other two girls had their boyfriends with them. Boyfriends weren't normally as good as mothers, considering many girls resented their boyfriends for getting them pregnant in the first place. If not that, they were unsure of whether or not to have the baby, and the guys were usually the ones to talk sense into them. In any case, many times, the tension between couples made the atmosphere sizzle. This afternoon, though, wasn't so bad.

Only Eve's voice continued ringing through his head. *A real live human being unfolding before your very eyes.* Why had he let that woman unnerve him? He'd wanted to become a doctor so he could help people, hadn't he?

And he *was*. He helped women to climb out of the pit of poverty. He made a way for many girls to go on to a college education, to successful careers. He prevented child abuse. He brought hope to people who thought their mistakes were permanent. He gave second chances. People who disagreed with that were close-minded and selfish. *A miracle, a miracle, a miracle!* Yes, it could be a miracle to some. And it could be a disaster to others.

The constant barrage of that woman's maternal bliss running through his head made the rest of the day seem to stretch longer than usual. Relief flooded him when he could finally clock out and drive home. When he pulled into his driveway, his wife's beautiful face peeked out the window. She'd been waiting for him.

Chapter 6: Beth

How long had Beth spent waiting on the living room sofa, peeking out the blinds to the front window every time the roll or screech of tires assaulted her ears? She got up only a few times, dashing to the bathroom to reapply her lip-gloss. As soon as she'd found out the news, she'd slipped on a sundress, curled her hair, and applied fresh makeup. So her husband would remember how beautiful she looked when she told him.

This would definitely go down as one of, if not *the*, most memorable moment in their lives. People took mental pictures of such moments, and she needed Trent's to radiate beauty forever.

She'd slept in later than she should and rushed through a shower. No time to style her hair. She threw on her clothes, grateful for casual Fridays at the firm where she worked as a legal secretary. Just before leaving, she'd made a stop at the bathroom. This was her monthly ritual: pregnancy tests. She bought them online in bulk and paid top dollar for them—not the over-the-counter brands, but the kind doctors used, the kind Trent recommended. Those tests would let her know, almost before her body itself knew, if their fertility treatments had paid off.

For nearly the first year, she woke early and went straight to the bathroom to take the test. Then she closed her eyes and counted slowly, methodically, while holding her breath. Gradually, she became so used to negative results that she couldn't stand to make it a big deal. The more she anticipated those mornings, the more devastated she became. So, for the last year, it'd been her habit to take one on the way out the door. Like it was not a big deal. Easier on her heart this way. Only today . . . well, today had been different.

She'd glanced at the test while grabbing her keys from the dresser. One step toward the door. Two. Then she froze. Backing up in what seemed like slow motion, she'd looked again. And again. Sitting down on the edge of the bed, tears brimmed in her eyes.

Shaking, she called work. Told them she wouldn't be in, that she felt kind of sick. Close enough to the truth. Her stomach had been flipping uncontrollably and the room tilted when she stood. And, of course, she'd be sick soon enough. She'd started to dial Trent's cell phone but thought better of it. What kind of news was that to get in the middle of rush-hour traffic? No, she'd tell him when he got home. And she'd make it special.

Throughout the day, she took three more tests. She wasn't sure why. They were the most accurate ones money could buy; surely the first one had been right. But each time she saw the results, her smile grew wider.

Maybe it wasn't a good idea to skip work. Though her excitement made being productive in front of the computer nearly impossible, the day stretched out endlessly with so much time to wait for Trent. Her nerves didn't allow her to eat much, but she forced down a banana and made herself an egg for lunch. After all, she had someone else to feed now. She browsed through baby name books and daydreamed. At one point, she took a brisk walk around the block. Other than that, she sat. Waiting. Wondering how their lives were going to look with a child in the picture.

Beth and Trent met as sophomores in high school and married four years later. He was the only one in his group of college friends who remained married. They idolized him. Mr.

Self-Made Man and his gorgeous lady, always by his side. Of course, their relationship wasn't without its rough waters.

Like the time Beth ended up pregnant as a junior in high school. Too much partying. What about Trent's plans for med school after college? She needed to work full time to help get him through schooling. A baby—well, it would have changed everything.

Trent comforted her the best he could and assured her he would pay for the termination. Then they could go on as planned. After he was done with his schooling, they could have as many children as they wanted. By then they'd have enough money to support them and give them the life they deserved.

She consented without much persistence on his part. It was the right thing to do. It had to be. After it was over, they were much more careful about birth control and scaled down their social lives to focus more on their studies and on each other.

Of course, things hadn't gone exactly as they planned. After Trent finished med school, they agreed to try to get pregnant. Only it didn't happen. Shocked and heartbroken, they'd tried for almost two years before seeking the help of a fertility specialist. If the fertility treatments didn't work, they would look into implantation.

But the treatments had worked. They were finally going to have a baby.

Trent's car pulled in the driveway about thirty minutes earlier than it had the day before. Must have been a good day. His smile widened as he got out of the car. Good. He was in a good mood.

It was anyone's guess what his expression would be when he got home. It depended on whether people appreciated him for the fine doctor he was or criticized him in arrogance and ignorance. Not everyone understood the importance of his job, and the weight of other people's opinions of him could make him cave inward on a bad day. But this was not a bad day.

She stepped away from the blinds and swung open the front door. Sweeping her in his arms, he kissed her hair. Pulling back, he studied her face, then her dress, then her face again.

"You look stunning. Why are you dressed up, hon? You look amazing, but don't you get to dress down on Fridays?" The words crept out, as if he didn't want to insult her by asking why she had put extra effort into her appearance.

"I didn't go to work today."

His face dropped.

"I'm okay, honey. Don't worry. Nothing's wrong. Come inside."

He followed her and perched on the edge of the couch, as if he might break something by throwing it off balance.

"Why didn't you go to work today?"

"I decided to take the day off. I got a lot done. I took a walk, made the bed, found out that we're pregnant . . . " Smiling, she watched his mind register the last statement.

Trent's eyes widened, and his jaw dropped. "We're . . . we're . . . " he stammered, shaking his head in wonder.

"We're pregnant, honey. We're going to have a baby. Finally." The tears that had sprouted all day came back with full force. Through the cascade, his slack jawed gape morphed into a broad grin. Relieved, she fell forward into his arms.

"We're pregnant. We're pregnant." He pulled back and looked into her eyes. "You're sure?" His smile and embrace suspended, as if on pause for her response.

"Positive. Like the tests."

Neither of them said anything for a long while. Thoughts and possibilities hummed through the silent air. They sat there silently as the room grew dimmer and dimmer with the fading of the sun.

After a long while, Beth said, "What's happening inside my body right now?" Wonder filled her, from her toes on up. There was a life inside of her!

Trent sat back, arms draped over the back of the couch. "Hmm . . . you're only four weeks or so. It's an embryo right now. It doesn't look like a baby yet. It's made of two layers. Your placenta is forming, and your amniotic sac is there already. The stage is being set for it to grow into a baby." He slid a piece of stray hair behind her ear.

"I don't like calling the baby 'it.'" She scrunched up her face at the word.

"What would you prefer? Should we say 'the baby' every time?"

"No. I think we're having a girl, so let's say 'her.' Then if we find out it's a boy, we can change to 'him.' You don't think that would scar her, do you?"

Trent laughed deep and full. "No, babe, I don't think that would scar *her*, but it might really mess you up if we find out it's a boy."

"When can we find out?" Thank goodness for her husband's expertise. It didn't feel awkward asking questions of him. If it were a doctor she didn't know, she might have satisfied her curiosity through books or the Internet.

"When you're about twenty weeks. You've got awhile." His eyes danced, his smile enchanting.

"No sooner?" Surely he could pull strings.

"Not unless you have an amnio, honey. And they don't normally do that unless there's a risk factor that would call for it." He stroked her disappointed face. "Don't pout, hon. You like surprises." His touch was soft and gentle. The powdered latex gloves he wore day after day kept his hands velvety smooth.

"I guess I feel like I've been patient long enough. I'm tired of waiting." She let out a dramatic sigh.

"I know, but it will all be worth it." He let out a soft chuckle. "There's nothing better than bringing a life into the world," he mumbled.

"Hmm?"

"Nothing. Just something a lady said to me at lunch today. She said, 'There's nothing better than bringing a life into the world.'"

She couldn't dissect his tone. Melancholy? Annoyance? Frustration?

"Was it one of those protesters?" Heat rose in her belly. Letting out a curse, she stood. "Religious baggage. Of course, pregnancy's great if you're ready for it, but they have no right to criticize you for helping women who aren't. All I hear on TV anymore is their ridiculous obsession with overturning Roe versus Wade. Don't they understand what will happen if they get their way? It will only go underground. They're not saving anyone. They're only putting millions of women in danger of unsanitary conditions!"

Trent shook his head. He might not like her getting herself worked up over the criticisms, but she couldn't help it. She was her husband's defendant. He put too much stock in people's opinions. "They have no right to criticize you. Don't they know—"

"Beth, hold on, hon. It wasn't a protester. Just a pregnant woman making conversation."

She'd been shifting her weight from foot to foot? She hadn't noticed. She sat back down.

"There was a wait at the restaurant. This woman sat at my booth while she was waiting for her table. I told her I was a doctor, and she went on and on about the miracle of life. She wasn't criticizing me. She didn't even know what kind of doctor I am." His expression revealed no clenched jaw or furrowed brow. Everything was okay.

She paused a minute. "Well, that's a little strange, don't you think?"

"Pregnancy can make you a little strange, babe. People say and do things they wouldn't normally do when hormones are involved."

"I guess you're right." Beth tilted her head. "I just can't see myself doing anything that bold, hormones or not. And I meant what I said, by the way. No one has a right to criticize you. You are a brilliant doctor. You help women out of hopeless situations. I don't want you to ever think otherwise."

They spent a few more minutes in the silence of their whirling thoughts.

"What do you think about Eleanor?" she asked finally.

He scrunched up his nose.

"Ellie!" she said in her defense. "Ellie is a cute name."

"Not if it's a boy . . . sorry . . . not if *she's* a boy." He laughed.

She rolled her eyes in mock contempt.

"How about we go out to dinner tonight to celebrate?" Trent said.

A smile spread across her face. "I was hoping you'd say that. I didn't start on dinner. Let's go to The Palms. But babe?"

"Huh?"

"Just the two of us, 'kay? No crazy pregnant ladies. Except for me, of course." Her eyes met his and she grinned.

He winked. "Deal."

Chapter 7: Lisa

The hardest part of the whole ordeal would be telling her parents she was pregnant. She'd gotten away with wearing baggy shirts and sweatpants for the past four months. Paranoid about disguising the growing bulge, she must have studied herself in the mirror thirty times a day, trying to figure out whether anyone would be able to tell. She hadn't told anyone, didn't want anyone to know. Even her best friend Britney hadn't known her secret for those months. She'd ask questions and give her opinion. Far too much for Lisa to deal with.

If she told anyone, it would become more real. She hadn't even told Mitchell for the first three and a half months, frantically pushing away his physical advances for the latter part of that time. If she didn't say anything, maybe the problem would go away.

Now, one night after she had met Eve at the clinic, her emotions ran ragged. She'd cried almost continuously throughout the day. She rode waves of relief that she wasn't going to go through with the abortion. She wouldn't have to add one nightmare onto another. But now she had to break the news of her pregnancy to her strict, religious parents.

She and Mitchell were supposed to have dinner at her parents' house that night, but she called to cancel because she didn't know if she could make it twenty minutes at that table without bursting into tears. She had to tell her parents eventually, but it was better to wait until she could proclaim her news with confidence, until she could keep her voice steady.

But she had never been able to withstand her mother's not-so-subtle guilt trips. Somehow her mother persuaded her to come. That was always her way.

Lisa spent the drive to their house tugging her seat belt tighter around her and fiddling with her purse.

"Cut it out! You're making *me* nervous. I can drive, you know?" Mitchell's attempt to hide his irritation fell short.

If she had to guess, she'd say it wasn't only her fiddling that made him nervous. For the first time in their six-month relationship, she'd voiced an opinion and held to it. That day at the clinic, she had ceased to be his puppet. She'd wiggled out from beneath his thumb. She would have been proud of herself if only she wasn't so afraid of him.

She knew his kind. It was when they were not in control that you found out they were not tame. He hadn't tried to rein her in yet, but she wouldn't put it past him. The threat of his physical strength, always implied in the past, might become a reality. She braced herself.

How had she come to this point? She'd been a good girl for nearly all her life. Her parents had raised her on a steady diet of Sunday School and strict discipline. She'd learned quickly to do what she was told . . . outwardly, at least. Her parents were relieved after having two other daughters who defied them at every turn.

Her compliance also earned her the position of the favorite daughter. Though her parents wouldn't admit it, it was obvious to those inside and outside of the family.

"Aren't you proud of your little sister, Dawn? She made the honor roll for the third year straight!"

"Lisa is going to really make something of herself. You watch your younger sister, Lydia. Watch and learn."

She stuck to the "good boys" throughout her years at Bristol High, going on group dates to PG-rated movies and school dances. She played the part until the day she graduated from high school, when Jim Newel approached her at the graduation party. With sandy blond hair brushing his brows and a delectable dimple on his left cheek, most of her classmates coveted this football star. Hard to not be flattered that he'd noticed her at all.

Three months later, she was pregnant and horrified. She eeked out the news to Jim.

He shrugged as if it were no big deal. "No problem, Lisa. I know a guy."

What? What kind of guy?

Oh. Her pulse throbbed in her neck. Abortion? An option? He spoke about it with the same ease he would talk about going out to dinner. *Don't worry about dinner. I know a place. Don't worry about the baby. I know a guy.*

She could trust him, right? Because surely, she couldn't trust herself.

She went to the clinic with him numbly. She'd just begun classes at Markley. She had a future to think of. After all, she was the good daughter. She was going to make something of herself. Everything would be fine. Jim said so.

The nightmares began that night of her first abortion. Nonsensical nightmares. Though she hadn't been far enough along for the child inside of her to have recognizable appendages, in her dreams she watched the baby be torn limb by limb from her womb on the movie screen of her mind. She heard babies crying when all else was silent.

Jim broke up with her a month later, but not before spreading the word about how easy she was. The torment of it all drove her deeper into her books. Despite the concentrated effort, her grades began to slip. She had to stop the incessant guilt. She started going to parties and living the lifestyle of the people she met, looking for anything to distract her from the nightmares.

Chapter 7: Lisa

After a few one-night stands, she met Mitchell at a club. He said all the right things. Flattered and flirted with a magnetic smile. When he was still there in the morning, she counted him a keeper. Two months later she was pregnant again, but how could she admit it? She didn't want to go through with another abortion, but were there any other feasible options? She had to end it before her parents found out. She couldn't herself face them.

When she finally told Mitchell, he hadn't taken it nearly as well as Jim had. He yelled, tipped over a table, kicked a dent in the wall. Said he'd figured she was on the pill and that he thought she was smarter than that. Then he reined his anger in, apologized, held her for a while and said he'd pay for everything. What option did she have? She'd always complied with the decisions of others, molding herself to their hopes, dreams, and ideals in hope for acceptance.

"What ya thinkin' 'bout, babe?" Mitchell's tone was a forced kind of casual.

She turned her face toward the window and rolled her eyes. He'd interrupted her thoughts.

"Nothing." The last thing she wanted to do was to open up to *him*.

"We don't have to tell them tonight, ya know. There's still time to change your mind."

Hard to say what annoyed her more: the fact that he was still holding out for her to change her mind or the fact that he had said "we." She'd bet all the money she had that she'd be telling the news without much help from him.

"She's going to know. She's my mom. She knows when something's up."

"She's not gonna know. You've got her convinced you're gonna be a medical missionary when you grow up or something. She thinks you're a good girl. She won't have a clue."

"I am a good girl."

"That's not what I heard," he said in a sing-song voice, running his hand up her leg.

She slapped it away. "Shut up. Do you think I wanted this to happen?"

His grip tightened on the steering wheel. "I'd think that if you didn't, you would have been more careful."

"I meant my life. It wasn't supposed to be this way." She yanked on her seatbelt again.

"You don't wanna be with me? Is that it?" He gave a sharp jerk on the wheel as they turned a corner, then slammed on the brakes, bringing them to an abrupt stop at a stoplight.

A gentle answer turns away wrath. Where had she heard that?

"I'm sorry. I'm afraid my mom is going to freak. I'm so glad you're supporting me in this."

He didn't say anything else for the duration of the trip.

Her mother's head peeked out from behind the curtains as they turned in the driveway. Lisa's mom ducked behind them quickly as if she wasn't anxiously awaiting their arrival.

Lisa took several deep breaths and peeled herself from the seat. She stepped out of the car and stood there for a moment. Mitchell came up behind her and put his hand on the small of her back.

"They're *your* parents," he whispered into her ear. "*You* lead the way."

Why couldn't she have a man who would be a pillar of masculine strength? One who would light her way instead of pushing her into the great unknown. Did such a man really exist or was it merely another mirage paraded before her heartstrings by the media?

She rushed to the door, escaping his hand. She blew out a breath. How ridiculous to have to ring the doorbell, as if her parents needed to be alerted to their presence.

"Lisa, you're here!" Her mother's innocent smile grated. "Hello, Mitchell. Nice to see you."

Chapter 7: Lisa

Her dad nodded to them from his recliner as they entered the living room.

"Well, dinner's ready," her mother said. "Let's make our way into the kitchen, shall we? I trust you're feeling well, dear?"

"Uh, yeah; why do you ask?" Had her mother guessed? But the morning sickness had worn off several weeks ago. And this pregnancy was not nearly as nauseating as the last one had been. Was every pregnancy different? Would she ever know?

"Oh, well, I assumed that the only reason you'd try to cancel on me would be because you weren't feeling well." Mother seldom looked anyone in the eye when talking to them. She flung most of her jabs and innuendos while walking away from them to some all-important task. She likely had spent much of her life daydreaming of having the boldness for face-to-face confrontation but had never quite made it to that point. And Lisa took after.

"I had a hard day." Understatement of the century.

"Why's that, dear?" Mother swung around to briefly meet her gaze.

Mitchell, who had been standing three steps behind her, silent until that point, broke in. "Oh, Mrs. McCuly! Is that a roast on the table? It's my absolute favorite."

"Why, yes, it is. I wasn't sure if you liked roast or not. Of course, Lisa's always liked everything I cooked. She's always been a good eater, never picky as a child. I don't have to work too hard to please her. She's always been my grateful child."

Lisa shot Mitchell a sarcastic smile. There Mother went again, putting Lisa on a pedestal. It was a long fall down.

Each bite of that God-forsaken roast dropped like lead in her belly. She forced herself to finish every bit of it to avoid commentary on her eating habits. They needed to get the announcement over with. Wait, no. It could wait until after dessert.

Finally, when Mother had cleared all the plates but before everyone left the table, Lisa gripped the bottom of her chair and dove in. “Mom, Dad, I need to tell you something.”

Mitchell shot her a wide-eyed look, as if he hadn’t truly expected her to go through with it. As if he was in the majority who didn’t know her secret.

Her mother took small, steady steps from the sink to sit back in her chair. “Yes, Lisa?”

“I’m—” She swallowed hard. “I’m pregnant.”

Her mom brought a quivering hand to her mouth. Her dad stared straight ahead, a small twitch at the corner of his eye the only movement in his expression. Lisa, the favorite daughter, had just wreaked havoc on her parents’ dreams for her.

Mother sucked in a noisy breath before speaking. “I knew we shouldn’t have allowed you to go to that school! Those secular universities—you’ve only been there a short while and they’ve already corrupted you.”

Lisa cast a glance at Mitchell. The university? How was her boyfriend getting off so easily? Because he complimented her cooking?

“You’re going to have to get married.” Her dad’s clear and direct voice sliced like a knife.

Lisa’s stomach lurched. Morning sickness was nothing at all compared to this. She didn’t look at Mitchell to see his response to that suggestion. Even though the idea repulsed by her, seeing horror in his eyes would sting to the core.

“Sexual immorality,” her mother whispered to herself.

“No, Dad. I’m placing this baby for adoption.”

Mother continued to mumble, staring at a small stain on the tablecloth. “How could you do this? You were always so well behaved. And you went to Sunday School every week.”

“Adoption.” Her father’s monotone gave no indication of whether he approved or thought such a thing ridiculous.

“Adoption?” Her mother abandoned her self-dialogue for the conversation at hand. “Do you realize what all is involved with the process? How do you know the baby will be placed in a decent family?"

Mitchell leaned forward. "We've met the lady who's gonna adopt her."

If she had been holding his hand, she would have dug her nails into it. But he hadn't offered his hand to her, and she wasn't about to reach out for it.

"Met her? How could you have met her already?"

Mitchell gestured as if Eve were standing in front of them. "She was at the abortion clinic, and she said she'd adopt the baby—"

"Abortion clinic!" Mother's voice rose an octave as the sheltered world she'd built around her daughter shattered. "Abortion? You were"—she clasped her hand to her heart—"you were going to *murder* your own baby?"

Lisa gulped down hot tears, shoving images from her nightmares to the back of her mind. "I'm not going to have an abortion. I'm going to have this baby and place it for adoption." She kept her voice firm, even though her hands trembled. She needed to dispel any thoughts of such a high crime. But her emotions refused to be subdued, and she wept.

"I'm so disappointed in both of you." Her father's voice dripped with disgust. "You're on your own in this one. You reap what you sow. Can't be coming around here begging for help."

"Chris!" Mother's eyes welled up and she turned her attention toward him, as if pausing the current scene for a sideline conversation. "She's your daughter. You can't throw her to the wolves."

"She won't learn her lesson if she's coddled."

"But she just found out she was pregnant." Her mother spoke through clenched teeth to her father before turning her attention back to Lisa. "Did you find out today, hon?" Her tone softened.

Lisa's gaze dropped to her lap. "A few months ago."

"Months? How far along are you?"

"Four months or so."

"Four months? Four months? Have you been to a doctor?"

"No," she whispered.

"You need to see a doctor."

Lisa bit her lip. Sure, a doctor would deliver the baby, but the process of check-ups and the progression of it all hadn't entered her mind.

"I don't have insurance," she said, almost to herself.

"Oh, that's right." Mother lowered her voice. "Your dad's insurance with his new job doesn't kick in for another month." Her mouth twisted. "I suppose they won't insure you anyway with a pre-existing condition."

Her father spit out his words. "Don't expect us to pay for it. You're going to have to figure out something." How had she gone from Daddy's little girl to a reproach to him in one evening?

"Mitchell said he'd pay for everything." Lisa feigned confidence. Surely, he wouldn't dare contradict her in front of her parents. Besides, he had to see that she had no other options left.

"Whoa . . . uh, when did I say that?" His expression shifted from unease to subtle anger with the furrow of his brow.

"You said," she whispered with veiled hostility, "you would pay for it all."

"That's *not* what I meant, and you know it." His voice was hushed but clear. She had overstepped a line. He turned to her parents, an apology plastered on his face. "Of course, I would if I could, but I don't have the money. My job isn't giving me many hours, you see . . . " He sat back, leaving his excuses hanging as if they would explain themselves.

Lisa's father was unmoved. "Figure out something."

Chapter 7: Lisa

"There's public aid . . . you know, state health insurance. I'm sure Lisa would qualify." Mitchell threw a hand out as if tossing crumbs to birds.

"No daughter of mine is going to rely on the government." Her dad's eyes went from cold to frigid. "Don't even consider it. I raised you to stand on your own two feet and you can be sure you won't be stepping foot in my house again if you lean on Uncle Sam. You'd better figure out another way."

"I will. I'll figure it out." She swiped at her tears with her sleeve. She would. Somehow.

"Are you taking vitamins? You need to be taking vitamins. I can't believe you haven't even seen a doctor . . . "

As her mother droned on, Lisa's thoughts whirled. Until that point, she had been attempting to take things one miniature step at a time. Suddenly, she lifted her gaze to see a giant canyon before her. Money. She needed money.

"What will your sisters think?" Mother raised a hand to cover her mouth.

"I have more important things to think about, Mother."

"Don't you even try to manipulate us, you hear? You're on your own." As if his last statement was a gavel, her dad dismissed himself from the table and her life.

"You know they've always respected you, Lisa. Dawn in particular. She always strove to follow the example you set. I wish you would stop thinking about yourself for one minute and think of how your actions affect those you love." Mother jumped up and scurried to the sink to rinse off dishes. They clanked as she placed them into the dishwasher.

"I don't know what they'll think." And Lisa didn't care. She had to wiggle out from underneath the incessant guilt.

"You know what *I* think?" Mother paused as if her question wasn't rhetorical.

"No, Mom. I haven't the slightest idea." Dry tearstains made Lisa's cheeks feel like parched ground. Exhaustion fell over her. She needed to make a swift exit.

Mitch scooted his chair back. Good. He had the same idea.

"I think they don't have to know." Mother slammed the dishwasher closed and wiped her hands on a towel.

"It'd be pretty hard to hide it around the holidays, don't you think?" Lisa closed her eyes. If only she curled under her down comforter at home.

Her mother's chair creaked as she sat again at the table. "Perhaps it would be better for everyone if you didn't come around for the holidays. Maybe you should go . . . somewhere . . . you know, get things straightened out in your mind."

Lisa's eyes flew open. "You don't want me around for Christmas? You want me to go away?"

"It's just that Dawn and Lydia have rebellious tendencies already, and they'll both be home from college for the holidays. You made a mistake, a horrible mistake. That's bad enough. If you corrupted your older sisters too, well, I don't know how I would handle that." She shook her head. "Plus, they'll tell your cousins, who will tell your aunts. You don't want the entire family to know your shame, do you?"

"I've got to go." Lisa stood so fast her vision swam.

"Think about it, won't you, Lisa? You've always been reasonable. One mistake wouldn't change that, now, would it?"

She didn't stay to answer.

Mitchell stepped on her heel as she opened the front door. His presence comforted her a little, since she felt too physically tired and emotionally drained to drive. She slept on the drive back, clinging to the deep emptiness that claimed her.

How could she face what was ahead? If only she could sleep for a long, long time. And wake to a new reality.

She might have given Mitchell a piece of her mind about what a coward he was if she wasn't so tired. Instead, she took it for granted that she could tell him later. But in the morning, she awoke to find a note scrawled on an index card saying he was making a new start somewhere else, as if running away could change the child's DNA.

How easy it was for him to leave the whole mess behind. It stung, but there were other thoughts that plagued her more. She would spend Christmas eight and a half months pregnant, broke, and completely alone.

Chapter 8: Eve

When I tried to press the off button on my cell phone, my hands trembled, and I hit three other buttons first. Hopefully, those three beeps didn't give away my lack of confidence to the person on the other end.

"Who was that?" Gideon asked. He'd walked in just in time to know I had been on the phone but too late to catch any of the conversation.

"I need to sit." The soreness in my back rivaled the ache in my mind.

"Come in here." He motioned for me to join him on the couch, but I didn't budge from kitchen table.

"Can you come here instead? Bring me paper, will you?"

"Sure. What's going on? Who was on the phone?" He slid a package of sticky notes across the table and coasted into the chair across from me.

"Oh, I meant paper. A notebook. Bigger." Hunger gripped me out of nowhere. I needed to eat. Anything. "And those pretzels over there. Do we have any chocolate?" I rested my forehead in my hands. Why had life gotten so complicated?

Gideon rose and gathered the needed supplies. So gracious. How did he put up with me? A "good wife" would joyfully greet her husband at the door and ask how work went. I couldn't even ask for paper without being picky.

He smiled as he placed a legal pad, pretzels, and chocolate in front of me. With a wink, he produced a pen from behind his ear. "Unless you were planning on writing with chocolaty fingers, you might need this."

And just like that, he put me at ease. Temporarily. Our children would have a good father. At least one of us could keep it together.

"I was talking to Lisa. Her parents aren't on board with this decision. Remind me, how much of my delivery will your insurance cover?"

"Are you worrying about money again? Insurance will cover eighty-five percent, hon. We've got nearly enough to cover the rest in savings. God will make up the difference. Don't stress out about it." He brushed my cheek with the tips of his fingers.

I closed my eyes, relishing his touch. Then I took a deep breath.

"We need three thousand dollars."

"Is that what the adoption costs will be? She called you back?"

"No. We're paying two thousand for the social worker and home study, plus another four thousand for legal fees. She's asking for three thousand more."

"What's the extra for?" His calm demeanor never vanished, as if we were a high-income family and not dependent on a youth pastor's income.

"Lisa doesn't have insurance. Her parents aren't going to help her, and they don't want her to get Medicaid for religious reasons. And her boyfriend Mitchell left her last night. She . . . " My voice wavered as tears threatened to push their way out of my closed eyelids. "She said if we want her to have this baby, we're going to have to pay for her doctor's visits and her delivery. The social worker said that might be the case, but I'd hoped . . . Can you believe this is actually one of the cheapest ways to adopt? Besides through the foster care system, I mean."

I scribbled figures on the paper with shaking fingers. Five thousand plus four thousand plus two thousand, plus five hundred for my own delivery, plus diapers, clothes, formula . . ."

Gideon halted my frantic financial assessment by placing his hands on my own.

"Eve, look at me." He spoke with such gentleness. My tear-filled eyes met his, seeking a pool of security to dive into. "When you set yourself to do what God's inviting you to do, there's always a cost. Is this baby worth fifteen thousand dollars?"

"Of course, she's worth it, but that's not the point. Where are we going to get the money?"

"Is God poor? Is five thousand dollars a big deal to Him?"

"No."

"If she's worth it, if He can do it, and if we really believe this is His will for our lives, we need to trust Him."

I pressed my lips together before answering. "How can you do that? How can you be so calm about everything?"

"I spent my lunch hour reading Matthew six." He shrugged. "Do not worry about your life. Look at the birds of the air and the flowers of the field. He cares, and He's got this." He reached over and ripped the sheet of paper out of the legal pad. Tearing it into shreds, he grinned.

As he stood to throw the pieces away, I surveyed the pretzels and candy. "Actually, I think I want chicken."

"Why don't you go sit on the glider outside and spend time in the Word. I'll cook chicken for dinner. Fried, baked, or grilled?"

His kindness undid me. "Oh, Gideon, I don't even know what I want to eat. I don't know what I'm doing. I don't know how to trust God for a measly amount of money. How am I going to do this?"

He kneeled on the floor beside me. Lifting my wet face with his hand, he tucked my hair behind my ear. "How are you going to do this? Eve, whose voice are you listening to? This isn't about *you* having to *do* something to make God proud. He's already so proud of you. I know you feel weak right now, but it's okay. He's got you. God has given you His heart for the unborn, and you're on a journey with Him. That's precious. There's eternal reward in walking with Him and getting to know Him more each step of the way."

I nodded, still crying. *Thank you, God, for a husband who will speak truth over me.* "Lemon chicken. I want lemon chicken with that seasoned rice. You remember?"

He laughed and the ache inside eased a little. "I remember. Go drink living water. I'll take care of dinner."

I spent the next hour mulling over the same passage Gideon mentioned. By the time the aroma of chicken was strong enough to lure me inside, I was a little more at peace. I treasured each bite as the flavor danced over my taste buds. We had never had a lot of extras, but we had everything we needed. The Lord took care of us. He always provided. Why would He stop now?

After a delicious dinner, we leaned back in our chairs, not ready to move.

"Can we talk about your conversation with Lisa, or would that upset you?" Gideon asked.

"We can talk." I blew out a breath. "I feel horrible for her. She's trying to do the right thing, but her dad isn't talking to her, and her mom's trying to convince her to stay away until the baby is born so that her family doesn't find out she's pregnant."

"Where does her mother expect her to go?"

"She doesn't care. Far enough so that she doesn't cause the family shame."

"And she said we were going to have to pay for everything or she wouldn't have the baby?"

"Mitchell was willing to fund an abortion but wouldn't lift his finger to help her keep the baby."

"You're angry." His voice didn't condemn me, but it stopped me in my tracks.

"I guess I am." Angry and . . . bitter? "This baby is a human being, and no one's acting like it. The biggest issue at stake is family pride or convenience. Even my mom thinks I'm crazy, Gideon. You know that? She thinks I've completely flipped." The peace from earlier slipped away as the issues loomed before me.

"Let's not be angry, Eve."

"I can't help it. I don't even know where it's coming from. I'm angry at everyone. At the abortionists for making money off someone else's death. At Lisa's parents, at Mitchell, at Lisa for not even offering to get a part-time job to help with the expenses. I'm angry that adoption costs so much and that my parents and friends don't understand." I huffed. "I'm not normally like this, am I? Do you think it's the hormones?"

He leaned forward and rested his elbows on the table. His eyes bore into me. "It's so easy to get angry, but don't do it. You can fight against it, Evie. You can refuse to give into it. There's a lot going on in your body right now, but much of it is only revealing what's in your heart. Let's pray."

His words stung. I closed my eyes. *Is what he said true, Lord?*

The answer came as a gentle whisper inside. Yes. Anger might have been manifesting more readily because of my pregnancy, but I had anger inside of me.

Where is it coming from? What lie am I believing?

That I had to fix everything and make it all right.

Oh, no. Not the savior complex again. I chuckled.

"What is it?" Gideon asked.

"Nothing. The Lord's showing me, again, that I can leave it all in His hands and trust the He is good. I don't have to try and fix everything that's broken."

"Just say yes to the next thing He asks You to do."

"The next yes."

"Which is?"

"To pray."

Gideon took my hand and led me to the couch. His grip tightened as we prayed together. We asked God to have mercy on us and on our country. We prayed for the Lord to reveal His truth and to comfort those people who were trudging through pain because of listening to Satan's lies. We prayed God would expose the deception surrounding abortion. We asked for His emotions on the subject so we could pray with Him as friends. As we interceded, Zephan kicked inside me, as if joining in our prayer with his feet.

As our prayers finished, I leaned into my husband, exhausted. I closed my eyelids and wished myself in bed under the covers.

"Ready for bed?" Gideon spoke softly, his lips brushing against my hair.

"You might have to carry me. I'm not sure I can make it all the way down the hall."

"Carry you, huh? That might prove more difficult than when we were first married."

"Are you saying I'm fat?" My eyes remained closed.

"Two people are more difficult to carry than one." I sensed a smile in his voice. How comforting that I could discern his expression without looking at his face.

"You should say something sentimental, like you'll carry me in your heart always. You know—like from a greeting card." I returned his unseen smile.

He took my face in his hands then, and I pried my eyes open. "Evie, you're beautiful. I knew you were an amazing woman when I married you, but it's a joy seeing you grow and blossom before my eyes."

I took his affection in, savoring the safe place I found in him and knowing it was but a whisper of my King's affection for me. "I love you," I said.

Gideon's gentleness gave me the strength to lift myself off the couch and walk towards the bedroom.

"Are you coming or not?" I called behind me. "There's no way I'm going to carry you!" His laugh resounded, and the stress from earlier melted away.

Chapter 9: Trent

Trent smiled as he lazily gripped the stirring wheel. Going home was the best part of his day. Always had been. But now, that Beth was pregnant . . . Wow. Even better. The way she greeted him with laughter and eyes beaming. He pressed on the accelerator.

When he pulled into the driveway, he found Beth waiting on the porch swing.

No one understood him like Beth, and no one validated his existence the way she did. He hadn't a clue how big the aching chasm inside his wife had been until an unborn child filled it.

She smiled as he climbed out of the car

Wrapping her in his arms, he kissed the top of her head. They walked inside and stood before the kitchen table where stir-fry waited on the plates normally reserved for company. Candlelight flickered, bathing her in a warm glow.

"I felt the baby move." She lifted a shoulder. "I thought it could count as a special occasion."

"Honey, I don't think you felt the baby move. It's too early. You're only eight weeks along."

"No, I felt a flutter. It's supposed to feel like butterflies. Isn't that what you said? Well, butterflies flutter. I felt a flutter."

The corner of his mouth twitched as he suppressed a smile. "I don't mean to be a kill-joy, but right now the baby is still tiny. Most women don't feel movement until eighteen weeks or later."

She planted a hand on her hip. "What was the flutter then?"

He raised a brow. "Probably gas."

"You mean to tell me I busted out the good plates for gas?" A sheepish grin crept across her kissable face.

He leaned forward and nuzzled her shoulder. She smelled like roses. "When you feel the baby move for real, you'll know the difference."

"How do you know? You've never been pregnant."

"I've been told." Best not explain how he'd been told. A couple of weeks ago, a woman in her early twenties had come in for a late-term abortion. When he had asked her why she had waited so long, she told him she had made an appointment early in her pregnancy but had thought she felt the baby move. *Now I know it wasn't moving at all. This*—she'd put her hand on her abdomen—*is moving.* He gave his head a small shake to slough off the memory.

"Well, we should use these plates more often anyway." Beth rubbed her hands up Trent's arms, sending his senses tingling. "Why have china if no one ever uses it?" She stepped back. "I'm starving."

So was he, but not for dinner. Pregnancy was attractive on her.

As she plunged into her meal with fervor, he watched her, unable to keep a smile off his face.

"What?" she mumbled, mouth full.

"You still don't have any morning sickness?"

"Not yet."

"Well, if you don't have any by now, you might not get any." He took a bite and relished the sweet and savory mixture. Maybe he was hungrier than he thought.

"Seriously? I thought everyone had morning sickness."

"Most women do to varying degrees, but a few never get sick at all. I guess you're one of the lucky ones."

"I always thought of it as a rite of passage." She took a drink and shrugged. "But I won't complain."

He spent the rest of the meal explaining the role of the hormones surging within her. She leaned forward as she listened, as if soaking it all in. Though she hadn't experienced morning sickness, she'd felt exhausted over the past few days. He didn't mind turning in early to watch re-runs in bed and listen to her breathe as she slept in his arms.

"So is the baby moving even though I can't feel her?" she asked out of nowhere. The television murmured on low volume in the background.

"I thought you were asleep." Trent tousled her hair.

"No, just thinking with my eyes closed."

"Well, to answer your question—yes. She's moving around like crazy, twisting her little arms and legs like nobody's business."

"But she's too little for me to feel her." Beth yawned. "She's got arms and legs now? Last week you said they were only buds."

"Every baby is different, but they change so much from week to week in the beginning. There are a lot of fine details to be formed still. Her fingers and toes are most likely still webbed, but they are there."

"That's amazing." She lifted herself onto her elbow, suddenly awake. "She has arms and legs and is moving all around? I can't believe all of this is going on inside of me and I can't even feel it."

He chuckled. "You'll feel it soon enough. In no time at all, I'll be able to put my hand right here"—he rested a hand on her stomach—"and feel a kick."

"I can't wait." She laid back down, wiggling until she was firmly pressed up against him.

"Neither can I." He meant it.

Chapter 9: Trent

***

The pleasure of the past night faded as Trent pulled into the parking lot at the clinic the next day. Evidently someone had organized a rally because picketers packed the sidewalks surrounding the clinic. Yelling and jeering, the crowd waved their neon-painted signs. He glanced up just enough to see one woman's eyes glaring at him. What a way to start the day.

On the far side of the parking lot stood a handful of those silent protesters yet again. They looked out of place in the havoc the others were causing. Had they missed the memo that today was the day to scream?

He drew a deep breath and exited the car. Head down, he rushed toward the employee entrance.

"Baby killer!" A man flung an insult in his direction, voice shrill.

Trent didn't give the man the satisfaction of looking up. Once safely inside, he let out a moan. Why did they have to ruin his morning like that? They should be at work doing something productive. He threw his wallet in his locker. Great. Now he was starting the day out annoyed and impatient. Those emotions normally didn't set in until late morning.

He left the locker room and headed to reception. After glancing over the list of that morning's clients, he hurried into his first patient's room.

"Hi. I'm Doctor Rhine." He forced a smile as he shook the girl's hand. Her hand hung limp in his as she shifted on the table. A strand of brown curls fell over her eyes, and she tucked it behind her ear. "The nurse will join us soon."

"I'm Lydia." Her voice came out small.

He glanced around the room. Hmm. She was alone. Almost everyone came with someone. "Hi, Lydia. Do you have any questions for me this morning before we get started?" He breezed through the standard question. Hopefully, she'd simply shake her head, and he could get things over with.

"I've never done this before." Her shoulders slumped, a telltale sign of shame. His job was to unburden her of any guilt. All patients met with a counselor before he performed the procedure. Most, like Lydia, still had reservations.

"I understand, but the procedure is safe, and you'll be on your way home in an hour or so."

"What does the baby look like? I mean, does it look like a baby or just a blob?"

Reservations were one thing, but these were the kinds of questions the counselors were supposed to answer.

"You had an ultrasound when you first got here, correct?"

"I couldn't look." Her head hung low.

"I see." Softening his voice, he dug deep inside himself, searching for empathy. He'd gotten into this profession to help women. She needed help out of her unwarranted shame. No doubt a family member or church friend had said something to burden her. "How far along are you?"

"Eight weeks."

*Eight weeks***.** He froze, remembering. *I don't think you felt the baby move. It's too early. You're only eight weeks along.* Beth's sparkling eyes alight with wonder, eight weeks pregnant with their child. His child.

Lydia stared at him with wet cheeks. He leaned against the counter, not trusting his legs to hold him up.

"If you're only eight weeks along, you could take the abortion pill instead." Eight weeks was borderline for such medical abortions, but his insides shook. He needed to escape to his office and collect himself.

She shook her head. "They said I would have to have someone there with me in case of complications. I—I don't have anyone. I live an hour and a half away, and this is the closest clinic I could find." Her excuses were inconveniently legitimate.

"I understand. Don't worry. The procedure will only take a few minutes and then the nurse will wheel you to a comfortable recovery room." He hadn't forgotten her original question. He was avoiding it.

"But the baby? It doesn't look like a baby, right? I mean, it's not like it has hands or feet or anything."

Nausea rose within him, and he pretended to study her chart while answering. Where was the nurse? He needed a distraction. But no such luck. "No, it is just a fetus at this point. There are slight buds where the arms and legs would be, nothing more." *Hypocrite.* He flipped through the pages, eyes down, stomach lurching.

"Okay." She breathed a sigh of relief.

He nearly did too, thankful for the end of questions. Thankful to be able to get it over with so he could get himself together.

Just then, Mary knocked, then breezed in. "Sorry about that. Got caught up with something. I'm Mary, your nurse."

Lydia nodded in her direction, then brought her penetrating gaze back to Trent.

"All right. Lay down there and we'll take care of this. It will only take a few minutes." He pulled on latex gloves and sat as she lay down on the table.

Her soft voice once again assaulted his ears. "So, it can't move or anything, right? It's only tissue?"

He swallowed hard.

"Just a few twitches due to nerves is all."

She said nothing more, and he rushed through the routine pelvic exam. "Would you like the extra pain medication?" *Please say yes*. How aggravating when women refused and then complained of pain.

"Yes." Tears coursed down her face.

Mary offered Lydia the medication and then stayed by her side, holding her hand. Mary previously had two abortions and was quite compassionate with first timers. Her presence, along with the medication, relaxed Lydia.

"I'm going to numb your cervix with an anesthetic and then dilate it. You might feel slight cramping. Breathe deep and slow." Her weepy breaths did nothing to decrease the shaking of his hands.

Get it over with, Trent. He prepared himself.

"Now I'm going to insert this tube into your cervix and connect it to the vacuum aspirator. It will terminate the pregnancy." He had a little trouble with the insertion. His nerves rankled him. Why was he having such a silly reaction? He'd been doing this for years on hundreds of women. Why was he suddenly shaky?

Finally, he finished. "It's done. Mary will escort you to your recovery room. Have a nice day." His voice rushed, and he missed the trashcan when throwing away his gloves. Clumsy. Without thinking, he stooped and picked them back up, depositing them into the trash.

He looked at his hand and his chest clenched. Blood smudged it from picking up the glove. He excused himself and dashed to the bathroom. As he scrubbed his hands, the wave of nausea returned. He vomited in the toilet.

What was with him? How could he let something so simple get to him? It's not like it was a late term. But he couldn't erase Beth's face from his mind. Beth, thinking she'd felt the baby move. Beth, enamored with all the intimate details of the life blossoming inside of her.

A knock sounded on the door. "Trent, it's Mary. Are you okay?"

"I'm not feeling so well."

"Do you want me to call Brett and ask him if he can come in today? You didn't look so good in there."

"Yeah, call Brett." He continued scrubbing his hands, though the residue of the blood was long gone. He should go for a run and put the entire day behind him. That is, if his stomach would settle down.

"I'll do that. Why don't you rest in your office for a little while?" Her footsteps retreated, not stopping for his response.

He wouldn't rest in his office. He had to get away from the clinic. Far away. Shutting off the water, he took a deep breath. He dried his hands, went to his locker to grab his keys, and jogged to his car, hoping to outrun whatever it was that plagued him.

Chapter 10: Eve

Waking proved more difficult than it used to, and I arrived at the clinic later than I planned. Determined not to let it throw me off, I waddled forward as quickly as an eight-months-pregnant woman could to join the group from my church. I took a strip of LIFE tape from the group leader and found my place.

When a burden for Trent fell upon me, I spent a half hour praying for him. *God, break in. Open up his eyes to see the reality of what he's taking part in. Expose Satan's lies. Show him the truth.*

I prayed silently, eyes closed, heart awake, too engrossed in prayer to count the women entering the doors. A hand touched my shoulder. I looked up to see my friend Angela angling her head to the front of the clinic. Trent, still in his white coat, rushed to his car. *Oh, God! Did You answer my prayer?*

Follow him.

No time to second-guess myself. I pulled off the tape, stuck it to my jeans, and hurried to my van, keeping an eye on his gray sedan. He sat without starting the ignition for a minute, which gave me time to reach my vehicle before he pulled out of the lot. It wasn't until I put the van in reverse that I stopped to question what I was doing.

"God, what if he sees me and thinks I'm stalking him? Oh, I *am* stalking him," I half-prayed, following the sedan at a distance while keeping him in eyesight. "Am I nuts? This would make a great headline for the paper. God. This is You, right? Not a crazy pregnancy thing?" I prayed while trying to keep up with Trent. Thankfully, he made few turns and stuck to the speed limit.

His car swerved onto a narrow side road and then an even skinnier gravel road. I dropped back more. Without the distraction of the other cars speeding by, he might notice my pursuit. He parked in a sandy clearing in front of a lake. I pulled over on the edge of the road, safely hidden by trees and brush.

Where were we? It looked so familiar. Realization struck. We were at Deer Creek Lake, only the main entrance was on the other side where there was sure to be people of all ages walking, biking, whizzing past on roller blades, flying kites, and all the normal activities for a July afternoon. Gideon and I never used this back entrance. Here, the lake lapped in a serene, eerie way.

"Okay, God. What now?" I squinted through the trees. Trent's head lay against the steering wheel.

Wait.

I continued to pray and watch him from a distance. A few minutes later, he got out and stood, gazing at the water. I unbuckled my seat belt.

Wait.

His mouth moved as he shifted his weight from foot to foot. He covered his face with his hands and leaned against the hood of the car as a frustrated cry pierced the air.

Go.

I got out and shut the door quietly. Taking a few deep breaths to calm my nerves, I sauntered his way as naturally as possible. *You led me here. You must be doing something.* I focused on this hope, not allowing my mind to wander to the sheer lunacy of what I was doing.

Father, he needs You. He needs hope. I slowed my pace. *I only want to say what You want me to say, Holy Spirit.* Tears and sweat covered every inch of his face, but Trent never looked up.

"Excuse me." I stood an arm's length away. His head snapped up. "Are you okay?"

"What?" His forehead crinkled. "Aren't you the lady from the restaurant?" His voice, though full and aching, didn't crack.

I nodded.

"I'm . . . I'm having a rough day. I came here to be alone." His gaze diverted back to the lake.

"I guess I've ruined your alone time, haven't I? It seemed like you needed someone to talk to." I leaned against the car, securing my place in the conversation.

He looked at me then. What was that in his expression? Certainly not amusement, but not quite annoyance either. He didn't speak for a few minutes, and I didn't push. Instead, I used that time to ask the Lord for guidance yet again.

"Do you always make yourself at home at other people's tables and cars?" His voice seemed far off, in another world.

I raised a shoulder. "Only recently."

"What was your name again?"

"Eve."

"Oh, yeah." His gaze seemed to follow every ripple of water, as if they had answers he sought. "Well, Eve, I don't think I could confess to *you* what's on my mind right now."

"Confess? Like a sin?"

"Some would say so. I never thought so, but today . . . I don't know anymore."

"We've all sinned." I relaxed and allowed my words to come naturally.

"You probably believe life begins at conception, don't you?"

"Absolutely." I brushed a stray hair off my face.

Chapter 10: Eve

"If I told you I made a living suctioning out fetuses with a vacuum extractor, you'd think I was a murderer, wouldn't you?"

"Yes." I stared at his profile. His jaw shifted. "But the Bible also says if you are angry with your brother without a cause, you're in danger of judgement. So, we're even there."

He glanced up at me, brow furrowed, then averted his gaze to the sand beneath his feet. "How can I be so overjoyed by the life growing inside my wife's womb and then go to work and perform an abortion?"

"Your wife's pregnant?"

He nodded.

"Your first?"

"Yes." A slight, weary smile flickered across his face, only to fade into tension. He bit his lip. "And no. She had an abortion in high school. We would have had a twelve-year-old by now."

"Could this be a sign it's time for a change? Your wife getting pregnant, I mean. Now that you know how wonderful having a baby can be, you could leave the clinic behind."

"It's not that easy." Anger tinged his reply.

"No, it wouldn't be easy. Someday, though, you're going to stand before God, and He places a high value on the life of the unborn. *That* wouldn't be easy." I sucked in a breath as Zephan shoved his foot under my rib.

"Are you saying I deserve to rot in hell? I've heard that before." He raked his hand through his hair.

"Yes. You deserve hell."

"I thought you were coming over here to make me feel better." He let out a dry laugh and shook his head.

"I deserve hell too." I ignored his last statement. "My heart's a mess. All kinds of gunk in there that Jesus and I are working through together. We're all separated from God without Jesus. I'm so glad He made a way for me to be forgiven and for us to be close again. He gave me life in exchange for death." Clouds shifted and light glittered across the water.

"That's different. Some things are beyond forgiveness." He turned to me again, eyes hard with a challenge. "You know what I did today? I outright lied to a woman. I told her the lump of tissue in her didn't have arms or legs, couldn't move. I lied. Last night, I told my wife the opposite. But I lied to this woman and then suctioned out her baby. I stopped its heartbeat, its movement. I stopped its heartbeat." He snapped his fingers. "Like that." He shook his head. "Now if my wife were to have a miscarriage, we would mourn. She'd be devastated. We'd cry and see it as the death of our child. Ironic, isn't it?"

I tried to suppress a cringe, but it must have shown.

"You're disgusted at me." He took a step back.

"There's nothing you have done that's beyond forgiveness."

"I've crushed little skulls," he whispered.

"Nothing is stronger than God's love." I kept my voice and gaze firm. He shook his head, but I continued. "Leave the profession. I know it wouldn't be easy, but you're a bright doctor. There are better uses to your talents. Do you remember when you were a child? You must have written a third-grade essay or something—'What I Want to Be When I Grow Up'?"

"Lady, I don't know who you are or where you came from. I have no idea why I'm sharing all this with you." He looked me over then, as if snapping out of his vulnerable mode into something more suited to his nature. I followed his gaze to the red tape that adorned my jeans. Oops. Forgot to take that off.

"You're one of them." His voice rose along with the color in his cheeks.

"One of who?" I crossed my arms.

"One of those religious nut protesters. You knew all along, didn't you?" He took two steps away from me.

Chapter 10: Eve

"Define 'religious nut protester.'" An amused smile began to creep up on my face, but I reined it in.

"What do you mean, define it? Why can't you people mind your own business? Every day I go to work, every day there's someone yelling at me, hate radiating out of their every pore. Don't you people work? Don't you have anything better to do?"

"I don't yell. I pray. And no, there's nothing better for me to do."

"I don't understand you people. You stand there with that tape over your mouths and expect to change what? The law? Women's freedom to choose?" His eyes lit in challenge.

"There's a higher court than the Supreme Court. There's a greater authority than our government. God alone can change hearts."

"So pray at home. Go ahead. Ask God to change things all you want. Just don't do it outside my work!"

"Oh, I pray for you at home too, Trent."

"For me?" He spit out his words. "For me? Don't waste your time!"

God, give me the words. I had no problem discussing abortion with other believers. Talking to Trent was like navigating uncharted territory, but surely the Lord wanted to use me to speak to him. "It's not a waste of time to me. There is an almighty, sovereign God who knit you together in your mother's womb. He gave *you* life and breath. He made you for a purpose, with great dreams in His heart for you. You're not living those dreams, and I won't stop praying for you until you do."

"A purpose? What purpose?" Anger and bitterness did an ugly dance in the tone of his reply.

"To love Him. To be loved by Him." I smiled.

"You mean to cower."

"No. I mean to love Him, to have a relationship with Him who first loved you. He's not a far-off, angry God. When you enjoy Him and you know you're enjoyed by Him, that's when you become alive."

His face twisted, but his voice was calm and controlled. "Look, you don't know me. I don't know where you get off following me and preaching to me. The only thing you've convinced me of is the fact that you're insane. You need to go back to wherever you came from, or I'm going to notify the police."

"I'll leave, but I want to know one thing first." I straightened myself to stand facing him.

"What's that?"

"Do you have nightmares?"

"Everyone has nightmares." His reply was harsh, but something else flickered in his eyes.

"Next time you dream about one of those babies, consider that perhaps God is trying, in His mercy, to turn your heart away from your profession and towards Him."

"You can leave now." He spoke through clenched teeth.

I walked away. It took all of my will to not steal a glance back in his direction as his car door slammed and gravel crunched underneath his tires.

The toll of the conversation hit me as I slid into my van. Tears flowed then, slowly at first but picking up speed. I cried there on the side of the small gravel road. *Oh, God, did I do and say the right thing? He just got angrier and angrier. There didn't appear to be any softening towards You at all. Did I botch things up?*

Zephan shifted within me as if to reassure me. The Lord didn't need me to do things perfectly. Only to do them in love. I pressed my hand to my stomach, relishing the feeling of his little body pushing up against my palm.

"My womb is a safe place for you, little man." I spoke softly, rubbing my bulge. I couldn't help but smile. As the tears slowed, I started the ignition. "What now, God?" I asked, looking at the clock and seeing I still had two hours before Gideon would be home.

I shifted into drive and headed toward Lisa's apartment.

Chapter 11: Trent

Trent drove around aimlessly for an hour and a half. If only he could forget the entire day. The questions, the blood, the *woman*. Attempting to turn his mind to other things proved futile. If he thought about Beth and the baby . . . well, that only served to make the situation worse.

He didn't want to go home in such a state of disarray since Beth would be home in three hours. She could read the slightest trace of anything negative in his expression. He couldn't hide from her scrutiny. So, he drove around and around the same city block, trying to clear his head. But Eve's words nagged him, almost as if she were sitting in the car with him.

I pray at home for you too.

Why would she pray for him? He only performed a service because it was in demand. What would he solve by leaving the clinic? They'd only hire someone else. Women would still choose to terminate their pregnancies. Everything would continue as usual without him. Did she ever consider that? It's not like he pressured women into having abortions. They wanted to. They were beating down the doors.

Since Eve advocated prayer so greatly, he gave Eve's God a piece of his mind.

"It's not my fault."

A thought crossed his mind, as if in answer. Whose fault is it?

"It's the women's fault! It's the men who get them pregnant. It's their parents' fault for not teaching their teenagers to use birth control. It's legal! Blame the government. Blame the voters. Blame the devil. Just don't blame me. I'm only giving them what they want."

What do you want?

"I want to work in peace. I want to make a decent living so I can support my wife and child. I want to be left alone. Leave me alone!"

What was he doing arguing with random thoughts? As if God would talk to him while he drove in his car. What did God sound like anyway? How could people claim to know His thoughts?

His cell phone vibrated on the passenger seat. He ignored the call. It had to be Beth, and he needed to get himself together before talking to her. She'd be on her lunch break, calling to see how work was going so far. He laughed to himself. How would he explain this one?

Someday, though, you're going to have to stand before God who places a high value on the life of the unborn. That wouldn't be easy.

He slammed his hand on the steering wheel to jolt the contrary thoughts far away from him. Turning up the radio, he tried to drown himself in the sound of the drumbeat. He sang along with the words, but her voice still haunted him. Stand before God? If that was true, he was sure God would let him state his case. Wasn't He a God of mercy? Wasn't that what people like Eve said? If He was so good and compassionate, surely He'd understand.

"It's not my fault."

She'd said herself that nothing was beyond His forgiveness.

Leave the clinic.

"Shut up, lady!" The air in his car stifled him. "You're making me as crazy as you are. Now I'm hearing voices and talking to myself."

What could he do? How could he drown the voices out? He pulled into the parking lot of a bar. He hadn't gotten really drunk since high school, save maybe once or twice in college. Back then things had seemed simpler. A few beers wouldn't hurt. Beth wouldn't even notice.

***

"You've been drinking." Beth's voice, normally pleasant, now grated. She stood with her hands on her hips, blocking the hallway that led to their bedroom.

"A little. No big deal."

"I can't believe you. You were supposed to be at work."

How could he get by so he could bury himself underneath the covers and sleep the next ten hours away?

"I was at work. Then I left. I had a few beers. Now I want to go to bed."

"What's going on with you?" Her voice wobbled, teetering on the edge of emotional collapse. "My husband is a respected doctor. He doesn't leave work. He doesn't lie and say he's sick, and he *doesn't* go out drinking in the middle of the day."

He squinted against a beam of sunlight. "Who told you I was sick?"

"Mary called asking if you were all right. Apparently, Brett is flying out to California for vacation tomorrow, and she wanted to make sure you'd be at the clinic."

"I'll be there."

"That's not the point. The point is that you left work, claiming to be sick, and you were supposed to be *here*. I had to lie to cover for you. I said you were sleeping when I really had no idea where you were. I was about to call the police!"

Chapter 11: Trent

The dam broke then, and she wept.

He tried to put his arms around her, but she pushed him away.

He scrubbed his hand over his face. "I'm sorry, hon. I had a really hard day, and I don't want to talk about it right now. I didn't mean to scare you."

"Why are you hiding things from me?" She gulped down sobs.

"I'm not hiding anything from you."

"Then what were you doing today? Why'd you leave work?"

"I left work because I felt sick." Would she let him hold her? She did but was stiff in his arms. "I drove to the lake to get fresh air, and this crazy protester stalked me. I was upset. I had a few beers. Now I'm home where I belong." He kissed her forehead.

"Ugh!" She pulled back in disgust. "You reek like alcohol. I'm going to be sick." She raced to the bathroom.

What kind of lowlife was he? He even made his wife sick. He trudged to the bedroom, slipped off his shoes and pulled the comforter up to his chin. He should be more compassionate, but exhaustion drowned him. In the other room the toilet flushed. Footsteps approached. Beth sat on the bed, and though his eyes were closed, he could feel her gaze on him.

"A crazy protester stalked you?" She sounded skeptical. Could he blame her?

"Yes," he mumbled through the pillow.

"Why were you feeling sick in the first place?"

"Must have been something I ate."

"What'd you eat that you don't normally eat?"

"I stopped for a breakfast sandwich on the way to work."

"Your plate was in the sink. You ate your omelet this morning and then got fast food?" He was sure her eyes scrutinized him. If only she was more gullible.

"I didn't finish eating the omelet. I didn't have time . . . was running late."

"But you had time to go through the drive through?"

"I went to the one by work."

"You *never* go *anywhere* by work."

"Not normally . . . I . . . I was in a hurry and knew that one wouldn't be crowded." Couldn't she just believe him and let it be?

"I hope you're not lying to me, Trent."

"I love you."

"I love you too. I'll let you go to bed, but you'll have to explain tomorrow." She dragged her slippered feet on the hardwood floor. When the door closed, he breathed a sigh of relief. How to mentally prepare for the next day's interrogation? There were several possible excuses and explanations, but how would they stand against Beth's intellect? She likely wouldn't believe any of them. He fell asleep without any clear solutions.

***

When Trent stumbled out of bed to slam his hand on the alarm clock, Beth was already awake. She was sitting up in bed, her hands folded awkwardly in her lap, waiting.

"Good morning, babe." He stood in front of the bedroom door, head pounding. Could he avoid an interrogation?

"Good morning." Her eyes scrutinized him.

"You're up early."

"I couldn't sleep. None of what happened yesterday makes any sense to me." Her lower lip trembled.

He sat at the foot of the bed. "What do I need to explain more clearly?"

"Everything. You were drinking. You haven't had more than a beer or a cocktail at a party since we were in college. You're not twenty anymore."

"I know. I don't know what came over me. I was so angry and upset. I didn't know what else to do." He squeezed her big toe as a peace offering, but she yanked her foot away.

"What did the lady say to you to make you so upset? You deal with those people all the time. What made this different?"

"She followed me to the lake, for one. She came over, leaned on my car, and jumped into my conversation."

"So? That is supposed to justify getting drunk?"

"No. I can't justify it. It was dumb." Would that smooth things over?

"Wait. She jumped into your conversation with who?"

"With myself. I was standing by my car talking to myself." He shrugged. That sounded ridiculous.

"What were you saying to yourself?" Her eyes hadn't softened towards him.

"I don't know. I lectured myself for leaving work, I think. I've never walked out early before."

A muscle tightened in her jaw. "So, you'd talk to yourself before you'd talk to your wife? You'd talk to a *protester* before you'd talk to your wife?"

"Honey, you're—" He couldn't tell her she was overreacting. He had to defuse her anger, not fuel it.

She quirked a brow. "I'm what?"

"You're right. I don't know why I didn't call you."

She stared at him, as if trying to pry the truth out of him. When he said nothing more, she nodded towards the bedroom door, dismissing him. "You'd better get ready for work."

"I love you, hon. I do. Forgive me for being such a moron." He stood and moved around the bed toward her.

"I'm trying to give you the benefit of the doubt here, but it seems there's something you're not telling me. Our child is going to need us to have good communication, a strong marriage."

“I know. I’ll work on communicating more clearly.” He kissed her forehead and headed toward the bathroom. “And I promise never to go drink like that again.”

“You’d better not!”

While he showered, he prepped himself mentally for another day at work. He needed to forget the entire ordeal of the day before. He would not go into work a wreck. He was a professional, and he’d act like it. No more crazy “conversations with God.” He’d go to work and do his job.

Strong and focused now, he walked into the kitchen to find an omelet waiting for him on the counter. Beth had started the coffee and poured orange juice.

“Thank you.”

“I didn’t want you to run out of time again,” she said with a wry smile. She sat across from him at the table and ate her bowl of cereal. Neither of them said much, but the hostility had dissipated.

“I need to get going.” He drained the last of his coffee and got up to put his dishes in the sink. “I’ll be home right after work. Maybe you can pick up a movie for us to watch tonight?”

“I can do that.” She came over to him and wrapped her arms around him, clinging to his shirt. “Please . . . just love me.” She shook in his arms.

“I do.” He held her face in his hands, gazing at her fragile features. “I will always love you.” They kissed, and she leaned into him. He must have earned her trust.

She walked him out to the car and watched him drive away. Hopefully, everything would return to normal at work, at home, and inside his own head.

Chapter 12: Ashira

Ashira began making plans to flee as soon as she found she was with child once again. If the child was another girl, Reuben might be merciful, letting her keep and raise her daughter. If, however, the child was a boy, he would require her to relinquish the child to the gods. When giving Shai to Molech did not bring the rain, he'd commented that perhaps Molech was unmoved by a female. Males were a greater sacrifice. Ashira's heart could not risk another great loss, so she planned her escape.

While her husband slept, she riffled through their food supply. There wasn't much to pack. Only a bit of bread. How would she sustain herself on the journey to Jerusalem? What would she do when she arrived? She knew little of trade and had few resources. She fingered the three golden bracelets around her wrist and the silver necklace, gifts Reuben gave her when times were not so hard. She could trade them for food once her small ration of bread ran out.

With or without resources, it would be a dangerous journey to make alone. Their village near Anathoth was not even a day's walk from Jerusalem, but men were known to raid and rape lone women, and Ashira would have no one to protect her. She could not say she was unafraid—only that she feared one danger more than the other.

Her husband shifted on their pallet. She stilled. If he woke, he would ruin her plan. His snores came quiet and soft. He was a sound sleeper, but she must be careful. Best not waste any more time. She pried open the door and stepped into the dark of night, carrying nothing in her sack save the meager supply of bread.

Though not far, Jerusalem was a busy place, with much buying and selling even in times of drought. Reuben would have a hard time finding her among the throngs of people, and she planned to remain well-hidden. Where would she stay? She knew no one in the great city. She didn't have plans beyond getting there.

She cast one last look over her shoulder at the house she and Reuben shared. Surely, this wouldn't be the last time she saw it. Once the skies yielded, there would no longer be a need for him to sacrifice her child. She could return home, beg for forgiveness, and raise her child together with her husband.

Perhaps Jeremiah the prophet was the true reason she headed for Jerusalem. He was born and raised in nearby Anathoth. Reuben and Ashira heard him preaching sometimes when they went there to trade or visit relatives. When he began to prophesy doom for the people, the crowds persecuted him, and eventually, he left for the capital city.

At the time, no one wanted to hear of coming destruction, not when so many other prophets proclaimed peace and safety. The God of Abraham would not forsake them, they said. They were His chosen people, and Jerusalem was His chosen city.

She was unsure what to think or whom to believe. Every time Reuben went to Anathoth, he would condemn Jeremiah and threaten to take part in stoning him if the prophet wouldn't relent. The more Jeremiah angered her husband, the more curious she became. When they finally drove him away to Jerusalem, she pretended to be relieved but inwardly worried that rejecting the prophet was yet another sin heaped upon their heads.

The other prophets were wrong. The drought did not lift as they foretold. If they had ears to listen and eyes to see, they would have found Jeremiah's words true and the others' false.

The answer to their rescue was not in Molech's hands or the hands of the prophets who worshiped him while speaking in the name of Yahweh.

Her feet pattered on the path and a light breeze tousled her shawl. The night was quiet, serene. She was alone with her thoughts. Perhaps the prophet of doom understood what the rest of them did not. When she got to Jerusalem, she would seek him and find out.

The stars twinkled above her, unaware of the peril of her journey. She'd traveled this way before for the feasts, though always in company. The journey alone was more ominous. Something crossed the path in the distance, and she sucked in a breath. A robber? No, a deer It scurried off and she continued.

As a child, she heard stories of Yahweh and the great miracles He performed in leading her people out of Egypt. But by the time she was old enough to marry, those stories were told less often among her people. Instead, there were stories of Baal, Molech, and the gods of neighboring countries—gods who were not as restrictive as the God of their fathers. These gods would let them live as they pleased, not under law, as long as the sacrifices pleased them.

The multitude of foreign gods drew Reuben's interest. "Why have only one God, when you can have many?" he'd said early in their marriage. She never questioned his reasoning. Until the drought came. They worshiped many gods, and not one of them could save? And when became clear Reuben intended to sacrifice their firstborn child, Ashira doubted all the more. What kind of god demands such a thing? At least the God of Abraham, Isaac, and Jacob didn't require innocent blood for answered prayers.

How could she respect Molech after the horror of seeing her daughter burned alive? Surely there was a better way. If she could find Jeremiah, she might find truth in the stories of old, the stories of deliverance from slavery and a journey through the wilderness.

She barely made it out of her village when new questions assaulted her. By the gods, what was she doing? By the gods? Or by the one true God? What was true and what was false?

She'd rehearsed her plans over and over, seeking any alternative. No, there was not another way. When Shai was born, she'd begged and cried, pleaded with Reuben for the life of her child. Her incessant "nagging," as he called it, only strengthened his resolve. He'd already become a hard man by then, demanding and unfeeling. Only it hadn't always been that way.

Ashira smiled as their wedding and the days preceding it came to mind. Though her parents arranged their marriage, she never resented them. They chose him because he was a strong and hard-working man, but Ashira held her own reasons for accepting him. His laugh and merry eyes danced their way into her heart. He was tender and carefree, despite his hard-working nature. She was proud to become his wife and looked forward to raising a family with him. He would be a good father, instilling in their children the value of work while also giving them room to enjoy life.

Then the drought changed him, hardened him. He took much pride in his work, but when the skies held back their rain, the fields didn't yield much. There was little to bring in, little to take pride in. Reuben prayed to a myriad of gods and sacrificed to the Queen of Heaven at the high places. The more days that passed without rain, the more desperate he became until, in his mind, there was no other option. Sacrificing their child was his last resort.

Gone was the merriment and laughter that characterized their marriage at first. Gone was the tenderness with which he used to comfort her. Instead, his eyes held nothing but fierce determination. He would see to it that the rain came, no matter the cost. Ashira's tears didn't move him. She hardly recognized the man he'd become, but she remembered the man she once loved.

Surely that man would return with the rains. She could only pray for a quick end to the drought.

Only who should she pray to? What gods would listen? How would she find the truth?

She tightened the shawl around her against a cool breeze.

Surely the rains would come before the time came to give birth. But what if they did not? Perhaps she was mad for taking this journey. She might save the life of the child within her, or she might forfeit her own.

The darkness pressed in. She rushed forward, eager for the semblance of safety of the great walls of Jerusalem. An ache arose within her as she trudged toward the city. She'd never felt so alone. Her large family always surrounded her as a child, and by leaving her husband, she left them as well. The journey to the city seemed longer on her own.

When the walls of Jerusalem came into view, the city seemed even larger and more breathtaking than she remembered. If there was ever a place to escape to, a place of safety, Jerusalem was it. Its impenetrable walls stretched high above her, the picture of strength and safety. Though she was certain many gods could be found within the city, Molech's burning arms could not touch her or her child there.

Once within the city walls, she looked for shelter. She should attempt to find an inn that would accept one of her bracelets as payment, but weariness washed over her. The lateness of the hour left the city quiet. Shivering against the cold, she searched instead for a secluded crevice or alley. Finding a small niche, she pressed her back against the hard stone wall and slid down to sitting. She bit her lip, peering this way and that. All was quiet. Still. Dark. Surely, she was safe.

Yet, her heart hammered in her ears. She rested her head on bent knees, too weary to keep her eyes open any longer. In the morning, she would look for the prophet who might hold the secret to their land's future.

Chapter 13: Eve

"Hey, honey?" Gideon called out to me from the kitchen. "Did you vacuum the nursery? She's going to be here any minute."

Vacuum the nursery?

I chuckled. "No."

"Well, can you?" Gideon sounded borderline frantic.

I met him in the kitchen, where he was sweeping the floor that I had swept twenty minutes earlier. "I don't think it needs to be vacuumed. I mean, no one has been in there to track anything in."

"But it's where the baby—babies—are going to sleep. Don't you think she'll take a really close look at it?"

"I doubt she's going to dust every corner to make sure we have a spotless house, Gideon. It's a home visit, not a cleaning contest." Anyone would be nervous, and I wasn't immune. But this adoption was God's idea. Surely, He would complete what He started.

"I don't know what to think. What is she going to ask? What if I blank and give a stupid answer? Don't they have enough information about us? We filled out a mountain of paperwork. You'd think they'd be out of questions by now." He fumbled with the dustpan, and it dropped with a clang.

"And you're always telling me not to worry." I tried for a joking tone, but seeing my husband so ill at ease caused apprehension to bubble up inside of me. What if we were rejected? What if they thought taking on another baby would be too much for an already pregnant couple?

No. I couldn't go there. God orchestrated all of this. Esther was meant to be with us. The Lord's hand was in this. I need to rest in Him. Trust. Rest.

As Gideon bent down to sweep invisible crumbs into the dustpan, the doorbell rang.

We froze.

"It's her," he whispered.

"It's going to be fine." My smile wobbled.

He looked from the door to me. "Should I answer, or should you?"

"Let's both go."

"Good idea. That will give her the impression of a happy family . . . a happy marriage. Not that it's not the truth. We do have a happy marriage. I just meant—"

"Calm down, honey. It's going to be fine." I hadn't seen my husband that nervous since the night he proposed.

Together we opened the door and greeted the social worker. What did I expect? Perhaps an older lady with a tight bun and wire-rimmed glasses that would slip down her nose. Instead, a woman no older than myself smiled at me. Her loose blonde curls glinted against the sunlight.

"Hello, I'm Marsha Leer, the social worker assigned to your case. I've spoken to your wife several times over the phone," she said to Gideon. "It's nice to meet you in person." As she shook our hands, I relaxed.

I invited her in, and she sat in the recliner. Gideon and I sat on the couch across from her, hand in hand. Gideon scooted as close to me as he could get. *Oh, yes, honey. Be sure to give her the impression that we're happily married.* I stifled a chuckle and gave Ms. Leer my full attention.

She pulled a file folder stuffed with forms from her briefcase. More paperwork. At least she would be the one filling it out. "Let's get started with the couple interview first.

I'm going to go over a few of the questions you answered about yourselves and your family dynamics. After that we'll do the individual interviews, and then you can show me around so that I can make sure your home meets safety standards and can accommodate a child."

I nodded and squeezed Gideon's sweaty palm, as if to repeat my mantra of "It's going to be fine."

At first, the questions were simple. Describe your family dynamics growing up. How were you disciplined as a child? What is your fondest childhood memory? Things like that.

Then they got a little more personal.

"How do you and your husband handle conflict in your marriage?"

Conflict? Um . . . What was that carefully-thought-out answer I had written down earlier in the process. I opened my mouth, but nothing came out.

I needed to say something, but what?

Gideon interrupted my hesitation. "Eve is really good at expressing her feelings. Normally when we disagree, we take time to pray about the issue separately, and then we come together and talk about it."

Whew. He bailed me out. But was that the "right" answer. Did it sound trite? Unrealistic? What would she think about the prayer part? Was it even true? Sometimes I raised my voice—even yelled. Gideon and I didn't fight like that often, but we weren't perfect. Should I confess that to the social worker, or would it make me a bad candidate for motherhood?

"What are ways that you deal with stress?" Ms. Leer interrupted my thoughts with another equally difficult question.

"We pray," I said. We pray? What if she has something against *religious people*? "And I go for walks. I pray while I'm walking." Great. That helped. Should I say more? Give a better answer? But Ms. Leer moved on.

Chapter 13: Eve

"Do you have any plans to extend your family size through birth or adoption in the future?"

Gideon and I looked at each other with question marks in our gazes.

I squeezed his hand. "Uh . . . well . . . "

"We're not sure," Gideon said. "Not for a while, we think. I mean, we'll have our hands full with these two babies. Not too full, I mean. Only that we want to take things one step at a time." He let out a nervous chuckle.

"Probably eventually," I added. "Just not right now." Obviously.

Ms. Leer's smile spoke reassurance. She placed the packet she'd been looking through back into the file folder.

Oh, good. We were done.

Then she pulled out a different packet. "Now, Gideon, I'd like to ask you to step out for a few minutes so I can interview Eve separately." Oh yeah. Not done. "If you have a cell phone, Eve can call you when we're all finished."

He nodded, released my sweaty palm, and slipped out the front door, leaving me to face the barrage of questions alone. My stomach sank as I studied his vacant spot.

"All right, Eve. Can you tell me how your family feels about this adoption?"

"My family?" They thought I was crazy. I couldn't tell her that but hated to lie. *God, what do I say?*

"Yes, your parents and siblings. How do they view your choice to adopt at this time?" She tapped the packet with her pen.

"Um . . . well . . . they don't really understand why we're choosing to do this, but I think they'll come around. It was a shock to them is all. They'll get used to the idea. I'm sure they will." Did I sound sure?

She scribbled away at her paper. "Okay, can you explain why you are choosing to pursue adoption at this time?"

"Do you mean because I'm pregnant?" My voice wavered.

"It's a standard question we ask each family."

Oh. "Gideon and I talked about adopting children before we were married, and we both agreed we wanted to pursue it. We did plan on waiting a couple years after having our own child, but when I met the birth mother, I knew it was the right thing to do. She needed someone to adopt her baby, and she's all alone without any support system. I had to help in any way that I could."

Had to help? People who help bake casseroles or donate a little bit of money. This was more than helping. How could I explain why I felt compelled to offer to adopt her baby? "We felt the Lord wanted us to do this. Now that we've started the process, we can't imagine things turning out any other way. It's meant to be." Yes, that sounded better.

As the questions continued, my own words gave me confidence. *It's meant to be. This adoption was meant to be, wasn't it, God? It's part of Your plan, and if it's part of Your plan nothing can stop it.* By the time it was Gideon's turn for an individual interview, I no longer second-guessed every answer. I could still use a neck massage to ease the tension, but my faith grew, and my fear waned.

I passed Gideon on the front porch. His shoulders nearly reached his ears. His own fear must have been building as he waited.

As I watered flowers and pulled weeds, my prayers bounced back and forth between asking for peace for my husband and for Amanda—the waitress I'd met—and Samuel, who had made his grand entrance the week before. When I'd visited the two of them at the hospital, the gentle way Amanda spoke to and handled her little boy struck me. It was obvious she had fallen in love with her newborn, despite all the obstacles that stood between them. Now I prayed for strength and provision for Amanda. The road of single parenthood would not be an easy one for her, and I asked God to above all lead her to Himself, the One who would carry her burden.

By the time my cell phone vibrated, signaling me to go inside, I'd nearly forgotten the weight of what transpired inside my home. I entered and grinned at my husband in an attempt to transfer whatever peace I felt to him. It didn't seem to work. I offered Ms. Leer something to drink, and she accepted, giving Gideon and me a moment of reprieve before she did the home inspection.

"Okay, now if you'd like to show me around, I'd like to see where the adopted child will be sleeping first. Then I'll need to make sure you have a working smoke alarm, a fire extinguisher, child proof locks, that kind of thing." She followed us around the house, making notes. What was she writing? I dared not ask.

"And do you have an emergency escape plan in case of a fire?"

I nodded and explained our plan, thankful I'd done research online and knew to expect the question.

"Okay, the last thing I need is your income verification," she said. As Gideon took his paycheck stubs from a folder in the kitchen drawer, she shuffled through her file. "How are you planning on paying for the adoption expenses again?" she asked.

My mouth twitched. "We have some savings."

Gideon stepped beside me. "And we're trusting God for the rest."

Trusting God for the rest? That probably wasn't the answer they were looking for.

I cleared my throat. "We're having a fundraiser at our church. A dinner." There. That sounded more promising, didn't it?

Ms. Leer jotted down a few more lines and snapped her file shut. "Well, it was great to meet you, Eve, Gideon." She shook our hands again. "I'll be in touch."

We smiled and nodded as we walked her to the door and waved good-bye. As soon as Gideon shut the door, our faces dropped.

"What do you think?" Gideon's brows rose.

"It went okay, right?"

"Yeah. It went okay. She seemed nice enough."

We plopped down on the couch. "That was emotionally exhausting." I took note of the normal amount of space that now separated Gideon and me, in contrast to how we'd sat during the interview. Why had we felt so pressured to perform? To be the perfect couple?

"Isn't it crazy?" Gideon asked. "People having biological children don't have to fill out stacks of paperwork or have an interview. They don't have to prove anything to anyone. But adoption is a different story."

"Seems ironic, doesn't it?"

"I can't understand it. It's not like we have anything to hide, and yet I feel like I'm supposed to have all the right answers. We have a good marriage, right?"

"We do."

"And we're going to be good parents?"

"We are."

"So why can't I relax and be real? Why do I feel like I need to put on an act?"

"I don't know."

We were both quiet for a while. I replayed the interview in my mind. What did she think of our answers? What exactly was she looking for?

"Evie?" Gideon's serious tone caught my attention.

"Yes?"

"I didn't want to bring this up until after the home visit was over, but we really need to pray for our finances. We only have two more weeks to pay the first installment of the legal fees."

"I know." I'd been trying not to think about it.

Chapter 13: Eve

"We should have scheduled the fundraiser sooner."

I didn't reply. We hoped to receive a chunk of what was needed from the adoption fundraising dinner scheduled a month from now, but I couldn't imagine all the costs of the adoption being met though one dinner.

"We haven't gotten any more responses from the letter we sent out." He ran a hand through his hair.

"I need to give Lisa a check tomorrow for her first doctor's appointment, too."

Any relief from the home visit being over evaporated next to our financial needs. They loomed before me, menacing and overwhelming.

"Okay, enough worrying," Gideon said. "Let's pray. God already covered the cost of the home study. We never expected my Uncle Mike to send that check. So, He can do it again. He will do it again." And with that, Gideon led us in prayer, once again seeming confident in the Lord's provision. I followed his lead. I would trust in God's goodness and imagine baby Esther safe in my arms.

Chapter 14: Lisa

The doorbell awakened Lisa. She'd fallen asleep? She peered at the American history book sprawled in her lap. She was supposed to be studying for the big exam on Thursday, but . . . If she didn't get at least an 85%, she'd fail the class. If she failed the class, she'd be at risk of losing her scholarship. Why didn't her body understand such weighty matters?

Oh yeah. It had a growing baby to consider. Exhaustion seeped through every pore. Why'd she'd think taking summer classes was a good idea?

It rang again. Pushing the book aside, she hoisted herself to her feet. She opened the door to see Eve's glowing face.

"Hi, Lisa. Do you have a minute?" Eve heaved in shallow breath. Three flights of steps were no joke.

She rubbed her eyes. "I don't know. What time is it?"

"One."

"Yeah. I don't have class until two." She stepped aside to let Eve in. "Have a seat." Lisa motioned to the recliner.

Eve sat and flipped up the footrest.

"What brings you here?" Lisa plopped on the couch across from her.

"Oh, I wanted to see how you're doing."

Something about Eve put her at ease. Like she had no preconceived expectations to live up to when in her presence.

She blew a raspberry. "I'm tired and stressed, but other than that, I'm fine." She let out a short, humorless laugh.

"Tired, huh? That's a little strange."

"Why's that? Aren't all pregnant women tired?"

"Well, yeah, in the first trimester, but you're past that. Right about now you should be getting a burst of energy, I'd think. But then again, what do I know? This is my first, and I'm sure each pregnancy is different." Eve stroked her belly.

"I think it's because I'm not sleeping well," Lisa said. "I can't sleep at night, and all I want to do is sleep during the day. Go figure."

"Ahh. Finding it tough to get comfortable?" Eve looked down at Lisa's stomach, which she had stopped obsessively trying to hide.

"Mostly it's bad dreams. I should be used to them by now."

"Bad dreams? What about?"

"I don't know. Stuff. So, how are you feeling?" Lisa picked up a throw pillow and fiddled with the tassels on the end. No need to revisit such images in the day. Besides, then Eve would know she'd had an abortion before. What would she think of her then?

Eve paused before answering, as if deciding whether to accept the shift of topics. "I'm feeling great. Thanks for asking." Another pause. "You know you can talk to me, right? I'm here to help."

"I know." Lisa glanced up. "I don't want to talk about it right now."

"I'll respect that. So, what's got you stressed out?"

"Oh, school. Money. My parents. Life." Lisa shrugged. No big deal, right? She was the strong one in her family, the over-achiever. She should be able to handle them.

"One at a time." Eve held up a finger. "School. Is it hard to keep up with classes when you're so tired?"

"That and the fact that I find it increasingly more difficult to concentrate. My mind keeps wandering. I think about when

I'm going to go see a doctor, what the delivery will be like, and if I'll ever see my parents and sisters again."

"I see. That's part of the reason I wanted to stop by. The doctor part." She reached down and pulled a card out of her purse. "Here's my OB's number. If you already have one in mind, that's fine, but I love her. Her office offers a discount for women without insurance. And here's money to cover your first appointment." She handed Lisa a business card and a check.

Tears brimmed. "Why are you being so nice to me?" Sure, she'd asked Eve for the money to cover her expenses, but to hand-deliver the check? To help her find a doctor? All without a twinge of resentment? "My own family can't stand me. My boyfriend dumped me. My best friend has even been distant since I told her."

"Lisa, you've made a choice that had a lot of repercussions. It was the right choice, but it's been costly for you. I admire your strength through all of this. I want to do whatever I can to help."

Shaking her head, she tried to speak, but all that came out were a few soft moans.

"It's okay. Cry it out. This is one of the few times in your life that you can bawl like a baby and people will understand—or at least think they do."

She took Eve's advice and didn't hold back. Eve sat silent, speaking compassion without words. Lisa didn't know how long it took, or if she even cried "it" out. When the tears ceased to roll down her cheeks, was it more from exhaustion or lack of resources? When she was able to speak again, she could only say, "I don't deserve this."

She didn't deserve Eve's kindness or money. Then again, she didn't deserve her parents' condemnation or being deserted by Mitchell. When she was younger, she'd imagined a thousand different scenarios of what it would be like to be grown up. This was not one of them.

"We all deserve death. God gives us life. It's the story of the ages." Eve sat back again, biting her lip. "I'm sorry. It's the truth, but sometimes I go into preaching mode when I need to listen."

"No, it's okay." Lisa wiped her cheeks with the back of her hands. "I was raised in church. I've heard it all before."

"What does that mean exactly? Raised in church?" She lifted a brow.

"My family went to church every Sunday, sometimes more. They taught me all the Bible stories. Genesis, Exodus, Leviticus, Numbers, Deuteronomy, Joshua, Judges, First Samuel . . . Old and New Testaments."

Eve smiled. "That's an impressive list. But let me ask you this—which Bible story has meant the most to you in your life? Or what verse?"

"What do you mean? I know all of them." It was only a slight exaggeration.

Eve flipped the footrest down with a thunk and sat forward. "Which one has touched your heart the most? If you had to only pick one passage of the Bible, which one has moved you the closest to the Lord?"

What was Eve was getting at? "I don't know. I like the story of Moses, all of it. From the baby in the basket to the miracles in Egypt to the journey in the desert."

Eve's eyes brightened. "Maybe you're carrying a Moses."

"I thought you're convinced it's a girl."

"Gender has nothing to do with it. The midwives were supposed to kill all the Hebrew baby boys. They had a death assignment, but they refused. There were repercussions for them, too. But they cared more about what God thought than what Pharoah did, and they didn't let fear of what would happen to them stop them. Moses should never have been able to live. Yet he did and went on to be God's agent as a deliverer of an entire nation." Eve's eyes implored Lisa. "Your baby was appointed to die that day, but you chose life. Maybe this little girl squirming inside you will grow up to deliver our nation from spiritual slavery."

"You think big." Lisa's mouth twitched. Here she was trying to figure out how to tough it through the rest of her pregnancy when Eve had grand ideas for the little one's future.

"I have a big God." She sat back. "I can't help it."

Comfortable quiet enveloped them. For that brief amount of time, Lisa let her mind wander. What would the baby look like? What would her voice sound like? What toys would she like to play with? Not as profound as delivering a nation, but it was the farthest she'd ever thought ahead. Hard to imagine.

Eve's voice broke into her thoughts. "You don't have to answer this right away, but I was wondering how involved you would like to be with your child. Do you want to visit her, or are you planning on going on with your life?"

Her eyes snapped to Eve's face. She wouldn't be the one making such a decision, would she? Surely Eve wouldn't want her dabbling in her adopted daughter's life. That seemed awkward on many levels.

"I don't know."

"Like I said, you don't have to answer that right now. It's something to think about. I don't want to pressure you into anything either way, but I want you to know that ball is in your court."

"Wouldn't it be awkward? Like we'd be stepping on each other's toes?"

"It could very well be. Or it could come naturally. I don't know. I haven't done this before." She let out a soft laugh. "All I know is that this baby will have two mothers, and she deserves to have a relationship with both of them if you're up to it."

"I'll have to think about it." The immensity of the decisions overwhelmed her. Eve had helped her decide what doctor to go to, which had been her biggest concern. Now that decision paled compared to what loomed before her now.

Chapter 14: Lisa

Eve braced her hands on the recliner's armrests. "You have time on that one, but you'll need to think about getting to your class about now."

Lisa glanced at the clock. Forty-five minutes had passed? As Eve lifted herself out of the recliner, Lisa gathered her books and threw them in her backpack. She ran her fingers through her tangled hair. Her cheeks warmed. She hadn't been taking care of her appearance in the slightest. She walked Eve out the door and thanked her for coming by, for the recommendation for a doctor, and for the money.

"No problem." Eve patted her shoulder. "If I were you, I'd call her either today or tomorrow. She should get you in rather quickly considering you haven't had any prenatal care yet."

Lisa nodded, but her stomach flopped. What could she expect? Would the doctor ask questions? What would she think of her situation? Did she have to know?

As if reading her mind, Eve reassured her as they started down the steps. "The first appointment will be pretty long. They'll draw blood for tests, ask you about your family's medical history, and will probably do an ultrasound since you're far enough along for it. They'll only ask medically relevant questions."

"Okay." Lisa fingered the business card in her pocket. "Thanks for the reference."

She eyed Eve's belly. What would she look like *that* big? It looked so natural on Eve, but Lisa couldn't imagine.

"Call me if you need anything," Eve said breathlessly. "Or even if you just want to talk."

"Okay. I will." But no matter how comfortable she felt with her, she wouldn't call Eve to unburden herself any time soon. Some things were meant to bear alone.

Rushing off to her world literature class, she made a mental to-do list: Study for the big exam. Call the doctor to make an appointment. Start writing the term paper for this class. Get prenatal vitamins. Get sleep. Read the story of Moses again.

Someday maybe she could add another item to her list: dream again—about something other than school and doctor's appointments. That, however, was out of reach for the moment.

Chapter 15: Beth

For four days, Beth pushed away doubts about Trent's true intentions with a perseverance of steel. Although he distanced her from what was truly going on in his heart and mind, she gave him the benefit of the doubt. He'd come around eventually. He couldn't be hiding anything disastrous, like an affair. His tenderness toward her since finding out about the baby testified to that. He was simply dealing with deep, dark emotions. She was accustomed to his moods. This was just a large, gloomy mood.

Today he had taken off work for a few hours to accompany her to her first prenatal appointment. She suggested he deliver their baby, but he insisted this wasn't in their best interest. "I'm too emotionally involved," he'd said. He did, however, insist with as much tenacity that he be intricately involved in the process. He'd chosen her OB and the hospital she would deliver at, and he wanted to attend all her appointments. How sweet that he shielded her with his presence. She'd get the best possible care for sure.

Beth's knee bobbed up and down as she waited to be called back into the examination room. Waiting eight and a half weeks had been long enough. She wanted to hear the baby's heartbeat, to know that everything was okay. Thirty minutes passed, then forty. She read and re-read the parenting magazine on the end table but wouldn't be able to discuss one article in there. Trent sat by her, intermittently holding her hand and reading a newspaper. When the nurse finally called her name, Beth let out a long exhale.

After checking her weight and blood pressure, she had to again wait for the doctor to make it to her room. "This is ridiculous," she told Trent. "Do they always make women wait this long?"

He smiled. "It's because Dr. Yoseph is the best there is, babe. He's high in demand and worth the wait."

"I don't understand why, if I'm not going to be seen until eleven o'clock, they make the appointment at nine-thirty."

He kissed her hand. "Why do you think I requested three hours off? Besides, this is the longest appointment. They'll be a lot quicker from here on out."

When the doctor did finally make his appearance, she forgot her complaints, lost in the myriad of questions. She answered questions about her parents' health and all previous hospitalizations.

"Is this your first pregnancy?" Dr. Yoseph asked.

"Yes."

"No, honey." Trent gave her hand a squeeze. Directing his response to Doctor Yoseph, he continued. "This is her second. She had an abortion previously."

Beth narrowed her eyes at her husband. She could strangle him. How embarrassing.

But the doctor continued with his questions. "Did you have any trouble conceiving this child?"

"Yes," she said. "We tried for two years before going on fertility treatments. We started those six months ago."

"Unfortunately, that's common after an abortion. We'll keep a special eye on this baby. Many women have perfectly normal second pregnancies." He stopped abruptly and began to study her chart.

"What's that supposed to mean?" Fear rose within her.

Trent shot her a pleading look.

"Sometimes women who've had abortions previously have complications. But as I said, many women go on to have perfectly normal pregnancies. No spotting?"

"No."

"Good. I'll go ahead and do a pelvic exam, and then we'll schedule another visit in four weeks." He snapped the folder shut with a tight smile.

"What about hearing the heartbeat?" She bit her lip. Was God going to make her pay for aborting her first baby by taking her second? Not that she'd ever really believed in all of that "judgment of God" garbage people always threw at her husband. Sure, there was a God, but He certainly had better things to do than hover over the human race, ready to lash out at any "indiscretion." No need to alter her life for an almighty distant deity. Still, the constant barrage of stories Trent had told her about protesters' beliefs niggled at her.

The doctor's pale blue eyes were all business. "We'll do that next visit. Most of the time, the baby is too small to hear a heartbeat on the Doppler. Trying to do so can cause undue fear on the part of the mother."

Trent broke in the conversation. "What about an internal ultrasound? Can she have one of those?"

"We only do them for women suffering complications. Your wife is not having any symptoms to make me think it would be necessary." He directed his attention to Beth again. "If you develop any disturbing symptoms or have any questions, please give us a call. Contact us right away if you have any bleeding or cramping."

She frowned but nodded. She had to wait another month for the assurance all was well? Far too long.

"Well then, if that's all of your questions, I'll do a quick pelvic exam and you can be on your way."

Beth pressed her lips together. If she spoke, she'd start to cry.

Chapter 15: Beth

Trent was quiet on the ride home. He seemed lost in a world of thought. Soft rock emanated from the radio so quietly Beth could barely make out the songs. She reached out to turn up the volume but stopped herself.

She needed to draw Trent out. "What are you thinking about?"

"Oh, nothing." He looked at her and smiled, but his eyes remained cloudy. Lines creased his forehead and the edges of his eyes. "I'm sorry, hon. I know you're disappointed about not getting to hear the heartbeat."

"Is he right? About the possibility of complications?" She winced. Did she want to hear the answer?

"Any pregnancy has the risk of complications, babe. They might be a little bit higher for women who've had abortions in the past, but it can happen to anyone. You have no reason to think anything will go wrong. You've got the makings of a great pregnancy." He spoke in the same tone he'd use with a client. As much as Dr. Yoseph's professional distance irritated her, hearing the same tone from her husband was too much.

"Why didn't you tell me?" Her voice teetered between anger and complaint.

"Tell you what?"

"That the abortion could cause problems later on. You kept that from me all these years?"

"I wasn't keeping anything from you. Nothing's really proven. Most women go on to have perfectly normal pregnancies afterwards."

"But he said—"

"He was being overly cautious. That's a doctor's job. You're going to be fine, Beth. This pregnancy is going really well."

"All this time . . . when I couldn't get pregnant, I thought there was something wrong with me. Really, it could have been from the abortion? I can't believe you didn't tell me that was a possibility."

He sighed. "Like I said, nothing's proven. No one's for sure that abortion and infertility are even related, much less that abortion causes it. Relax, babe. You're pregnant and everything's going to be fine."

She fiddled with her seat belt. "Couldn't you do an ultrasound on me?"

He paused. "I guess I could. You could come by the clinic right after we close." His voice wavered, as if he had reservations about the arrangement.

"What's wrong?"

"Nothing's wrong. That should work fine." She couldn't decipher his expression. She changed the subject, lest he retreat into silence again.

"So, you're sure Dr. Yoseph's the best? He didn't seem extraordinary to me."

"I'm sure. He's made quite a name for himself. Give him a chance."

At least words were flowing between them again. She needed to keep him talking. "So, how big is she now?"

Trent grimaced but didn't skip a beat in answering. "She's still only a little bigger than an inch."

"Are you annoyed at me or something?"

His lower lip protruded. "No. I don't know if I have any new information for you, though, hon. It seems like you asked me a few days ago." He made momentary eye contact with her, flashing a slight smile.

"I guess I did. I like hearing it." She almost apologized but stopped herself. She didn't have to be sorry for her excitement.

"The baby has little arms and legs, little fingers and toes. She's got little ears and a little nose. Her heart's divided into four chambers. Now she's got to grow and fill in the fine details." He placed a hand on her leg. There. All was well between them.

She let herself relax for a minute, then another thought disturbed her. “Why did you have to tell him about the abortion?”

He quirked an eyebrow “Are you embarrassed?”

“It doesn’t seem like any of his business. It’s personal.”

“He’s your doctor, Beth. Everything’s his business. It’s important he know it all. Besides, he doesn’t care. He hears it all the time, I’m sure.”

He pulled into their driveway. “Have a good day at work. I’ll see you around five o’clock at the clinic, right?”

“Yeah. I love you.” She leaned over and planted a kiss on his cheek.

“I love you too.” He met her kiss with one of his own, full on the mouth, taking no captives. Her toes curled and warmth spread within her. Smiling, she got out of his car and into her own, reminiscing about that kiss all the way to work. Maybe soon things would be back to normal between them.

***

When Beth pulled into the parking lot of Trent’s clinic, the secretary was pulling out. Trent’s car stood alone in the parking lot. An eerie feeling crept over her. Did Trent’s hesitation have anything to do with being in the building alone? She parked by his car and surveyed the area before getting out. It seemed like she was alone, but a lurking protester could jump out of nowhere.

The door was locked. She knocked and waited a minute, but Trent didn’t come. She knocked louder. Then louder. Every nerve tingled. A couple of Trent’s friends from med school had died when a maniac bombed their clinic. She pounded at the door, heart pounding in her ears. Then she fished her cell phone out of her purse and called him.

“Hi, honey. You here?” His voice came out calm, in stark contrast with her insides.

“Yes, I’m here. I’ve been banging on the door for five minutes.”

“Oh, sorry. I’m in the back. I’ll be right there.”

When the door creaked open and his face popped out, her breath finally slowed.

He cast a gaze in each direction, scanning the parking lot, then closed and locked the door behind him.

“Come back here.” He motioned for her to follow him.

Beth had never been inside the clinic before. She glanced in all the rooms on her way down the hall. Tables with stirrups. Rolling stools. Much like the doctor’s office she’d been in earlier. It was so quiet; her shoes made thunderous sounds as she walked.

“In here.” Trent nodded towards a small room with a similar setup.

“Thank you, doctor.” Her smile trembled with the release of adrenaline moments before.

“I won’t make you wear a paper gown, unless you want to for fashion’s sake.” He went to the other side of the room and wheeled the machine forward. “I don’t normally do these, but I remember how it works. It’ll give us a good listen to the heartbeat.”

A couple minutes later they saw their child on the monitor. Beth squinted, then let out a breathy laugh. A pulsating bulge. A miniature heart? Trent turned up the volume and it sounded like horses racing to a finish line. Glorious.

“Is everything all right?” She propped up on her elbow. “It seems to be awfully fast.”

“One hundred and seventy beats per minute. Perfect.” His face shone, and for a moment she forgot the fog that had recently landed between them. They grinned at each other, immersed in the sound of the life they had created together.

Chapter 15: Beth

"So, everything's all right?"

"Everything's great. That's it. Let me clean this up and shut 'er down, and we can get out of here."

While Trent cleaned up, Beth put her pants back on and wandered down the hall. She came to a door on her left with Trent's nameplate on it.

"Is this your office?" she shouted down the hall.

"Yep."

Leaning inside, she turned on the light. Towers of neatly stacked papers graced his desk, everything in its place. No surprise there. She plopped into the chair behind his desk and opened his middle drawer. Immaculate. She started to close it when a letter peeking out from behind a manila envelope caught her eye. Neatly handwritten. Definitely not Trent's writing. The sure sign of a female.

She sat quiet for a moment, listening to make sure Trent was still at work in the room. Then, extracting the letter, she held it low in her lap and read.

Dear Trent,

It's Eve. I'm sure you remember me. I wanted to jot you a note to let you know my phone number in case you need anything. I know we didn't leave things well, but I'm hoping you're considering altering your career choice and going forward into the dreams I know God has put on your heart. If you returned to work, I have no doubt you've been unsettled. You know it's not the right place for you to be. If you need anything—prayer . . . anything—call me.

Truly,

Eve

Beth glanced at the number on the bottom of the letter. It was from a local area code. Her hands shook as she read the letter again. She couldn't make sense of it. Who was this woman? Where had Trent met her? She'd been so sure he wasn't having an affair. Now, though it didn't seem like affair material, the personal tone of the letter disturbed her.

Footsteps sounded down the hall. What should she do? Hide the letter or confront him? Did she want to know the truth? Was it worth erecting more walls between them? He reached the room before she could decide.

"I'm ready when you are." He poked his head around the door.

She stared at him, mouth parted.

"What's wrong?" Coming closer, his gaze landed on the letter in her hand. "Can you believe the nerve of that lady? First she stalks me in a restaurant, then she stalks me at the lake. Now she's writing me letters telling me to call her for prayer." He shook his head as if it was ludicrous, but his eyes held agitation.

"Who is she?" Beth's voice wavered as her gaze dropped.

"Remember I told you about that pregnant protester who followed me from the clinic to the lake that day I wasn't feeling well?"

"Yes, I remember."

He flung an arm in the letter's direction. "She evidently didn't intend to stop there."

"What does she mean about changing your career?" She kept her voice quiet. Things between them were too fragile to risk breaking them with loud words.

"She wanted me to quit the clinic and find other work. I told you she was a protester." He sounded defensive, speaking too quickly.

"I'm trying to make sense of this. It sounds like you had a conversation with her." And this mystery woman knew more about what had been going on in her husband's heart than she did.

"If you can call that a conversation. Most of it was me trying to convince her to leave. She wouldn't budge until I threatened to call the police."

"Do you want to change your career?" She fixed her eyes on the mystery woman's neat penmanship, not ready to meet his gaze.

"Now why would I want to do that? I'm making a great living here helping women get on with their lives." His voice trembled slightly. If she had been in a rage, she might have missed it.

"And you have no reservations?"

"No, honey. She's trying to plant ideas in my head, is all. She probably thinks the world would be a better place if the only abortions going on were behind the scenes, illegal and unsafe."

Beth nodded. That made sense. Different people used different tactics. Some tried to yell doctors like her husband into guilt. Others tried more subtle manipulation.

"Are you going to call her?" She folded the letter.

"What? No. Why would you ask that?"

"You kept the letter." She forced herself to look at him.

He hesitated, shaking his head. "Evidence, honey. In case I need to get a restraining order. I wasn't going to do anything about it. The woman's pregnant and looks as if she's due any day. It's not like she's a threat to my safety or anything. But if she doesn't leave me alone, I will have to call the police."

She nodded again. She couldn't argue with his logic. Still, it seemed there was something he wasn't telling her. Maybe not something hidden about his relationship with Eve, but rather something deep in his heart that disturbed him. The same thing that had driven him to that bar.

She glanced at the number one last time, committing it to memory, then placed the letter back into his desk. "I'm ready to go."

As she stood, he came and put his arms around her.

"You knew when you agreed to marry me I wasn't going into a hassle-free profession, yet you've stood by me, supporting me all these years. I'm so glad I have you with me to weather all these situations." He kissed her hair and handed her a picture. "There's our little bean." He pointed to the black and white sonogram photo and smiled slightly. It did indeed look like a bean, only with tiny extremities.

"Amazing."

They walked out to their cars arm in arm. She pressed as close as she could to him. If only she could get closer, into his heart. Hopefully he would choose to open up to her soon.

Chapter 16: Lisa

Lisa entered the crowded Italian bistro to find her friend already seated. Britney's hair had grown out since high school but remained unconventionally spikey. Colorful tattoos covered both arms and her nose ring glinted under the overhead light. She still stood out in a crowd.

No wonder Lisa's parents had never approved of her. Mother had nearly choked when she found out the girls had both gotten into Markley and wanted to room together in the dorms. *That* was a hard no. But Lisa hadn't minded the apartment Mother footed. It made certain kinds of fun even easier. Her stomach rolled at the thought.

She needed to focus on why she was here. To salvage this friendship. Was that dramatic? Maybe she'd imagined the distance growing between them since her pregnancy announcement. Britney's suddenly busy schedule could be a coincidence.

"Hey, Brit." Lisa's smile trembled.

"Hey. How've you been?" The corner of Brittany's mouth twitched. Maybe this wasn't a good idea after all.

"Okay, I guess." She replied without thinking. How honest should she be?

"You're . . . showing." Britney motioned to her bulge, eyebrows raised.

"Yeah. It's getting hard to hide now."

"I guess so. You look tired."

"I am. I haven't been sleeping well."

Chapter 16: Lisa

The waitress came by to take their drink orders. As she bustled away, Britney said, "I wouldn't be able to sleep either. It would freak me out to have something growing inside me."

Lisa's mouth parted. What should she say to that?

Britney waved a hand in front of her. "Sorry. That the mommy thing isn't for me."

"It's not really for me either. I kind of got thrown into it, I guess."

"You don't think you'll keep it, do you?"

Lisa shook her head. "No. I told you I'm giving it to Eve."

"Well, you know." She shrugged. "People change their minds about those kinds of things. It's not going to be easy."

"Believe me, I have no intention of keeping it. I have a life to get on with, and I wouldn't know the first thing about taking care of a baby. I don't think I'm built for it. I'm not oohing and ahhing over each little development. I don't feel that bond mothers are supposed to have. It's like I'm sitting on another bird's egg." But she could feel that bond if she let herself. Couldn't she? Wouldn't she?

The waitress stopped by, placing iced teas before them in a flash and flapping out her order pad. Since she'd offered to pay this time around, when Britney opted for the shrimp, Lisa ordered a chef's salad out of limited resources. She shouldn't really be splurging on lunch out; this friendship mattered.

"I guess I always pictured you having a bunch of little brats running around your heels. I think it'd suit you," Britney said.

"Maybe someday. I'm too young. A few years and a husband would probably change things." She sighed. "But who knows? I haven't gotten anything figured out anymore."

"So, is it a boy or a girl?" Britney swirled three packets of sugar into her tea with her straw, concentrating on the tornado-like motion.

"I don't know yet. I'm supposed to go to the doctor soon. Eve gave me money for it and everything. I guess I need to make an appointment." She bit her lip to keep from begging Britney to come with her. She couldn't picture dragging her friend into an OB office, no matter how close they'd been in the past.

"Make the appointment then."

"I know I need to." Lisa clenched her hands in her lap.

"Then do it."

"It's just . . . I'm kind of paranoid about doctors now. Ever since . . . you know. I'm scared to death."

"But this is different. For one, it's legal and safe. It's a doctor's office, not a backwoods trailer."

"He was cheap. And Jim's friend."

"I don't care." Britney pointed a finger at her. "That was idiotic. Women don't have to do those kinds of things anymore—not when it's perfectly legal to go to a clean, safe clinic."

"I don't want to talk about it." Lisa's voice came out harsh. What kind of repercussions would such a conversation have when she lay in bed? Images of what had happened in that trailer consumed her dreams most nights. She'd told Britney about her nightmares once, but she didn't want to talk about them again.

"Apparently there are a lot of things you don't want to talk about anymore," Britney muttered.

"What's that supposed to mean?"

"I'm having a hard time with the fact you kept this from me for three and a half months." She looked down again, seemingly fascinated with making fingerprints on her glass.

"Is that why you've been distant lately? Because I didn't tell you?" Lisa kept her voice soft, but underneath she seethed. Britney had no idea what she'd been through.

"Distant?"

"Yes, distant."

Britney quieted as well. After a couple moments, she met Lisa's gaze. "I don't know. I guess it hit too close to home.

What if it were me? What would I do? I mean, your nightmares are enough to make me want to steer clear of having an abortion, but I don't think I could do anything else. I've been with so many guys, so many more than you have. Why you and not me?"

"You're on the pill."

"Jenny was on the pill too. She still got pregnant."

"She probably was too drunk to remember to take it. It's nearly foolproof." Lisa tried to reassure her friend, but the question took root in her mind. Why her?

"Well, what about Tracy? She was on the shot and still got pregnant."

"Okay, so maybe nothing's foolproof. But you're careful. You should be okay."

"Can I ask you a question?" Britney said after a moment.

"Shoot."

"Why weren't you on something?"

She brushed imaginary crumbs off the table. "I don't know for sure. It took my mom seven years of trying and multiple treatments before she got pregnant with me. After hearing that story over and over again, I guess it seeped into my conscious that getting pregnant was hard to do. It never occurred to me that it would happen to me. Then . . . well, then I never wanted to set foot in another doctor's office for the rest of my life."

Britney twirled her straw around. "I'm sorry to break it to you, but you're going to be seeing a lot of your doctor in these next couple months."

"I know. I'm just afraid to face it."

"Why don't you ask Eve to go with you? She started this whole thing."

Lisa scrunched up her nose. "I'd feel strange doing that. She's already done so much for me."

"Just an idea."

Their food came then, and their conversation dwindled to American history and modern psychology. Britney complained of tough coursework, but Lisa knew better. Britney was soaring through, acing her classes, and becoming the favorite of all her teachers. Meanwhile Lisa, who had always beat her out in the grades department, struggled to pass.

Her cheeks warmed. She couldn't tell her friend this. If she hadn't gotten herself into this mess, she'd be in the same state as Britney—unburdened by finals that wouldn't hurt and couldn't much help an already-thriving GPA. And she wouldn't have to worry about losing her scholarship.

"You really should ask her, you know." Britney's voice broke through Lisa's thoughts.

"Ask who?" Hadn't they had just finished speculating on whether two biology professors had a thing for each other?

"Eve."

She fiddled with her napkin. "I don't know about that. I already feel like I'm asking too much of her."

"Asking too much of her?" Britney's eyebrows rose to an unearthly level. "What about what she's asking of you? She's asking you to bear her child for nine months, go through horrendous labor, and then hand it over and pretend like nothing ever happened. The way I figure it, you've got the right to ask a few things in return."

"First of all, I forbid you to use the term 'horrendous labor.' Secondly, she's giving me the option of staying involved with the baby." The waitress returned to drop off the check. Lisa tried not to gasp when she saw the total.

"What do you mean 'stay involved'?" Apparently, Britney was oblivious to the fact that the price of her shrimp meant Lisa would dine on ramen noodles for the next week.

"She said I should consider how involved I want to be. I guess I could choose to visit and see her if I wanted to. Or I could leave her be." Her mind hurt from thinking about such momentous decisions.

Britney's brows shot up. "That's weird."

"It could be weird."

"Could be? Come on, Lisa. You'd see your little girl or boy, who looks like you, and take her to the zoo? Only you couldn't discipline her and wouldn't have any authority over her. You'd have to ask Eve permission to see your own child. What would you say when the kid would start to ask questions? 'Why don't I live with you, Mom?' Could she call you 'Mom'? Eve would be her mom. What would she call you? 'Ms.'?"

"I don't know what to think. I guess there are plenty of people who do it."

"Well, you wouldn't catch me doing it, is all I'm saying. You've got to make up your mind. Is she going to be your kid or Eve's? She can't be both."

Lisa didn't reply. What could she say? Britney had a point, but she also didn't want her child to turn eighteen, track her down and vent her anger that she'd never known her birth mother. She'd read about such encounters in magazines and trembled at the thought of a now-grown child asking, "Didn't you love me?" How was a mother supposed to answer such questions? She didn't know which way to move to avoid regret.

"Anyway, call Eve, would you? Tell her you're nervous about going to the doctor and you'd appreciate it if she could come to the first appointment with you. She might even be honored."

"I'll think about it." The waitress came back with the credit card receipt, and she signed it, mentally wincing at the amount. "We'd better get off to class."

"Yeah. It's my last human anatomy class. I might throw a party after the final."

"I'll come as long as there's something non-alcoholic to drink," Lisa said with a smile.

"Sure. I'll supply chocolate milk especially for you and Junior." Britney smiled back, and for a moment, it was if nothing had changed. "Hey, Lisa, I'm sorry for being such a jerk. I know you'd stick by me if I was in your situation. I shouldn't have bailed like I did."

"No worries." Their walk slowed as they neared the door, as if neither wanted to part.

After she left, Lisa debated whether she could fit in a quick phone call before her class. Stomach quivering, she opted to wait until after. Her procrastination distracted her during the final review.

She was daydreaming when the class let out, the rustle of papers around her alerting her to their release. She slid her book into her backpack and headed toward the door. One of her classmates stopped her before she could leave.

"Oh, I didn't know you were pregnant!" the girl cried.

"Yep. I am," Lisa's gaze shifted toward the hallway.

"That's great! I'm pregnant too. I'm not showing yet, of course. I'm only seven weeks along. My name is Debi." She thrust her hand out for Lisa to shake.

"I'm Lisa." She shook Debi's hand, keeping one eye on the door.

"It's great to meet you. My fiancé and I are thrilled to be having a baby. He's excited—really he is—but he can't understand like another *woman* can, you know? So I saw you and thought, there's a gal who can understand."

Lisa nodded, though if this nearly-married girl was looking for a sympathetic ear, she needed to look elsewhere.

"Maybe we could do lunch sometime?" Debi continued. "I found this great buffet. I usually don't like buffets, but I'm telling you this one is good. Since we're eating for two, we might as well go to an all-you-can-eat place, you know?"

"Maybe we can do that. Right now, though, I've really got to go. I'll see you Friday." Lisa smiled and made her escape.

Chapter 16: Lisa

"Okay, see you Friday, Lisa!" Ms. Perky (soon to be Mrs. Perky?) called down the hall.

Lisa turned and offered a slight wave. Picking up her pace, she made her way towards her apartment with one hand on the cell phone in her pocket. Once safely inside, she took a deep breath, flipped open her phone and dialed. If she put it off any longer, she might not do it at all.

Eve answered on the second ring.

"Hi, Eve. It's Lisa. I had a question." Her voice trembled and her hands shook.

"What can I do for you?" Eve asked in her typical, friendly way.

"I was . . . u-uh w-wondering if you might . . . if you might want to c-come to the doctor with me? I kind of have a thing about doctors—"

"Well, let's see. When is your appointment?"

A slight rustling in the background signaled the pages of a calendar or daily planner.

"Well, y-you see," Lisa stammered, "I haven't m-made an appointment yet." She struggled to find justification but, finding none, let her silence do the talking.

"Oh, I see. I'm busy Thursday and Friday morning, as well as next Wednesday afternoon. Other than that, I think I could swing it. Why don't you call me and let me know when your appointment is?"

Lisa stared at the phone for a moment, trying to decipher the tone of Eve's voice. It sounded . . . normal, as if Lisa had made a perfectly reasonable request and not imposed one too many times on Eve's kindness.

"Are you sure?" she asked. "It's not an inconvenience?"

"You're a person, Lisa. Not an inconvenience. Besides, we've got to get my baby to the doctor, don't we? I told you I'd help any way I can."

Something in Lisa stirred at Eve's declaration of possession over her womb. She wasn't offended but felt awkward, as if caught with stolen goods.

"You're not curious as to why?" she asked, almost to herself.

"I told you I wouldn't push. I figure when you're ready to talk, you will."

But she wouldn't. She vowed it. The shadows she saw in her dreams were too dark for Eve's happy little world.

"I'll give them a call, then call you back."

After they hung up, Lisa stared at her phone a few minutes longer, wondering at what a woman like Eve was made of. Had Lisa ever done anything out of unselfish motives in her life? Her lips twisted as she dialed the number to the doctor.

"Hello, Complete Women's Obstetrics and Gynecology. How may I help you?" The voice on the other end sounded efficient and businesslike, making her stomach turn yet again in a nervous twitch.

"Yes, I'd like to make an appointment." She tried to sound confident.

"Are you a returning or new patient?" The woman asked this as if it was the hundredth time she had asked the question that day. To her, Lisa was probably another incoming call.

"A new patient."

"Which doctor would you like to see?"

She fumbled to pick up the business card off the kitchen table. "Uh, Dr. Rosa?"

"What insurance do you have?"

"I don't have any insurance." Shame coated her words.

"You'll be paying out of pocket then?" the receptionist asked. As if there was another option.

"Yes."

"The first available appointment is Friday at one o'clock."

Panic coated the back of her throat. "I can't do that. I have a final."

Chapter 16: Lisa

"The next available appointment is Tuesday at one o'clock."

Lisa did a quick inventory of her finals schedule. She had Tuesday afternoon free. Her stomach unclenched.

"Yes. That will work."

"May I have your name, number, and address?"

She recited her information, breath steadying. Good for her. She made the call. She voluntarily offered to go see a doctor. Now all she had to do was drag herself there.

"Okay, Ms. McCuly, I have you down for Tuesday at one. Please call at least twenty-four hours in advance if you need to cancel or reschedule."

She clicked her phone off and sank into the couch cushions, the tension of the day pulling on every ligament and muscle. "This is why a prego needs a husband," she mumbled to herself. "To give her a massage if nothing else."

After calling Eve back, she leaned against her bathroom door jam. Should she take a bath? Nope. Too exhausted. She didn't have the energy to make it to the tub, much less lug herself out of it. She laid her head on the couch's stiff throw pillow adorning, and she drifted off into a dreamland complete with unfeeling receptionists, perky redheads, and chef salads.

The dream that was strangely missing was the one that had become so familiar—she could play it over and over again in her head like a favorite movie. That evening, there were no men in white coats. There were no babies being torn limb from limb. There was no screaming, no blood, no tears. It seemed that the only way to dissipate the doctor of her dreams was to make strides to replace him with a new one—a doctor who would deliver this baby alive.

Chapter 17: Ashira

"Woman! Wake!"

Ashira lifted her head, blinking back the haze of sleep. Where was she?

"You shouldn't be here. It's not safe." A man's voice, low and measured.

Her muscles tensed, readying to flee, but then the undercurrent of care in his tone settled over her.

"I have nowhere to go," she said, squinting to make out his features in the flicker of lantern light. A dark, neatly trimmed beard. A narrow nose rising between two small, nervous eyes. How foolish of her to leave the security of her home.

"Come with me."

She had no better options than to follow the tall figure around the bend and into a small stone house. She slipped her sandals off before stepping over the threshold. Once inside, he turned to her and said, "I'm Josiah. My wife is Rizpah. She is asleep, but she will attend to you in the morning. You may stay the night on the mat in the corner."

"Thank you."

He said no more and turned into the far room. Latticework covered the two small windows behind her, blocking out even the minute sliver of moonlight. Only a candle flickered on the table in the center of the room. Her back and neck ached from the journey and from sleeping in a hunched over.

Chapter 17: Ashira

She slid her bag to the floor and stretched her stiff limbs. The house smelled like leather and yeast. She tiptoed over the cold floor to blow out the candle, then let her eyes adjust to the darkness. When her feet found the mat, she dropped to the floor and pulled the flax blanket over her, not caring how hard the floor was beneath her. Sleep found her easily, despite the unfamiliar surroundings.

She awakened to the sun and to the clanging of pots. A petite woman worked in the kitchen, long hair hanging loose around her shoulders.

"Hello?" Ashira's voice came forth timid, so ashamed was she of her presence in the stranger's home.

"Hello." The woman glanced at her. "I regret I do not have much to fix for you. In days past, I was known for supplying a feast to whoever might pass our way. Now, though, we do not have much to offer."

"I understand." Ashira pulled her heavy woolen abayah snug around herself.

"Josiah said you were sleeping on the street corner."

She nodded. "I arrived in Jerusalem last night and had nowhere to go."

"And why, might I ask?"

"I was fleeing from my husband."

Thank goodness she didn't ask why. No telling whether Rizpah's allegiance was to Molech, Baal, or the God of their Ancestors. It was not uncommon to pledge allegiance to all three and more.

"What are your plans?"

"I do not know. I only wish to hear Jeremiah. Perhaps then I will understand what I am to do." Ashira stood and tidied the blanket on top of her mat.

"Jeremiah the prophet?"

"Yes."

She scoffed. "He prophesies nothing good for us, only death and destruction. I do not understand why anyone would wish to hear those words. Listen to Hananiah instead. He speaks well for us."

"But what if Jeremiah's words are truth? Shouldn't we give ear, even if they are unpleasant?" She ran a hand through her hair and twisted it into a braid, then quickly replaced her head covering.

"You go and listen if you would like. I can show you the way. Only I will not give heed to his words nor be seen amid the crowd. There are those who would have him killed. Go and listen if you will." Rizpah waved a hand as if to shoo Ashira off. "You may return tonight if you have need."

Some who would have him killed. Like her own husband. Ashira thanked her and ate the small barley cake Rizpah offered. It was not enough to fill her, but the sweet taste satiated her craving after the tiresome journey.

Rizpah asked not her name, and Ashira did not offer it. In her position, it was better to be unknown. She walked with her host to the market in silence. Around them, donkeys brayed, vendors shouted their wares, and buyers haggled. Rich spices mingled together—hyssop, basil, and thyme. They passed booths with exquisite pottery, with goat cheeses and olive oil, with various household gods.

"Walk that way a little." Rizpah motioned to her right. "He will be there, speaking to the few who will listen. Can you find your way back?"

"I believe so." Ashira followed the path Rizpah had shown her, peeking through the sea of people and straining to hear the voice of a prophet amongst the marketplace chatter. How would she find him if there was not a crowd? She was not used to such commotion, to the daily life of the city. If only she were taller so she could see more clearly. If Reuben were here, towering over the crowd, he would have no trouble finding the man. Only if Reuben were here, she would not want him to find the prophet!

Finally, she spotted a man standing on the street corner, surrounded by a small crowd. If she had never seen the man before, she might have continued walking, convinced he could not be a person of importance. But she recognized his unkempt hair and fiery expression. Whereas the other prophets wore fine apparel, linen or even silk, Jeremiah wore only a plain woolen simlăh. The rough material crudely sewn together protected him from the elements but did little to elevate his prestige in the eyes of the villagers. His voice, however, rung with authority. Ashira stood on the outskirts of the small crowd, curious and eager to hear what he had to say.

"This is the word of the Lord that came to me concerning the droughts," the prophet proclaimed. "Judah mourns, and her gates languish; They mourn for the land, and the cry of Jerusalem has gone up. Their nobles have sent their lads for water; they went to the cisterns and found no water. They returned with their vessels empty; they were ashamed and confounded and covered their heads. Because the ground is parched, for there was no rain in the land. The plowmen were ashamed; they covered their heads. Yes, the deer also gave birth in the field, but left because there was no grass. And the wild donkeys stood in the desolate heights. They sniffed at the wind like jackals; their eyes failed because there was no grass."

"It is true," she mumbled to herself. No matter what others said, his words were true. The other prophets spoke of hope, but she could see no hope. She wanted to believe good was on the horizon—but to what end?

"What of the other prophets?" a man close to the front shouted. "They say 'You shall not see the sword, nor shall you have famine, but the Lord will give you assured peace in this place.'"

"Ah, but the Lord says, 'The prophets prophesy lies in My name. I have not sent them, commanded them, nor spoken to them; they prophesy to you a false vision, divination, a worthless thing, and the deceit of their heart. Therefore, thus says the Lord concerning the prophets who prophesy in My name, whom I did not send, and who say sword and famine shall not be in the land, but by sword and famine those prophets shall be consumed.'"

At this, the crowd erupted. Shouts of blasphemy flew forth among much jeering and arguing.

Jeremiah's words rose above the din. "Let my eyes flow with tears night and day, and let them not cease for the virgin daughter of my people has been broken with a mighty stroke, with a very severe blow. If I go out to the field, then behold, those slain with the sword. And if I enter the city, then behold, those sick from famine! Yes, both a prophet and priest go about in a land they do not know."

Ashira shuddered at his words, for indeed they were of doom. Had famine only begun to touch their land? Would things indeed get worse? What of those slain with the sword? And what did he mean the prophets and priests would go about in a land they did not know? Certainly, the fate of Judah would differ from the fate of the Northern Kingdom. Israel had gone into exile, but Jerusalem would not be taken, would it? It was God's own city and contained His holy temple. Surely God would not forsake His own.

Jeremiah continued speaking despite the murmuring of the crowd. Men whispered to one another, faces radiating pride and superiority. A few women huddled to one side, their eyes wide with worry.

"Thus says the Lord, 'Behold, I am fashioning disaster and devising a plan against you. Return now every one from his evil way, and make your ways and doings good.'"

His voice came as a mournful cry, a desperate begging. Return, he'd said. Surely there was hope if they would return to the God of their ancestors, the God of Abraham, Isaac and Jacob. If only they would tear down their idols, cease their sacrifices to gods made by human hands, and follow the laws of the God who had led them out of Egypt, He would relent. A glimmer of hope coursed through her. Yes, the prophet spoke doom, but it was avoidable doom. If only . . .

The murmur of the crowd escalated into a roar. Men argued with their neighbors, some threatening to stone Jeremiah. She took a few steps back to distance herself from their response.

"That is hopeless!" The man next to her shouted above the commotion. "So we will walk according to our own plans, and we will every one obey the dictates of his *evil* heart." He laughed as he said so, as if it was improbable that his heart be evil.

Bile rose in Ashira's throat. The prophet called for everyone to repent, but she was powerless to control the reactions of the crowd. She could not make them turn and could not avoid the terror of which Jeremiah spoke.

Fresh tears stung her eyes. She turned and rushed away from the crowd's rebellion. She needed to be set apart from them, had to avert impending judgment.

Though they would not turn, she would. *O Lord. I will repent and walk righteously. No longer will I burn incense to idols. No longer will I look to gods of stone for deliverance. I will look to You.* But what should she do? Return to her husband?

She spent the afternoon praying and walking about the city, keeping alert for Reuben. There were booths filled with carved idols. Despite the famine and poverty, people continued to buy the abominations. They would rather starve bowing down to wood and stone than repent and live. Indeed, the hearts of mankind were evil, their intentions impure. *Oh, Messiah! When will You come and deliver?*

Chapter 18: Eve

I rushed into the doctor's office at ten past one in a frenzy. Quickly scanning the seats, I spotted Lisa clutching the arms of a chair, wide-eyed and white-knuckled.

"I'm *so* sorry. I can't believe I'm late."

She moved a magazine off the chair next to her, motioning for me to sit.

"I can't believe I'm here," she muttered.

"Well, I'm glad we both made it." I smiled at her to ease the tension that drew visible lines on her forehead.

"I almost left when I saw you weren't here." Her voice had an odd edge to it, as if she were upset at something other than my tardiness. What was that reaction about? One moment Lisa would be closed-off and wary, hiding behind sardonic humor; the next moment she was pitifully grateful for a kindness and vulnerable. I tried to be patient and understanding, putting myself in her place, only it was hard to understand where she was coming from. *Lord, I can't do this in my own strength.*

"I'm sorry," I repeated.

"Where were you?"

"At the clinic. I meant to leave early, but I got the opportunity to pray with this woman and I lost track of time."

"At the clinic? That's a regular thing for you, then? Are you looking for another baby in case this one doesn't work out?" She smirked.

"Yes, it's a regular thing. Our church prays there every morning, Monday through Friday. I try to go at least three times a week. And no, I'm not going to scout out another baby. I think two will keep my hands full for a while." I kept my voice level. Best not to get defensive. Whatever wounds this girl had festering inside her, my sarcasm wouldn't heal them.

"Why do you do it then? Why were you there that day?"

"I go to pray. It's as simple as that. I pray for every woman going inside those doors, and for the doctors and nurses as well. What's that?" I motioned to the clipboard on her lap.

"It's only paperwork. Pray for what?"

"Pray for life. Did you already fill it out?"

"Some of it. I guess I'm a little overwhelmed." She shrugged, as if the forms on the clipboard in front of her were optional.

"Well, finish the forms first. We can talk about the prayer later."

She sighed and picked up her pen. Painstakingly, she completed the top portion, filling in her name and date of birth and writing "none" in the insurance portion. "That's one good thing about being uninsured." She cast a sarcastic glance my way. "Less to fill out."

Five minutes passed and she was still only a third of the way through the page. She shot me a pained expression.

"Do you want me to help you with that?" I asked.

"It's so much . . . information. I d-don't . . . " she stammered.

"Here." I took the clipboard from her. "I'll ask you the questions and you tell me the answers."

She nodded and sat back in her chair.

"This page is all about medical history. Do you know any history of medical conditions in your family? Heart problems, respiratory problems, cancer, anything like that?"

"I don't think so. My grandma had emphysema, but she smoked a lot."

"Anything else?" I asked scanning the page.

"No. I can't remember my parents ever being sick. I think they're immune."

"See, we're halfway done with this page already." I checked "no" on all but one box. "No asthma, right?"

"Nope."

"Okay, what about the father? Do you know any of his medical history?"

"How would I know?" she asked with a sneer.

"Do you remember him mentioning anything about his parents being sick or anything?"

"Mitchell didn't talk about his family—ever. He spent most of his childhood in and out of foster care."

"Okay. I'll write 'unknown' here then. No big deal," I said.

Apprehension radiated from her.

"Have you had any complications during this pregnancy?" I looked over the next page.

"I don't think so."

"No bleeding?"

"No. Nothing like that." She looked off into empty space.

"We're almost done. This asks about previous pregnancies—"

"Lisa," the nurse interrupted. Lisa and I both sat up with a start.

"The nurse or doctor will probably finish this with you," I whispered, handing her the clipboard. We stood and followed the nurse down the hall to the scale.

"Eve, I was surprised to see you out there. Who's this?" The nurse turned to regard both of our faces, puzzlement creasing her forehead. I couldn't quite remember her name. Susan, perhaps?

"No, Lisa's a good friend of mine."

Lisa's head snapped in my direction, making it clear—though not rudely—that this assessment of our relationship surprised her.

"Oh, good. That's nice of you to come along. Let me get your weight, Lisa. My name is Sandra, by the way."

Lisa limply shook her outstretched hand.

As the nurse checked Lisa's weight and blood pressure, her body stiffened even more. Why did such routine procedures unnerve her? I'd eagerly anticipated my first OB appointment, and here Lisa was looking pale and faint with fear at hers. *Lord, I don't get it. What else is going on with her? She won't talk to me, won't open up. How am I supposed to help her?*

"Your blood pressure looks good. Dr. Rosa will be in soon." With that, the nurse left, the door closing a bit too loudly behind her.

Lisa kicked her heels against the bottom of the exam table. I sat in the hardback chair next to the table and scoured my mind for something comforting to say.

"I really like Dr. Rosa. I know not all of her staff is extremely friendly, but she's wonderful."

My attempt was met with silence, besides the *bang* of her shoes hitting the table. Okay. I'd try again.

"So, you know that I think it's a girl, but what do you think? Do you have an inclination either way?" Hopefully they'd do an ultrasound, and I'd get to see the gender firsthand.

"I've been going with what you said. You seem so sure." She didn't make eye contact.

"I really think so, but then again, God has a sense of humor. He's got a way of surprising us."

Silence again. She bit her lip and looked as if she was about to cry.

"Was it something I said?"

She shook her head.

"You really don't like doctors, do you?" I put a hand on her shoulder, and she shuddered.

"That's the understatement of the century."

"For how long?" I asked, as the Lord stirred compassion in my heart.

"Ever since—" She stopped herself. "For a year or so," she whispered. She grabbed a magazine. Apparently, she had no interest in continuing the conversation. As she skimmed it, I said a silent prayer for her emotional healing. How could I get her to open up to me?

"Hey, this article is on adoption," she said a few minutes later.

"Oh, really? What's it say?"

"It's about this lady who adopted a baby from Korea. She seems pretty happy with her decision," she said dispassionately. What an odd comment. It was as if she placed adopting a baby in the same category as buying a product from a store. Like there were customer satisfaction ratings. She continued to read, and I continued to pray. It wasn't too much longer before a faint knock sounded at the door.

Dr. Rosa came in. "Hello, Lisa, I'm Dr. Rosa."

Lisa lifted wide eyes but didn't reach out a hand.

"Hi, Eve. It's nice to see you as well."

I smiled and nodded, keeping an eye on Lisa.

"Okay, let's see here." The doctor flipped between the paperwork and her chart. "When was your last menstrual period?"

"I . . . uh . . . don't know. I didn't have one . . . for a while."

"Your periods are irregular then?"

"Uh . . . yeah."

"Do you have a guess? How far along do you think you are?" she asked, voice gentle.

"I think I'm probably due at the beginning of January."

"That'd put you around eighteen weeks. We'll do an ultrasound in a little while to pin down an exact due date. You haven't had any other prenatal care?"

"No." Her answer came small and ashamed.

"Are you on any medication?"

"No."

"Do you smoke, drink, or do drugs?"

"No."

"Are you allergic to any medications that you know of?"

"No."

"Have you been taking a prenatal vitamin?"

"No. I meant to start, but I wasn't sure . . . " Her voice cracked, and I reached out to squeeze her hand.

"It's okay." Dr. Rosa glanced at our exchange. "I'll give you a prescription for one before you leave today. It's recommended women take them in early pregnancy to prevent neural tube defects, but many women don't find out they're pregnant right away, and most of those babies do fine."

Lisa nodded, the lines around her face easing a bit.

"Is this your first pregnancy?" Dr. Rosa continued.

"Yes."

"No miscarriages or abortions?" she asked without glancing up.

Lisa was silent. Her lip quivered, and tears sprang at the corners of her eyes.

I stood beside her, silently offering whatever comfort she would be willing to take.

"I . . . uh . . . " She looked at me, eyes pleading. "I had . . . an abortion a couple months before getting pregnant." She hiccupped, the attempt to control her sobs clearly a strain.

It all made sense to me then—the "bad dreams" she had mentioned, the fear of doctors, the hesitation to go into the clinic, the look she had given me moments earlier. She'd been pleading for mercy.

"I understand this must be a traumatic memory for you, Lisa. Why don't I give you a couple minutes? I'll come back in a bit, and we can finish going over your medical history then." Dr. Rosa slipped out.

Once she left, I took Lisa's hand. "It's okay. Go ahead and cry."

"I'm sorry," she managed in between sobs.

She was sorry? Of course, she was. I was too, though her past wasn't my fault. Still, it was as if I were her older sister, someone who should have been able to protect her, to shield her from the enemy's lies and then from his accusations. I was helpless in the midst of such great pain. If only I could erase the past.

"Oh, Lisa, I forgive you. Okay? I forgive you." I brushed her long brown hair out of her face with my hand.

"Are you mad? Do you think I'm a monster?" She wiped her face with the backs of her hands.

I handed her a tissue from my purse. Oh, I was angry, all right, but not at her. At the devil, the father of lies. *Oh, God! When is this going to end? When are You going to come back and put an end to Satan's schemes?*

"No, I'm not mad at you. I don't think you're a monster. The devil told you it would make things all better and deceived you. He's a liar, and you bought into his lies like so many others have." I kept my tone gentle. "It happens to all of us. I'm so glad you didn't go through with it again. Do you have nightmares of the clinic?"

"It wasn't at the clinic." Tears continued to come at a steady pace. "It was in a seedy trailer with a guy who had three tattoos—three that I could see, anyway." Her quivered again.

"It's okay, Lisa. You don't have to talk about this now, not here. I want to hear about it, though. After the appointment, you can come over to my house if you'd like. You won't have the pressure of trying not to cry. Does that sound good?"

She nodded, wiping her face again. Though she clearly attempted to rein in her emotions, it appeared that a word or thought could send her over the edge.

"Think about this baby, Lisa. In a few minutes, we'll know for sure if it's a boy or a girl. You'll get to see her wiggle around. Maybe she's sucking her thumb. They'll take a picture, and you can put it on your refrigerator." My attempt at a diversion was met with little more than a blank stare.

"Shouldn't you be the one with the picture on your refrigerator? It's your baby."

"Well, they'll probably take more than one." I smiled reassuringly. After a few moments, she nodded again.

"All you have to do is finish the health questions. She'll do the exam, and then we'll get to see the ultrasound."

"And then we can leave."

How could the ultrasound have no pull for her? Mine had been a long-awaited moment filled with eager anticipation. All Lisa seemed to care about was getting away. Was she distancing herself from the baby because I would raise it? Or was her lack of maternal instincts yet another repercussion from the abortion?

Lost in thought, neither of us spoke again until we heard a knock at the door. Dr. Rosa entered again, the clipboard in her hands and her expression soft with compassion. "Are we ready to proceed?" Her voice was gentle and cautious. What a gem.

"Ready as I'll ever be," Lisa said, head down.

Dr. Rosa continued, reviewing the basic family medical history I'd helped fill out earlier. Lisa rattled off the yes and no answers with no apparent reluctance, but she kept her eyes fixed on the floor, glancing up towards the door occasionally as if planning her escape. When the questions finished, Lisa's shoulders slumped in relief. The fearful look returned moments later when Dr. Rosa asked her to undress for the exam.

When Dr. Rosa again left the room, I met her gaze. "I'll wait in the waiting room for this part," I said. Her embarrassment must have won out over her fear because she let me make my exit without any protest.

As I sat in the waiting room, I asked God to heal the wounds the enemy so mercilessly inflicted on her. Lisa's pain ran so deep I felt helpless next to its sway. I couldn't claim to have been there, to know what it felt like, to be able to relate in any way. I knew painful consequences of sin, for sure, but nothing that reached such a magnitude. Lisa's sin haunted her day and night, giving her no rest.

In what seemed like mere minutes later, the nurse was at the door, saying that the technician was ready to do the ultrasound. I followed her down the hall to the back room, excitement building with each step. Lisa lay on her back, bare belly protruding. She offered a slight smile when I entered. Perhaps she was a little intrigued after all.

"I'm going to squirt gel here. It'll be cold." The technician—who I recognized from my ultrasound a few months ago—seemed tired and unenthusiastic. When I'd had mine, she was upbeat and lively, chuckling at my surprise to find only one baby in my womb. Now she seemed to be burdened with monotony. How could looking at life inside the womb ever get old? Perhaps anything could be taken for granted.

She moved the instrument all around Lisa's abdomen until the shape of the baby came into focus. We viewed the little heart palpitating, and she turned up the volume until a sound like horses galloping resounded. Lisa's lips curled up into a smile. The technician pointed out the head, arms and legs. The baby squirmed at the pressure on her habitat, and Lisa let out a soft chuckle.

"Did you want to know the sex?" the tech asked after taking the typical measurements.

"I think she'd strangle me if I said no." Lisa cast a joking look in my direction.

My grin widened.

"Say hello to your little girl."

"I knew it!" I thrust a fist in the air. I'd have one of each to raise and to love. I would get to experience the unique aspects of both masculinity and femininity. I'd get to throw balls and pick up army men and braid hair. How fortunate I was to be let in on Lisa's miracle.

"You always have to be right, don't you?" Lisa's eyes held a sparkle I hadn't seen before. For once, her voice wasn't filled with sarcasm or confusion. Strange how one tiny life could make such a big change in a woman's heart.

The technician handed Lisa four different pictures taken at different angles. "The doctor will go over the results on your next visit, but everything looks good. You're 19 and a half weeks pregnant with a due date of December twenty-fourth. Take this up front to make your next appointment. She'll want to see you again in four weeks." She handed Lisa a paper and left the room. Lisa wiped the jelly off her stomach with a tissue and followed me out the door.

"So, you could have a Christmas baby," I said.

She meandered, gazing at the pictures, apparently no longer in such a hurry to leave. "I guess I don't have anything better to do. If you can't spend Christmas with your own family, you might as well spend it in the hospital."

I frowned. Her unveiled bitterness made me ache for her and for the family that had so readily abandoned her. She had enough pain without holding onto such undeserved hurt.

"We'd love for you to spend Christmas with us. If you're not in labor, that is. I guess if you are, we'll spend it with you."

"You mean you're going to be there when I have the baby?" She pulled her eyes away from the baby's black and white profile and looked at me.

"If that's okay with you. I'd like to help you through it."

She gave me a quizzical look but said no more. After scheduling her next appointment, she followed me out the door.

"So, would you like to come over? We can talk if you'd like, maybe eat something. I'm craving pizza. Either that or I'm subconsciously lazy and don't want to cook this evening. We can pick some up on the way."

She hesitated, bit her lip, and then agreed. "I'll follow you."

Chapter 19: Lisa

Wow. Had Lisa really seen her little girl moving around inside of her? She rubbed her belly with one hand while keeping the other on the wheel. There was a real baby in there, not a little lump of cells. A baby that looked remarkably human, not much different from a newborn.

At every stoplight, Lisa stole a glance at the pictures. She needed to give at least one to Eve, but which one could she possibly part with? A half hour earlier she hadn't cared about seeing the baby at all. Now, fascination gripped her. She had never much doubted there was a God, a Creator of all things. If she had doubted, such unbelief would be crushed after seeing something so miraculous right before her eyes.

Before the ultrasound, it'd been easy to remain mentally and emotionally distant. After all, she didn't have the right to become attached to the life within her when she'd be giving it up within a few months. But seeing the ultrasound—the movement, learning that she was carrying a baby girl—that changed everything. Were the new feelings springing up inside her okay? Her baby gave her belly a gentle nudge. Was the baby pushing back? When would she be able to feel it?

She followed Eve's minivan into the local pizza shop's parking lot and waited as Eve got out and waddled inside. What an amazing woman. Every encounter with her confused Lisa. She'd never met anyone like her and couldn't classify her like she'd classified the rest of the people in her world. Eve was genuine. The first time she'd met Eve outside the clinic, it was clear Eve was different. She'd longed to be Eve's friend. Now, here they were. Not exactly friends but heading in that direction. Eve had said as much at the office.

Lisa looked at the pictures again in wonder. Her baby had toes and fingers. She had turned her head away from the probe, seemingly annoyed at the interruption to her world. A girl. What would her name be? Surely Eve had dibs on that, but it didn't stop her from wondering.

She went through a mental list of the baby dolls she had named as a child. Though her tastes had changed since that time, how ironic that she'd once had a baby doll named Evie. She'd been missing an eye and had long ago abandoned the clothes she'd come with for Lisa's own baby clothes. She smiled. She had pictured those dolls when she'd written that essay as a child.

Eve waddled back out to her van, cradling three pizza boxes and one smaller box. Lisa shook her head. How on earth could they eat three pizzas? When Eve had a craving, she went all out.

On the road again, worry began to take its toll. Lisa had set herself up, backed herself in a corner with that confession in the exam room. She had to talk now. There was no way around it. She wasn't afraid of Eve's judgment—the truth was out, and Eve had treated her no differently. But her stomach recoiled at the thought of dredging up the memories she'd fought so hard to bury.

A few car lengths ahead of her, Eve slowed her pace, almost as if she sensed Lisa's apprehension and was giving her a few seconds more to prepare herself. Lisa took deep breaths, as her mother once instructed her to do whenever she was stressed. Back then, her biggest worry had been the next test she had to take. A mere percentage of her already-high grade had been at stake then. With the nightmares and the stress she'd been under lately, now it seemed her very sanity hung in the balance.

She pulled into a driveway behind Eve's car, and for a few moments, her surroundings distracted her. Eve's house wasn't elegant in the expensive kind of way—a modestly sized ranch in a quiet neighborhood. Nothing special. But the beauty of the garden out front took her aback. It was worlds away from her mother's garden back home, in which different kinds of flowers were aligned neatly in rows. Eve's garden was wild and passionate. Vibrant, exotic colors intermixed with each other in no particular order, like a petal rainbow.

Eve emerged from her minivan with the boxes in hand. Lisa shook herself and got out to help her carry the load.

"Eve, your garden is gorgeous."

"Oh, thank you. Do you ever wonder what the Garden of Eden looked like? I guess if it's in my name, it's in my blood."

It took a minute for her comment to register. "Oh, yeah. Adam and Eve. In the garden." Did that give the impression they were on the same page regarding God? In reality, Eve seemed likely as elite and untouchable in her spirituality as the apostle Paul. If only Lisa could bridge the distance between them. She would try to hold up her end of the conversation if Eve started talking about God again.

The other woman fiddled with her keys. "I guess Gideon's still at that meeting."

"What does your husband do?"

"He's a youth pastor at our church. There was a big important elders' meeting today, but I thought it'd be over by now."

Eve opened the door and held it open with her elbow as Lisa wedged herself inside. Eve's home was modestly yet beautifully decorated with flowered patterns of different kinds. The mixture of colors and shades captured Lisa's admiration.

Chapter 19: Lisa

Eve followed her gaze around the room. "A person's house can tell you a lot about them. What does mine say about me?"

"You like flowers." Lame and inadequate, but she couldn't put the rest of her awe into words.

"That's a start." Eve smiled and nodded for her to come into the kitchen. She took two plates from the cabinet and slid one patterned with a giant auburn sunflower in front of Lisa. "Dig in. I couldn't help myself. I had a piece in the car."

Despite the awkwardness of the conversation that was sure to come after the pizza, Lisa laughed.

Over pizza and ice water, Eve entertained her with stories of gardening, painting, and decorating. Though the subjects never would have interested her before then, they intrigued her coming from Eve. Lisa's mom had kept a tidy house and a well-manicured lawn, but she'd never admired such things. Yet as she sat there with Eve, she longed for beauty. Her parched heart wanted to soak it up. In Eve's house, there was a possibility of a life lived the way it was meant to be from the beginning. A possibility of avoiding the ugliness and heartache of everything that lay outside of this microcosm of perfectness.

"So, Lisa, I don't want to pressure you into anything, but I do want you to feel the freedom to unburden yourself. I'd like to hear your story. Those heartaches are too big to carry on your own."

There it was. The invitation she'd been both dreading and aching for at the same time. Sometimes, especially right after the ordeal, she'd wanted to talk out her massive mess of feelings, but there was never a right time or place. So, she had buried them and struggled with them when the sun went down and the quiet lent itself to noises and images from the past. But how to start? What to say?

As if reading her mind yet again, Eve offered an entrance. "How did you feel when you found out you were pregnant the first time? What went through your mind?"

"Not abortion." Lisa sucked in her breath and struggled to remember what she had tried to forget for so long. "I remember being shocked. I knew theoretically it could happen, but that soon? With the first guy I'd ever been with? My mom tried and tried to get pregnant. It was a long struggle for her."

"So you abstained until then?"

"Of course. I was always a good girl. My mom went on and on about my virtue. I was raised in a Christian home. I'd always done the right thing. I guess I got tired of fighting it. It happened so fast. I didn't know what to think, and I followed my boyfriend's lead."

"He pressured you into an abortion?"

"I don't even know if there was much pressure applied. He acted like this kind of thing happened to him all the time. He was calm and in control, and I went along."

"All the way to a trailer." Eve's voice held no disgust, only deep sorrow. As if Lisa was her own daughter and she was aching along with her.

"He said he knew a guy. I didn't ask questions. He led me up to this rickety trailer, introduced me to his friend, and then waited outside. Dan—that was his name. Dan had on a white lab coat as if he were a real doctor. The place seemed clean enough, but I wasn't scrutinizing it too closely. I wanted it all to be over with."

"And . . . "

"It's never over with, Eve. The baby might be long gone, but it's never over with. The nightmares . . . I remember the blood, the pain, his completely uncompassionate attitude. He laughed at me, Eve. He said, 'I guess you got yourself into a mess,' and *laughed*. I hear that laugh at night in my dreams."

Chapter 19: Lisa

Lisa had been looking down until then, too ashamed to meet Eve's eyes. When she did, tears brimmed in them. Seeing Eve cry caused Lisa's eyes to well up too.

"Then my life was about doing anything I could do to stop remembering. I thought if I could cover up that first bad relationship with another positive one, I could forget. Instead, I got pregnant again. Mitchell begged and pleaded with me to go to the clinic. He kept saying there was nothing to worry about. 'You've done it before,' he'd say. I hated him for it, but I didn't know what else to do. So, I went with him to the clinic."

"I'm glad I was there. I thank God you turned around. Oh, Lisa, I'm so thankful you didn't have to go through that again."

"Well, I'd looked at the clinic's website the night before. It all sounds so great and easy. They don't tell you the truth. They don't tell you it will haunt you for the rest of your life. They don't even tell you it will hurt. Their slogan is *Compassionate Care*. If they had a shred of compassion at all, they'd tell you the truth."

"Maybe they're so blinded they can't see the truth." Eve's whispered comment aroused Lisa's defenses. Whose side was she on?

Lisa's eyes narrowed. "Well, somebody should say something."

Eve's gaze remained steady. Earnest. "Yes. Somebody should say something. What about you?"

She scoffed. "Me? Say what? To whom?"

"So much pain came out of your experience. Wouldn't you like good to come out of it as well? You could be a voice to women who wouldn't otherwise know the truth." Eve gave a slight tilt of her head before taking a sip of water.

"How?"

"You're on your school newspaper, right? You're majoring in journalism."

"I *was* on the newspaper. I took the semester off."

"And the next semester is right around the corner."

"I can't write about having an abortion. We're assigned to different topics." She shook her head frantically. Eve needed to back off. "I'm not ready to talk about it, okay? You're the first one I've ever told. My best friend doesn't even know the details or the ramifications." She sat back, seething at Eve's suggestion. How dare she try to guilt her into confessing her crime. It would kill her.

"Okay, then. Take time to think about it." Eve's voice was gentle, and Lisa dropped her defenses a degree. "But know this: 2,363 babies are aborted a day in America. That's 2,363 kids who will never have dance recitals or football games. That's 2,363 women who will ache deeply and go to drastic measures to dull that ache. How many women have nightmares like you do? How many live with regret? You take two years to think about it, to get over your fear, how many babies is that? How many women?" Eve paused for a moment, glancing to the ceiling. "Over a million and a half or something huge like that."

"That's not fair." Lisa shot up and paced around the kitchen. "You can't pin the hurt and pain of all those women on me."

"No. That's not what I'm trying to do. I'm trying to show you the good that could be done. If you had an impact on even a third of those people, that's over half a million women who could be spared because you dared to open your mouth. It's not your fault they're choosing abortion. But you see the danger they don't see. If you would warn them, imagine—what the enemy meant for evil, God could turn it around for good."

"I'm trying to get my life straightened out right now. I can't bear the weight of anyone else." Her feet itched to storm out the door, but she'd never had a friend like Eve. She needed to make peace between them.

Chapter 19: Lisa

Eve was quiet, staring into space in the direction of the corner cabinet. She took a deep breath and released a long sigh. "I'm sorry. I wanted to encourage you to speak up, not pressure you. I didn't mean to manipulate you with a guilt trip. I need to learn when to push and when to pray."

Lisa bit her lip. Which one of them was truly in the wrong? And what caused such a passion within Eve?

"So, you go to the clinic every week and just pray?" She fumbled to recover whatever comradery they'd found at the doctor's office.

Eve let out a slight laugh. "That's the problem with this generation. *Just* pray. Oh, Lisa, prayer is one of the most powerful things we can do. It's not a second-class activity to do when everything else fails."

"I meant—"

"No, I understand. I'm not bashing you. I guess it's a hard concept for people to understand in our culture. We stand there and pray, knowing the end of this monster we call abortion will not come with a posterboard sign or a shout. God has got to move. He's our only hope. He's the only one who can change the tide and turn this nation around." She was quiet for a moment, then said, "Do you remember the story of Daniel?"

Lisa nodded. "He was thrown into the lions' den because he prayed to God instead of to King Darius, but he survived because of his faith in God." There. Nailed the details of that story.

"Exactly. Daniel served a higher authority than human kings, and he knew the power of prayer. Daniel once said that God is the only one who can turn the hearts of kings. He raises rulers up and tears others down. He is the One who convicts hearts. And He longs to show His mercy and remove sin from us. Daniel saw a vision of God on His throne, above all other kings. And like him, we appeal to a higher court."

"Doesn't standing there silently make you feel so hopeless?" The concept floated out there somewhere. Perhaps one day she'd get it.

"I see what you're saying. Yes, in a way. I watch women go in pregnant and come out not pregnant, and I can't run up to them, shake sense into them, and turn them around. In that respect, it's a hard route. But standing there, I also remember the faithfulness and goodness of my God. There's always hope with Him." Eve locked eyes with Lisa.

A shiver slid down her spine. Did her statement have a double meaning?

"Why are you so passionate about this?" Lisa asked. "I know a lot of people who believe abortion is wrong, but I've never heard anyone speak of it like you."

"Do you believe abortion is wrong?" Eve's eyes, though kind, pierced.

"Yeah, I think so. In most circumstances." She shrugged.

"Most circumstances?"

"Well, yeah. I mean, if the mother's life is in danger, or the child is going to be born with defects, then maybe it's okay. I guess it depends on that mother's convictions."

"If it were up to you, I would have been aborted." Eve's soft voice cut right through Lisa.

"What? Why?"

"When my mother was pregnant with me, the doctor discovered I had a genetic disorder. One of my chromosomes was missing a leg. It's a very rare condition, but other children who were born with it had major problems. Some were vegetables, growing in age but not maturity. Most couldn't walk. Few could talk. The doctors strongly advised my mother to have an abortion. They said I would never be normal. I'd never be able to do the things other children would do. They didn't even know if I'd survive the pregnancy and delivery."

"But you're fine."

"Exactly. I was born perfectly healthy and normal. I hit all the milestones slightly late, but nothing major. I was a little behind in school for a while, but I caught up. No one would be able to tell I had anything wrong with me. The doctors were amazed. To them I was a life not worth saving. I have to wonder how many other women were told something was wrong with their children. How many other women were advised to consider abortion and went along with it?"

"So now you're a champion of the unborn."

"Even if I never had the ability to walk or talk, would I have been any less of a person? Life is the Lord's to give and His to take. I've asked Him to give me His heart for the unborn—to let me feel His emotions for them so I can pray out of that understanding—and He's been granting my request. He loves those little ones so much. And He loves their mothers. How could I go about my normal everyday life like nothing was wrong?"

"People do it all the time. They can't stop their lives over someone else's choices." Lisa kept her voice soft while stating that observation.

"I know. It's a tension. I need to celebrate life by living my own. I need to rejoice in this baby kicking inside of me. But I can't forget. There's a season to mourn."

"And I need to—" Lisa stopped, distracted by a strange feeling in the pit of her stomach. Instinctively, she placed her hands on her belly. "Is that . . . is that the baby?"

Eve grinned. "What does it feel like?"

"I don't know. Like a little pop?" Was that the word for it?

"It very well could be. You're right at that time."

Lisa sat still, concentrating and waiting. She took several deep breaths, keeping her hand still. After a few moments, discouragement sneaked in. "I don't feel anything anymore. Maybe it was only my imagination."

"I bet it was the baby. You'll feel her squirm occasionally. Soon, though, you'll start feeling those hard kicks around the clock. Just wait. It's amazing."

Lisa excused herself to go to the bathroom. What was going on inside her? How soon would her little girl make her presence known?

Wait no. Eve's little girl.

Should she ask Eve what the baby's name would be? No. She wouldn't dare. But that didn't keep her from speculating. Was Eve the kind of woman who would choose a traditional name, or an unusual one? Finding her way back to the kitchen, she had an idea.

"So, have you picked out a name for your little boy?" She attempted to keep her voice nonchalant, as if she was only mildly curious.

"Zephaniah. Zephan for short."

She inadvertently wrinkled her nose. Now *that* answered her question, leaving her with slight uneasiness over the name Eve would choose for the little one dancing inside of her.

"It means 'God has hidden' or 'God has treasured.' I didn't like it at first, either. I had prayed one day about what to name him, and that night I had a dream. In the dream a nurse handed me my baby and told me his name was Zephan. I woke up, sure it was a crazy pregnancy dream and not from the Lord. But that night I prayed again for the name the Lord wanted for this little one and I had a similar dream. In that one, Gideon came home and asked 'Where's Zephan?'" She laughed to herself. "The next night I said, 'Okay, God. If you really want me to name my baby Zephan, tell me how to spell it.' Then that night I had a dream in which I was looking at the birth certificate. There it was plain as day: Z-e-p-h-a-n. At that point, I stopped fighting it. Now it's grown on me."

Lisa stared at her, dumbfounded.

"What?" A rueful smile played on Eve's lips.

Chapter 19: Lisa

"Do you always dream like that? I mean, do you think God gives you certain dreams?" Of course, she remembered reading about people in the Bible who'd had divine dreams, but she'd never met someone who actually claimed such direct communication with God.

"I don't dream *all* the time. Not every night, at least. But yes, I do believe He can speak through dreams. He's the same yesterday, today, and forever, right?"

"I guess so. But it seems foreign to me. I don't think I've ever had a dream from God."

"Maybe you need to ask." Eve shrugged, as if it were that simple.

Lisa made a mental note to try it out, to see if it worked. But hopefully God wouldn't tell her a crazy name for her baby. Not that she had a say anyway.

"So," Eve began, "Do you have any preferences for a name for your girl?"

Lisa's mouth parted. "I-I thought that was your choice."

Eve shrugged again, as if it were a minor issue. "How about I choose the first name and you choose the middle name. Does that seem fair?"

"She's your baby." Lisa's voice caught in her throat. "I guess I don't know how all of this is supposed to work."

"To be honest, I'm not sure how it's supposed to work either. We'll figure it out one step at a time. You can't tell me you have no interest in her name."

"Oh, I'm interested, all right. Especially after hearing your boy's name." She smiled through watery eyes.

"I was thinking 'Esther.' Actually, I've thought that from the beginning, before I met you."

"When you thought you were having twins?"

"Yep." A smile danced at the corners of her mouth.

"I kind of like it."

"What about you?"

"I hadn't really thought about it. I mean, I didn't know I had a right to."

"Well, now you know. The middle name is your choice. Just don't make it too crazy." Eve winked then, and the tension from earlier was forgotten.

Lisa forgot to ask God for a dream that night. Instead, she tossed and turned, different names and spellings racing through her head. She spoke a few of them aloud in the dark, analyzing how they rolled off her tongue. At one point she thought she felt the baby move again and laid still once more. But no little movement rewarded her patience.

When she finally fell asleep, there were no breathtaking messages from on high. Instead, she found an even greater blessing. After an evening of dredging up horrifying memories, she didn't have one nightmare. Not one.

Chapter 20: Trent

Trent received a frantic call from Beth at four o'clock in the afternoon.

"I'm bleeding, Trent, and not a little. I'm scared, honey." His wife hiccupped through tears. "What should I do?"

"I'll be right home." Almost as an afterthought, he added, "Bleeding during pregnancy can be perfectly normal. There are plenty of reasons for it. Why don't you call your doctor's office and let them know? I'll come home right away."

It was a slow day at the clinic, anyway. He didn't have any other appointments and had been catching up on paperwork. He'd rather be home with Beth in case something went wrong. Though he knew what he'd told his wife was true—she and the baby were probably fine—the fear in her voice unnerved him. She'd been having lower-back pain earlier that week but no other complications. Back pain, too, could be completely normal.

Still, at twelve weeks, they weren't out of the danger zone yet. With her previous abortion, there was a greater risk of a miscarriage. That's the way things were. But they couldn't lose this baby. It would kill Beth, absolutely kill her inside. And if anything happened to Beth, he didn't know what he would do.

He slipped into his car and accelerated a bit more than normal when exiting the lot. To gain control of his tumultuous emotions, he said out loud, "We're having a healthy baby" His voice in the quiet vehicle sounded more confident than he felt. “This is normal. She’s going to make it to full term and be beautiful. And my wife is going to be fine.”

His cell phone vibrated in his pocket. He struggled to pull it out while keeping his eyes on the road. “Beth?” He swerved slightly.

“Trent? The nurse said to come in if we can make it before five.”

“I’m five minutes away now. It only takes ten to get there. I think we’ll be fine.” He clenched the wheel with sweaty hands.

“I’ll be ready.”

“I’ll honk.”

She might get her ultrasound from Dr. Yoseph, although she might not enjoy it.

He pulled up in the driveway and didn’t even have to honk. His wife stood on the steps out front, tears pooling in her eyes. He reached over to open the door for her.

“Don’t worry, babe. Many women bleed during pregnancy. It doesn’t necessarily signal anything’s wrong.”

“That’s what the doctor said, but something doesn’t *feel* right. I’ve been cramping and . . . It feels like something’s terribly wrong.”

Alarm filled his mind, but he forced himself to appear calm. She needed his strength at that moment. He clamped his mouth shut. Any questions about the severity of her cramping or if she’d experienced any other symptoms would be far from reassuring.

“I’m sure everything’s okay.” He put his hand on her knee and squeezing gently. “Most miscarriages happen earlier on. Once you hit fourteen weeks, the risk goes down dramatically, and you’re nearly there.”

“What will they do, Trent? How will they help?” She alternated between wringing her fingers and clutching the sides of her seat, her face twisted with pain.

"They'll do an ultrasound and check everything."

"Everything?"

"They'll check the baby's heartbeat, its size, the condition of the placenta, the fluid level—everything."

"And what if something's wrong? What will they do?"

"It all depends, hon. Let's not think about that right now. Everything is probably fine." And if not, most likely there's nothing anyone could do.

They rode the rest of the way in silence, drowning in their own separate worries. When they arrived at the office, he helped Beth out of the car and into the office. It neared closing time, and only one other couple occupied the waiting room.

He went up to the window to sign in, but before he could write Beth's name on the line, a nurse poked her head around the door. "Come on back," she said, waving them in. Did the rush in her voice and manner have to do with the late hour or the seriousness of Beth's condition?

They followed her through the hall.

"Dr. Yoseph will do an ultrasound first," the nurse said. "Afterward, he'll most likely do an exam, but that will depend on the results." She gestured for them to step inside an exam room. "He'll be just a minute."

Beth perched on the examination table, her eyes still blotchy and red, her lip bleeding slightly from where she'd been biting it. It was a habit she'd had ever since he'd met her, but he hadn't noticed her doing it recently. She'd been so happy since finding out she was pregnant.

Dr. Yoseph rushed in, chart in hand. "I understand you're having bleeding and cramping."

Beth nodded.

"We'll do an ultrasound to determine how the fetus is holding up first. Then we'll need to do a pelvic exam to see if you're dilating at all. Go ahead and lean back, unzip your pants, and pull up your shirt." She did so, and he squirted a liberal amount of gel on her abdomen.

Chapter 20: Trent

In less than a minute, their baby's profile graced the screen. It took another thirty seconds to get the wand in position. Then Trent saw it—a beautiful, pulsating heart. Dr. Yoseph turned a dial, and they could clearly hear the strong thump.

"The heartbeat's fine. It's 156 beats a minute, which is normal."

Beth cast a wobbly smile at Trent, then glanced at the doctor.

Dr. Yoseph seemed preoccupied with measurements, no further explanations forthcoming. Trent couldn't see the screen well from his angle across the room, but it looked as if everything was in proper order. Did the man remember they were waiting for answers?

Dr. Yoseph slid the wand back in place and handed Beth a tissue for the jelly. "The baby looks healthy. Follow me to the room down the hall and I'll check your cervix." With that, he stepped out of the room and on his way.

Trent helped Beth to her feet, and they followed as quickly as they could.

"Go ahead and undress from the waist down. I'll be back in a moment." He motioned towards the paper drape lying on the exam table before shutting the door behind himself.

"He must be ready to go home," Beth said with a nervous laugh. Trent's mouth tightened. Dr. Yoseph's pace was far from congenial, but it was after five p.m. at that point. And the man's time was precious. He was the best of the best.

Seconds after Beth finished undressing and sat back on the table, the doctor knocked on the door. Sliding onto his rolling stool, he snapped latex gloves on. "You'll feel pressure."

Beth sucked in her breath, shoulders tense. Trent almost told her to relax, that tensing up would make it hurt more, but what good would that do?

After a few moments, Dr. Yoseph sat back, yanked his gloves off, and sighed. "I'm afraid you're already dilating. Your body is getting ready to expel the fetus. At this point, there's nothing that can be done. My advice is to go home and rest. Avoid intercourse or any strenuous activity. It should pass within a day or so. When it does, we'll need you to come back. We'll check and make sure all of it was expelled. If not, we'll need to do a D&E."

"Pass?" Beth's eyes welled up.

"Miscarriage is unfortunately common in the first trimester. All you can do is wait."

"Are you sure?" Trent's voice sounded foreign to himself, husky from holding back tears of his own. "It's inevitable?"

"Yes. An inevitable spontaneous abortion. You can make an appointment for Monday on your way out. I'm sorry." With that, he was gone. Off to more important things?

A sob erupted from his wife as she reached for him and clung to his shirt.

"No. No. This can't be true. I can't lose the baby. I tried . . . I tried to get pregnant for so long. I can't lose her now." Her body convulsed.

He could remain in control no longer. He let his own tears flow too. Their baby was dying.

He wanted to offer words of comfort but had none to give. And staying in the sterile exam room was not helping. Handing her a tissue and taking one for himself, he gently reminded her to get dressed. "Let's get out of here and go home."

When they reached the front desk, Beth kept on walking. Trent paused, waiting for the clerk to finish typing so he could schedule an appointment.

"I have a nine a.m."

"That's fine." His voice dripped with defeat.

Beth caught his eye and glared through her tears. Following her to the door, he gave her a questioning look.

Chapter 20: Trent

Once they were out the door, she said, "How could you do that?"

"Do what?"

"Give up like that. You're planning on this baby's death. Just like that."

"Honey, I'm being reasonable." He winced, realizing how that sounded. If he was being reasonable, that implied she was not.

In a huff, she picked up her pace—then, as if remembering the doctor's warning against strenuous exercise, she slowed.

"I can't accept it. I have to have hope."

They rode home in silence and grief. Tears continued to slide down her cheeks, though she didn't make a sound. He racked his brain for a loophole, for a shred of hope he could offer that their child would be okay.

Only he knew about miscarriages. He induced them for a living.

The thought sickened him, and he struggled against a bout of nausea. What was the matter with him? Why couldn't he even think about his job any more without feeling uneasy? He'd always been able to deal with inevitable misfortunes and move on. But ever since that day he talked to Eve at the lake, something felt wrong—off-balance. He didn't know what it was or what to do about it. And now this. What was he supposed to do?

Beth didn't say a word after they came home. She went upstairs and shut herself in the bathroom.

Should he go to her? But he was still choking on his own sorrow. He fell onto the couch. They needed help. Some kind of miracle.

In an instant, he remembered the letter and rushed out to the car to find it. He had buried it in his briefcase, keeping it for evidence in case he had to file a restraining order for stalking. Frantically searching through the papers, his eyes fell on the feminine handwriting. There was the number of the only woman he knew who still believed in miracles. Crazy as he thought she was, desperation cut through the cords of rational thought.

He shoved the briefcase into the driver's seat, sat in the passenger's seat, and shut the door. His fingers flew across his phone.

"Hello?" Eve's voice was curious.

"Eve, it's Trent. I don't know if you remember me. I'm the doctor—"

"I know who you are. What's going on?"

"My wife's having a miscarriage. I thought . . . I don't know what I was thinking. We need some prayer or . . . or something."

He was out of his mind.

"May I come over?" She sounded . . . sincere? And serious.

He rattled off his address. How would he justify this to Beth? He'd invited over the woman who had caused such tension between them.

He went inside and paced. What could he say to his wife? How could he explain? He was desperate, that was all. But he was sure Beth would read more deeply into his actions than that. Summoning up his courage, he tapped on the bathroom door. He heard only quiet sobs. He knocked again gently.

"Yes?" Her voice was angry and heavy.

"Beth, someone's coming over."

"Who?"

"Do you remember that crazy pregnant woman?"

"How could I forget?" She did little to hide the bitterness in her tone.

"She's coming over to pray for you. I didn't know what else to do. I want to help."

The door opened to reveal Beth's puffy eyes and tear-stained cheeks. "You called her? And invited her over?"

Chapter 20: Trent

"I . . . I want to do everything we can to save this baby. Prayer couldn't hurt."

Her eyes softened as they met his own.

"I don't even want to ask why you had her number handy. I can't be mad at you right now. I need you too much."

She fell into his arms, clinging to him. He led her over to the couch, and they sat together hand in hand, waiting. When a car pulled up, they looked over their shoulders simultaneously.

"I better not sense any chemistry between you two." She crossed her arms.

"Don't worry, babe. You'll see there's nothing to be concerned about." He opened the door and let Eve in.

"Hi," she said. Turning to the couch, her eyes shone with compassion. "Beth, right?" Beth nodded. "Hi, I'm Eve. I've come to pray for you. I know the Lord loves you fiercely and believe He wants to reveal His kindness to you today."

"The doctor said it was inevitable." Beth choked on her own voice.

"God created this baby. It's up to Him whether she lives or dies. God has the final say, not the doctor." Eve spoke with the authority and confidence Trent had not been able to summon. "May I lay my hand on your shoulder?"

Mistrust radiated from Beth's eyes as she considered the offer, but after a moment, she nodded. Eve sat on the couch next to her, taking Trent's spot, and planted her hand firmly on Beth's shoulder.

"Father God, I come before You today, asking for the life of this unborn child. You have knit this child together in Beth's womb. This baby is fearfully and wonderfully made. I ask You, in Jesus' name, to break through in Beth's body with power. Have mercy on this daughter whom You love. Touch her womb, Lord. Show Yourself strong in her body. Reach down and make the wrong things in her body right. Have mercy, Lord. Have mercy."

Trent had been looking down, staring at his feet as Eve prayed. Startled at the emotion in Eve's voice, he looked up at her face. Her eyes were closed, but small tears made their way down her cheeks. Nothing about her seemed crazy or judgmental. She continued praying for a few moments, then asked Beth how she felt.

"I don't know."

Trent raised a brow at Eve. How was she supposed to feel?

After a moment, Beth said, "My stomach feels warm."

His eyes snapped from Eve's face to Beth's. Her stomach felt warm? What on earth did that mean?

Eve nodded matter-of-factly. "That's good. Sometimes we can feel heat in our bodies when there's a healing taking place." With that comment, she continued to pray.

Trent stood there, uncomfortable and out of place. He believed in God, even if he didn't believe the same way Eve did. He even believed prayer could work in different circumstances. Unusual things happened every day—things some might call miraculous. Still, he had always preferred to hold such claims at arm's length. In contrast, Eve seemed to believe these sorts of things could happen at any time to anyone.

He was so lost in his own thoughts that he didn't notice Beth's demeanor had changed until minutes afterwards. She was no longer crying. In fact, her face was peaceful, with the trace of a smile. She looked relaxed and at home with this woman she'd been so hostile toward moments before.

"Now how do you feel?" Eve asked again.

"I don't know. Different. I'm not so afraid anymore." When Beth opened her eyes, they shone.

"I want you to go check and see if you're still bleeding," Eve said. "I believe the Lord is doing something in your body."

Beth nodded and made her way to the bathroom with an air of anticipation. Trent turned his attention to Eve.

Chapter 20: Trent

"Have you ever seen a . . . miracle before, Eve?"

She smiled bashfully. "A couple people I've prayed for were healed—little things, you know? Migraine headaches, arthritis pain, that kind of thing. Nothing like the miracles that Jesus did, or the miraculous healings going on in other parts of the world, but enough to build my faith and make me believe God can do it and His heart is to heal."

What could he say to that? He kept his eyes pasted on the hallway leading to the bathroom, afraid for his wife. She seemed full of such ridiculous hope. To find out such news from the doctor was hard enough, let alone to be filled with hope yet again and have it possibly crushed.

"There is a woman from my church whose eyes were healed. One minute she couldn't see a thing without her glasses. The next minute, she could see 20/20 without them."

Trent didn't look at Eve's face but sensed a smile in her tone. What would it be like to believe as she believed?

They waited there quietly for what seemed like an hour. In reality, it couldn't have been more than five minutes. What was taking Beth so long? He finally rushed down the hall and knocked on the bathroom door. At the sound of fresh sobs, disappointment ran through him. Evidently, he had found some hope in that prayer, or he wouldn't have been disappointed.

"Beth? Are you okay?"

"Yes. Yes. Hold on. I'll be right out." What was that tone in her voice? He waited outside the door, ready to envelope his distraught wife in his arms the moment she made her exit.

She flung the door open moments later. The face that greeted him was tear-stained, for sure, but strikingly bright. She reached up and put her arms around his neck. He held her, rubbing her back and trying to think of something comforting to say. Her body trembled. He pushed her back to look into her eyes.

She was laughing! "It stopped. Trent, it stopped. I'm not bleeding. I don't feel any cramps. No pain at all!" She laughed again, sounding tired, but joyful. She hugged him again, then dashed past him to the living room.

"Eve, it stopped. I'm not bleeding!" Trent heard Eve's reply from where he stood in the hallway, too stunned to move.

"That's wonderful. Right now, Beth, I want you to thank Jesus for healing you. Say it out loud."

"Thank You, Jesus! Thank You, God!" Beth's voice resounded with exuberance.

Guilt gnawed at him for still doubting, but he did so all the same. Surely there had to be a mistake. Perhaps the bleeding let up temporarily. Maybe it already passed. She'd probably begin bleeding again tonight, and they'd have to go through the grief all over again.

"Thank you, Eve. Trent? What are you doing?"

"Coming." He forced himself to smile and return to the women.

"How can I thank you?" Beth asked.

"It's not me, Beth. God alone can heal. Take care of that precious girl of yours. She's a miracle." Eve headed toward the door, smiling at them both. "I need to get back home, but please call me if you need anything."

Beth nodded, still smiling.

Trent stared at the door as Eve shut it behind her, leaving the two of them alone to wrestle with the events of the day.

Though he put on a positive front for his wife, nerves clawed at him. When would she begin to bleed again?

Beth went on and on about the baby and possible baby names. She talked about decorating the nursery and how she wanted to register for gifts in the coming week. She wondered which one of her friends was going to throw her a baby shower and whether they'd try to surprise her. All the while, Trent's body radiated tension, though she didn't seem to notice. All those dreams—what a lot to lose for the second time.

Chapter 20: Trent

That night, Beth fell right to sleep. Trent lay awake late into the night. He tossed and turned, plagued by thoughts of Beth's smiling face, Eve's tears as she prayed, and his own doubts. In desperation, he even tried praying himself. When he finally fell asleep, he dreamed of an ancient man. Upon waking, he couldn't remember who the man was. Maybe it was even Jesus. All he remembered was that the man had placed his hands on Trent's eyes and commanded them to be opened.

Beth was already humming in the shower. He wanted to relax and join in her happiness but held himself back. Someone needed to be prepared when the inevitable happened.

Chapter 21: Beth

Monday came and went, and Beth did not go to the doctor's office. Instead, she lost herself in marveling over the life within her. She was carrying a miracle baby. Her little girl had to be special. Why else would God choose to spare her? Gratitude and expectation brimmed within her.

In a notebook at work, she recorded possible baby names. She searched through dozens of baby name websites, but nothing seemed right. Everything seemed too *ordinary* for a child who had been snatched from death.

No need to worry about Trent and Eve anymore. Eve's demeanor and her compassion towards Beth made it obvious she was simply seeking to right the wrongs of the world. If Eve considered abortion one of them, who was Beth to judge her for it? She might not agree abortion should be illegal, but she couldn't hold Eve's love for the unborn against her. It had saved her baby. Why should she be offended if Eve wanted to save others as well?

Eve called her a couple days later to see how she was doing. How astonishing that she *cared.* After being frustrated with the lack of compassion from her doctor, it was refreshing to have someone check up on her.

Of course, the nurse had checked up on her as well when she didn't show up for her appointment on Monday. When Beth said she wasn't bleeding anymore, the nurse stammered about how Beth still needed to come in for an examination.

Chapter 21: Beth

Beth ignored her request and instead made an appointment for mid-September—a month later. Of course she'd keep up with regular visits, but why waste a perfectly good afternoon at the doctor's office when she didn't have to?

However, Trent had convinced her to call back and make an appointment on Wednesday "for confirmation." Although he never outright disagreed with Beth's insistence that all was well, she had a feeling he wasn't buying it. She couldn't blame him. He was a doctor, after all. He was in the business of medical certainties, not miracles. She didn't need a doctor's appointment to confirm the fact that her baby was alive within her, but if it would make Trent accept the fact, she would swallow her pride and call the nurse back.

When Wednesday's ultrasound showed a healthy baby with a strong heartbeat, Trent's eyes registered surprise and pleasure. He shook his head as if he couldn't rationalize what had happened, but from that point forward, he took part in her excitement over the baby. He even went with her to register for baby items.

She told Eve about the ultrasound and Trent's reaction, still bubbling over with joy. After a few minutes of talking about baby clothes, Eve asked if Beth would want to give her testimony at Eve's church.

Why did she say yes? She hadn't been to a church since her aunt's funeral when she was in college. Her excitement must have won out over her usual reservations about religion. However it happened, she and Trent wound up sitting next to Eve and Gideon at their church two weeks later.

The nerves didn't set in until they arrived. For her, at least. From the way Trent paced back and forth and changed his tie three times, he had to be dreading the event.

"What if someone recognizes me? What if they say something hateful?"

Obviously, he hadn't had many pleasant experiences with religious people. Understandable. "You don't have to come with me, you know."

"Of course I'm coming with you."

The corner of her mouth twisted upward. Thank God he insisted. Going to church was strange enough. Going alone would be too uncomfortable.

"Ready?" She grabbed her purse.

"Now? No, I don't think so. We should arrive fashionably late."

She frowned. "But what if we have trouble finding Eve? I don't want to cause a scene looking for her after the service has already started."

"Beth, please." He tented his hands under his chin. "Please don't force me to make small talk."

Her purse dropped from her hands onto the couch. "I definitely don't want to have to do that. Let's get there five minutes early. Sound good?"

They did so, pulling into the crowded parking lot and filing in among the smattering of strangers. They managed to dodge the greeters at the door. While the smiling couple with name badges chatted with the people who came in right in front of them, Trent and Beth ducked in the sanctuary's side entrance. Soft music emanated from overhead speakers. They filed up rows of cushioned blue chairs and spotted Eve and her husband sitting in the second row from the front.

"That's great," Trent mumbled under his breath as he and Beth walked toward the couple. If he had had his way, they'd probably have sat on the edge of their seats in the back row so that they could slip out at a moment's notice.

They had a couple of minutes to exchange pleasantries with Eve and Gideon before the musicians came onstage. Then self-consciousness hit her. Should she sit or stand? Would people notice if she *didn't* sing? The music was catchy enough—much more tolerable than the hymns she remembered droning through the church when she was a little girl. She had few memories of being in a church, but every single one of them was negative. Why would people go to such a depressing gathering unless someone dragged them there?

She had always believed in God. But why was it necessary to alter her life in light of that fact? There had to be a Creator, but it wasn't like He stood around watching every little move of the people on earth. Surely he had better things to do. He couldn't be so uptight that He'd be concerned if people went on with their lives without obsessing over Him.

It wasn't God that she detested, though. It was those people who claimed to love God but who were so judgmental it made her sick. What right did anyone have to criticize how she lived her life? Or what her husband did for a living? It seemed that once people embraced religion, they got this holier-than-thou, arrogant attitude. Why couldn't they mind their own business?

She had gone to school with a Christian girl who looked horrified when Beth had told her she and Trent were living together. Her mouth even hung open for a minute, as if that were the most preposterous thing she'd ever heard. So what if they weren't married? They ended up getting married, didn't they? They were in love! Didn't that count for anything with those people? It's not like she was a slut sleeping with five guys at the same time. She was as committed to Trent then as she was now.

Trent nudged her. Had she been fuming on her internal soapbox?

"You look ticked. Smile. You're going to go on stage in a few minutes." His eyes twinkled, mocking her.

"Sorry," she whispered.

She turned her attention back to the music, resorting to the compromise of clapping but not singing. The singing went on and on, until she could barely hide her annoyance when they started yet another song. Trent caught her gaze, and she discreetly rolled her eyes, eliciting a smile from him.

Finally, it was over, and everyone sat. A burly man with a goatee went up to the front and gave a few announcements. Eve leaned over and whispered that they'd go up after he was finished. Beth's pulse raced, and she held herself back from biting her lip. What was she doing there? Who was she fooling? One sentence and they'd know she wasn't "one of them." They should have chosen the edge of the back row.

Eve leaned towards her and nodded. Choking down all reservations, Beth followed her down the side aisle, up the steps and onto the stage. Eve took the microphone from the man as if she was born with one in her right hand. If she had any nerves at all, she buried them deep.

"As you know, we like to begin each week with a healing testimony. We believe the Lord has the desire to heal, and His Word says to lay hands on the sick and they will recover. While that's happening mostly on a small scale here, we will not despise the day of small beginnings. In other places around the world, the blind are receiving sight and the deaf their hearing. The dead are being raised. The Lord is the same here as He is there, and we believe we will see more and more."

For a moment, Beth forgot where she was, lost in thought. Blind people were receiving sight? Where? How could that happen? The dead raised? How come she'd heard nothing about it? Was it a joke or a hoax?

"Over a week ago, Beth—a friend of mine—was healed through prayer. I asked her to come this week to share her testimony."

As Eve handed her the microphone, the audience erupted in applause. She hadn't expected such a reception, and it threw her off. Her carefully rehearsed speech flew from her brain. When was she supposed to begin talking? What was she going to say again? After a few moments, the clapping died down, and Eve gave her a slight nod. Taking a deep breath, Beth plunged ahead.

"Um, hi, I'm Beth. I'm fourteen and a half weeks pregnant with our first child. Last week I started cramping and bleeding, and my husband took me to the doctor. After examining me, the doctor told me I was going to have a miscarriage. He said that it was inevitable because I was already dilating. He told me to go home, that I'd lose the baby and I was supposed to go back Monday to have a D and C to make sure it was all out."

Though she knew from high school speech class that she shouldn't look at the audience, she found herself making personal eye contact with several members of the congregation. Their expressions were full of concern and compassion.

"When we got home, I couldn't stop crying. We had tried for a long time to get pregnant. It devastated me. Then Eve came over and prayed for me. I-I'm not used to people praying for me or anything, but when she did, I felt warmth spread across my abdomen. When she prayed, I stopped bleeding. It's been over a week, and I haven't bled since. The doctor did another ultrasound. My baby is alive."

Beth teared up, and quickly handed the microphone back to Eve. Shifting her weight from foot to foot, she looked to Eve for a clue of what to do next. Should she go back to her seat or wait?

"Let's praise the Lord!" At Eve's pronouncement, the room broke out in more applause and outbursts of thanksgiving to God. Beth tried to remain nonchalant, as if she was used to such exuberant displays, but how many steps would it take to escape to the safety of her chair? She took about three side steps towards the edge of the stage before Eve glided towards her and placed a hand on her shoulder.

"After the service, we'd like to pray for and bless Beth and her baby. If you'd like to be part of that, come up to the front left afterwards." As if suddenly realizing that she hadn't asked Beth permission to this, Eve glanced over to her and whispered, "Is that okay?"

Beth nodded. What choice did she have? She couldn't refuse in front of everyone.

Eve then handed the microphone to an older man with wispy white hair who Beth hadn't seen take the stage. They headed back towards their seats. Beth couldn't move fast enough. The older man gave an announcement about an upcoming prayer meeting, then prayed for the offering. As they passed buckets around, Trent put his arm around Beth's shoulder.

She looked around to see if anyone else in the room was touching. Was it appropriate? She shrugged his arm off and instead discretely grabbed his hand and gave it a squeeze.

"You did a good job," he whispered in her ear. She passed the bucket to him with a smile.

For the next half an hour they listened to a different man, this one younger than the last, preach on the Sermon on the Mount. Beth tried to pay attention, certain it would help to pass the time more quickly, but she couldn't focus. What it would be like to be prayed for after the sermon?

Time dragged, then seemed to speed up too fast. Was she relieved or nervous when the pastor wound down his sermon with a lengthy prayer? If only they could leave. She put a hand on her belly. The faster they could get to the end of the service, the more quickly she could do so. Safe on her home turf, she could enjoy her unborn baby and her husband without wondering whether she fit in or whether she was doing the right thing at the right time.

The service concluded, and a scattering of people across the room stood and stretched. Some picked up their belongings and headed for the door, while others turned around in their seats to whisper to the people behind them. Her eyes swept the room. Maybe everyone would leave and there'd be no one left to pray or bless, or whatever they wanted to do.

"You did a wonderful job, Beth." Eve's glowing smile radiated peace and contentment as usual.

Beth wanted to slap her and hug her at the same time. She was so perfect and compassionate all the time. Was she even human?

"Come on up front. We'd love to speak blessing over you and the baby."

Beth grabbed Trent's hand, and they followed Eve up to the front corner. By then there were small groups of people milling about. From the back of the room, a woman laughed. Soft music began emanating from the speaker by Beth's feet, apparently a clue to the others to either quiet down or file out.

"That was a beautiful testimony. Just beautiful." An older woman in a bright blue hat patted Beth's shoulder. "Brought tears to my eyes. Beautiful."

"Thanks," she muttered. Was that the right thing to say? Others gathered around them, some offering similar affirmation and others nodding in agreement.

"Let's pray for continued health and life for this baby. Feel free to bless her however you feel led." Eve laid her hand on Beth's shoulder, and others followed suit.

The air around her thinned, and the room swayed.

Trent gave her hand a squeeze, as if to encourage her through it.

Eve led off, asking God for favor for Beth and the baby. She prayed He would protect her womb, that the baby would grow strong, and that her pregnancy would continue free of complication and even the common aches and pains normally accompanied by pregnancy. As she prayed for joy and peace, Beth relaxed under the weight of Eve's voice.

Another woman picked up right where she left off, asking for a quick and easy delivery of a full-term baby. Someone else asked God to surround her with His peace and presence and to draw near to her during her pregnancy.

One after another they prayed, each with a weight of conviction equal to or greater than Eve's. Wow. By the sincerity in their voices, it seemed as if they truly did *care* about her baby—and even Beth, though they had never met her before, had no stake in her future, and didn't know how different she was from them.

A man's voice boomed forth. Beth opened her eyes to see who it belonged to. A large, burly man stood with his hand on Trent's shoulder, asking God to give her husband wisdom and the ability to love their little family well. He prayed for God to strengthen their marriage. Trent shifted his weight, obviously uncomfortable with the shift of attention onto him. His body lost some of its tension as the man finished and another woman spoke "destiny over the child"—whatever that meant. It sounded nice.

Beth focused on every word that went forth. Everything they were asking for sounded wonderful, even if she never would have been able to put it into such words. She felt oddly drawn to this group of people with whom she most likely had very little in common. Unused to people being concerned with the welfare of others—of strangers—an ache arose within her. Was this what it meant to love one's neighbor? How come she hadn't experienced it until now?

The prayers finished, and they bombarded Beth with hugs and half a dozen "Bless you's." She nodded, teary-eyed. Trent smiled at her and nodded towards the place where they'd sat during the service. She grabbed her purse from beneath the seat and they made their way towards to door. They took three or four steps at a time as others came up to her, telling her they were glad the two of them had come.

Finally, Trent and Beth made their escape. Once safely inside the car, Trent let out a monstrous sigh. "Funny how church can seem so much like hell, huh?"

Chapter 21: Beth

"I didn't think it was that bad." Beth clutched her purse in her lap.

"Not that bad? It was nearly two and a half hours long! There should be a law restricting the length of services." He shook his head, clearly irritated that she didn't chime in with agreement.

"Well, maybe it was a little long, but nobody else seemed to mind. What's it to you? It's not like you're going to join."

He looked at her quizzically. "By the sounds of it, you might."

"No, I'm not going to start going to church." Her voice was firm, but perhaps she wasn't opposed to the thought. "I thought the people were nice, that's all. I don't think they're bad people."

"No. Not on Sunday at least." He turned the stereo up, a signal that their conversation was over.

She opened her mouth, about to ask what he meant by that, but clamped it shut. It was clear where he stood with religious people, and she understood why. She'd come to Eve's church with similar feelings, after all. Better to keep her opinion of the morning to herself and to allow him to do the same. It wasn't worth an argument.

As Trent drummed his fingers to the beat of the music, Beth allowed herself to ponder the longing she'd felt in the midst of their prayers. Why did their words comfort her so much? Why did she, despite the fact she found the service long and boring, want to return?

The words to a song she had heard ages ago came to her mind. She softly hummed the melody, singing the words in her mind.

They will know we are Christians by our love, by our love. They will know we are Christians by our love.

Chapter 22: Lisa

"What I'm saying is that I'd like to do a piece." Lisa sat across from Lacy Stevens, the senior editor of the *Pride of the Press*.

Lisa had spent a few weeks resenting and resisting Eve's suggestion that she be a voice to other women considering abortion, but in the end, her conscience had won out. If only she'd known the side effects not listed in the fine print. If she could help educate other women about the emotional repercussions of abortion, all the research and writing would be worth it.

"A piece? Lisa, you know how it works. We give you a topic, and you cover it. If you quit because you were tired of covering the different events in the student body, I can assign you to something else, but you can't just choose whatever you want to write about now that you're back. Especially since this is going to be the first issue of the semester. We need to get these articles written fast."

Lisa sighed. How could she make her point and move forward? She had to be doing the right thing. But then, shouldn't it be easier?

"I want to write a piece about abortion."

Lacy cocked a brow. "A women's lib thing? I'd consider it if it was in conjunction with a current event or major case in court, but there doesn't seem to be much buzz about the subject lately." Lacy shuffled papers, a polite signal to abandon their conversation for more important things.

Chapter 22: Lisa

"No, I'd like to do an article on how emotionally harmful abortion can be to a woman."

"Whoa." Lacy sat back, snickering. "This isn't the avenue for that. I'm sure if you go to one of those crisis pregnancy centers or something, they could plug you into the right outlet." Her mouth curved in a cynical smile.

Lisa had the urge to tweak it with her fingers.

Her shoulders sagged. At least she tried. There clearly wasn't an interest. Sighing softly, she hoisted herself out of the chair, a task that became increasingly difficult by the day. Just then, a gentle jab poked her abdomen. Then another.

After that night of waiting for the baby's movements, they were gradually becoming more distinguished. She didn't feel them every day, least of all when she was waiting for them, but those movements were an undeniable reminder of the life growing inside of her.

A life which, at that moment, seemed to be prodding her not to give up. Lisa had to be a voice. Little Esther couldn't speak of how her life had been threatened by a lie. She couldn't utter a word of warning or a statement of her innocence. It was up to her birth mother to speak for her. And for the brother or sister she would never be able to play with, along with all the unborn friends she would never have a chance to meet.

"I'll tell you what." Lisa locked eyes with Lacy. "I will write the story and submit it to you by the prescribed deadline. If you read it and decide it's not for your paper, that's fine. But don't make a judgment until you see it."

Lacy threw her hands up. "Fine. Have it your way. But if you're serious about jumping back in, you're also going to have to cover the stories assigned to you as your first priority. You can't slack on your real work to pursue this . . . this *piece*."

Ignoring the sarcasm laced in her comment, Lisa nodded. "Deal."

Riding a wave of victory, she waltzed out of the building. Once her feet hit the pavement of the sidewalk, however, doubts rose. Where could she start? What would she even write? Should she do a factual article filled with stats and mind-numbing numbers or try for a feature-type of story with more of a personal feel? How would she summon the emotional energy needed to dive into the debts of a blood crime she wanted to look away from?

And she needed to do all this without letting her grades slip. She'd barely passed the summer semester and had been determined not to go that route again. One more C or D and she could kiss her scholarships goodbye.

Lisa slowed her pace as the boldness she'd felt moments earlier faded. Could she take it back? Erase what had happened? She couldn't write an article about abortion. If only she'd never gotten close enough to abortion's deadly chasm to peer into it. If only she was still innocent, the world a blank slate full of endless possibilities and little responsibility, a world of wonder waiting to be explored. She bit her lip until she tasted blood. If only she could rewrite the story of her life.

If she walked any more slowly, she'd be run over by other students bustling along without a care in the world besides their new class schedule. She only had to take one step after another until the article was written, no matter how painful it would be.

Back in her apartment, she shuffled to her laptop sitting on the kitchen table. Dread pooled as she sank into the chair and waited for her word processor to load. Then a blank page loomed before her. Her throat tightened and her palms sweated. How to start? Where to start? How could she be a voice for the multitudes when she was just finding a voice for herself?

She rubbed her temples, then snatched her phone and hit number four on her speed dial. One ring. Two. Three. She was going to have to leave a voicemail.

Chapter 22: Lisa

But then Eve answered, out of breath. "Hey, Lisa, what's up?"

"I should ask the same about you. You sound like you just finished first in a marathon."

"Close enough. I did walk a flight of steps."

"Are you trying to get that baby out?" Her mom once told her how she'd walked three miles to usher Lisa into the world. Her contractions had begun as she was rounding the last block.

"Not for a few weeks, at least. Two more weeks and I'll be considered full-term. At that point, I might try a marathon if you really think it would help."

"It helped my mom. At least that's how the story goes, anyway. Who knows? It may have been a coincidence."

"This time I left my cell phone upstairs. I spent ten minutes looking for it. Pregnancy brain. Now I have to catch my breath and go back down before my pancakes burn."

"Pancakes?"

"I had a craving."

Lisa smiled to herself. Surely, she'd never have the kind of cravings that caused some women to eat pickles on their ice cream or pancakes in the late afternoon.

"So, what's up?" Eve said.

"Well, I did it." She stared at the blinking black cursor on the laptop screen. "I went into the editor's office, told her I wanted a spot back on the paper, and told her I was going to write a piece on abortion."

"Good for you!" Eve's breathing became more labored. She must be waddling down the steps towards the smell of burning pancakes. "So, they were interested, huh?"

"Not exactly. Actually, she acted like it was pretty ridiculous, but we agreed that she would take a look at my finished article and make a decision at that point."

"So, now all you have to do is write."

If Lisa would have been there, Eve probably would be hugging her at that point. Or right after she turned off the burner. A few days before, she'd dropped by Eve's house and told her that she thought Eve was right, no matter how angered she had become at her suggestion at first. Eve's expression hadn't held a hint of "I told you so." Instead, it radiated the pride and approval she would expect a mother to have for her child after a hard decision had been made.

"That's the problem. I don't know where to start or what to say. If it's not well written, it's guaranteed not to be published. I don't want to waste time on a piece that will only see the trash can."

"I see. Well, I'll pray that God will give you the exact words to say. I believe this is of Him, Lisa, and if it is, it will get published one way or another. God is bigger than editors or people's opinions. You don't have to be paranoid about writing perfectly. Do what you can and allow God to be God."

"Yeah, but where do I start?" Strange that she no longer inwardly flinched when Eve brought up God. Though she hadn't started going to a church or anything, she had finally read the stories of Moses and Esther. Picking up a Bible after all that time felt right, somehow. Kind of like those friendships she'd heard about where two friends saw each other only on rare occasions but could still picked up exactly where they left off. Perhaps it was a poor comparison, since she hadn't actually *left* the Lord, but it *had* been years since she'd picked up a Bible and read it of her own free will. And it was the same as she remembered it from Sunday school: comfortable in a familiar sort of way.

"Why don't you take a look at the clinic's website? If your purpose is to counteract the lies surrounding abortion, you'll find them all written out for you there, I suppose."

Lisa sighed. Eve was right, but she'd rather do most anything else. "Okay. I'll start there."

They chatted for a few minutes about Lisa's upcoming OB checkup and about her Braxton Hicks contractions, which were coming with more regularity now. As they talked, she browsed the clinic's website.

Making small talk while exploring the page made it seem easier, as if the site didn't have the final say. After a couple minutes, however, Lisa had to hang up and devote herself to the task at hand. Eve once again reassured her that she was praying for her. Although Lisa took little stock in such pleasantries, she knew it was more than an idle comment—Eve would be praying, and that gave her the confidence to move ahead.

She found one page that gave more information about the clinic itself. Skimming through the information, different words stood out to her: Warm. Comfortable. Supportive. Safe. Compassionate. Non-judgmental. She might throw up. Was her experience so far removed because she had it done in a trailer and not a clinic? Would things have been different if she'd gone to this office? Would she still have the nightmares, the guilt? Would anyone take her seriously in this article, or would they think they wouldn't suffer as she had, as they went to a licensed center?

The questions plagued her, and a growing doubt nagged at her mind. Did she even have the authority to write such an article? She had to try, at least. She pushed the thoughts, feelings, and wave of nausea aside and continued reading. She clicked on another icon to view their mission statement. There it was again: the word "supportive." Right after the word "dignity." Their mission was to preserve women's emotional well-being throughout the abortion process. Sounded nice. And impossible.

A deep sadness welled within her with each sentence she read. She skimmed a page of frequently asked questions, lacking the emotional energy to read each statement in detail. The FAQ asked, "Is abortion dangerous?" That question hadn't even occurred to her until after the procedure was underway. Of course, it had been dangerous for her to go to an unlicensed "doctor," but she had a feeling the case regarding the clinic would be harder to prove.

The answer was, "Abortion is safer than labor." She stared at that statement for a long while. It didn't ring true, but how could she counter the statement?

Do abortions cause psychological problems? She didn't expect a flat-out "yes," but the words that stared back at her from the screen made her stomach sink: "It is rare for women to have psychological problems after an abortion. Most women are happy with their decision and relieved it is over."

Relieved it is over. Her own voice rang through her mind from a conversation with Eve. *It's never over.* Was it true? Was she a rarity? An oddball who couldn't seem to get over what she'd gone through? Were there truly many other women who went on with life without giving their past a second thought? Was there something wrong with her?

The tears began to spring up. She closed her laptop and buried her face in her hands. She allowed herself to sob. Her body convulsed under the weight of the pain.

Surely, she wasn't the only one, was she? After all, the clinic was selling a service. They were going to say whatever they needed to say to lure women through the door. Even if it wasn't true. It was marketing, like any other business. She couldn't be the only one. There had to be others out there like her. Maybe not everyone who'd had an abortion, but certainly somewhere out there were women who ached under the weight of their guilt and shame—women who wondered about the life they gave up, what their children would have looked like and how old they would be.

Just then, Esther thumped inside her. Lisa calmed her trembling body. She'd read somewhere that a woman's stress level could affect her unborn baby. She'd caused enough trauma for one lifetime. She forced herself to take deep breaths and subdued the urge to cry. How was she going to write this article? She couldn't begin to answer these questions or even write anything without falling apart.

She lay down on the couch, pulled a nearby blanket over herself, and curled up into as much of the fetal position as her belly would allow. Eve was most likely praying for her at that very moment, so she followed her friend's lead. She was a little rusty at praying, and her words were simple.

"God, I can't do this. I know I need to, but I can't. If You really want me to write this piece, You're going to have to help me. You're going to have to heal me. I can't do this on my own."

Her whispers seemed to nestle near the rafters of her apartment as she slid from sorrow to sleep.

Chapter 23: Ashira

Months passed, and she welcomed her new little boy into the world with a bittersweet pang. His father was not there to see his son. Yet, he was alive. Safe.

Phineas' newborn cry aroused Ashira from her slumber. "Shhh," she whispered, pulling him close to nurse. "We do not want to awaken Rizpah and Josiah, do we? Would that be the proper way to repay their kindness?"

Phineas quieted quickly and ate. The soft moonlight accentuated his miniature features. He took after his father with dark hair and a wide brow.

It had been nearly a year since Ashira arrived in Jerusalem. She'd meant to return home much sooner, but the skies would not cooperate. As long as the rains remained shut up in the heavens, her home village would not be a safe place for her and her son. Though she ached to see her husband and family, she had little choice but to remain in the great city.

Josiah and Rizpah had been kind and allowed her to remain in their home. Rizpah patiently taught Ashira her trade, and Ashira worked with her in the marketplace weaving mats in exchange for food and board.

"Isn't it odd that people buy such items during hard times?" She'd asked Rizpah one day at the market.

The woman shrugged and threaded the reeds on the loom. "Most try to live life as normal despite the drought."

"Do they think if they ignore the drought, it will go away?"

Chapter 23: Ashira

"They put faith in Hananiah's words that the rain would soon come. Prosperity is around the corner, my dear."

Oh, that it were so. When the Babylonians besieged Jerusalem a few months ago, the people had been momentarily shaken from their idolatrous practices. However, the siege lifted when the Babylonians feared the Egyptians would come to deliver Jerusalem. Things soon went back to normal. Though Jeremiah prophesied Nebuchadnezzar's army would return and destroy Jerusalem, most did not believe him, choosing instead to believe those who prophesied that the King of Babylon would return the articles taken from the temple.

Rizpah tucked a stray strand of hair behind her ear and continued working. "I believe the other prophets. The God of Abraham, Isaac, and Jacob will not desert their city."

"But you worship idols."

"I worship Yahweh too. He will protect us and cause us to prosper again."

So Rizpah thought Yahweh a good-luck token, not a true God. Ashira pressed her lips together. No use trying to persuade her differently.

When Ashira's hands ached from weaving, she'd ask Rizpah if she could take a moment to rest. "Go on," Rizpah would say kindly. "Go and listen to your prophet."

And she did. Ashira listened to Jeremiah speak almost daily. If only her people would hear his instructions and repent of their double mindedness. The throngs that surrounded her, however, were not receptive to his message. They came only to mock him. Idols were still sold on the street in mass numbers, and the worship of false gods was rampant. She could only pray that the people would turn before it was too late.

Listening for her husband, she would keep her head down whenever she was on the streets. She had seen no sign of him since she'd arrived. Thankfully, she'd not been found, but what if he was not even looking for her? Was he angry? Why did he think she left? Did he miss her? Had his heart hardened or grown more tender? She ached with loneliness.

As Phineas drifted back to sleep, Ashira stroked his fine hair. When would they be able to return home? *Lord, will You send the rain? I want to return to my hometown, but I lack the courage. Send the rains, Lord. Save us.*

Even as she prayed, doubt pooled in her belly. Her people were not turning their hearts towards the one true God. They were not forsaking their idolatrous ways. Would the Lord send rain to an unfaithful people? She amended her prayer. *Turn our hearts towards You, O God. Have mercy.*

***

The crowd around Jeremiah dispersed, yet Ashira lingered on the outskirts, hoping to hear another word from the Lord. It was late, and she needed to head towards Rizpah's home, yet she could not seem to leave. Phineas slept contently in a sling close to her chest. She had a few moments to spare, so she waited.

Jeremiah sat then, a signal to the few who were left that he was finished speaking for the day. Still, she did not move. His feet were caked with dust. When he wiped his brow with the back of his hand, he left a trail of dirt behind. He brought his canteen up to his lips and drank deeply, chin bobbing. Water dribbled from his beard.

"You wish to ask me something." Jeremiah's eyes locked onto hers.

She averted her gaze, uncomfortable with the intensity of his regard. Could he read her mind?

"It is not proper for me to inquire of you," she said. How could she, a woman, ask a question of this man?

"The Lord says to you, 'Return.'"

Chapter 23: Ashira

"Return?" Had he really said that? Had God given Jeremiah a message especially for her? "Return to my home? Return to my husband?"

"Your Maker is your husband."

"Yes, I know that now. He is the one true God, and there is no other."

"You have fled out of fear?"

"Yes. Fear for the life that was growing within me. My husband would have me sacrifice this child to Molech, and I could not bear it. I fled from my village, next to Anathoth."

He nodded.

Did he know this before she had spoken of it? Did he know about Shai? About her sin? A true prophet of the Lord might know all things.

"You need not fear any longer." His eyes peered deep. Perhaps even into her very soul. "Return and carry my message to the people there. They must repent before it is too late."

Carry his message? She sucked in a breath. "Forgive me for being so forward, but I . . . I have seen you speak in Anathoth, and your own people have never accepted your message in the past."

"Yes, true." The prophet sighed. The lines in his face deepened, the weariness of years calling out to people who would not listen. "I have often wished to be free of this burden of speaking judgment to the people. The Lord made it clear that most will not heed my words, and I will be an object of scorn all my days. But I must be His mouthpiece. I cannot keep quiet. His word is like a fire shut up in my bones. I must speak what He gives me to speak, regardless of whether others listen."

She gave a slight shake of her head. "I do not have such courage."

Jeremiah's unblinking gaze assured her. "The Lord will go before you. You must return."

Phineas shifted in his sling. The hour grew late.

"I must be going now." She nodded to Jeremiah and turned to walk to Rizpah's home. The conversation shook her. What was she to think? He said she must return. Did he mean now? Tonight? Tomorrow? *Lord, I wish to see my husband again, but I am so afraid.* Would she find his demeanor altered even without a change in the skies? If it would only rain, she might have the courage to go back. But the skies had not yielded, and she couldn't return. Not yet. Perhaps if she waited a little while longer . . .

Rounding the corner, she ducked into home. Josiah and Rizpah's home, not hers, though she'd lodged there for nearly a year. Her home was in her village and with her husband. A home Jeremiah had told her to return to. But he did not say when.

Rizpah sat at the kitchen table, kneading dough. "Ah, you're returning late, Ashira. What did your prophet say today?"

"Good evening, Rizpah." Ashira joined and removed Phineas from the sling to feed him. "Jeremiah spoke again of the return of the Babylonians."

"And you believe him? Surely you see now that he was wrong. They have left our city and will not return, unless it is to restore the items taken from our temple. Hananiah prophesied the holy articles would be brought back within two full years."

"Oh, Rizpah, must we go over this again?" Ashira kept her voice gentle. "Jeremiah says the Lord has not sent Hananiah and that he makes the people trust in a lie. I believe Jeremiah, and you believe Hananiah. It seems that we will not agree on this matter."

"Yes, indeed. Time will tell which prophet is true and which is false. Until then, we must find another matter to debate."

Rizpah smiled, and Ashira said a quick prayer for her opinionated friend. *After all the kindness she has shown me, Lord, do not let her be destined for the sword. Keep her safe when the Babylonians do return and lead her back to You.*

That night, Ashira tossed upon her bed, unable to sleep. Jeremiah's charge tumbled through her brain. She could not shake the feeling that she needed to leave Jerusalem soon, that Jeremiah had not meant for her to put the matter off. Yet how could she make plans to leave when it still hadn't rained?

Soon it would rain. And then she would return.

Chapter 24: Eve

I stood in front of the clinic on a Saturday morning. Today was the tenth anniversary of the clinic's opening, and many different protesters surrounded the building, waving signs and chanting slogans. I recognized a few protesters from other churches. Most I hadn't seen before. Though my church hadn't announced today as an official prayer day, most of the regular crew showed up. Even the pastor had taken time out of his weekend schedule to stand with us.

The heat of summer melted into the gentler temperatures of early fall, though September remained a week away. I shivered as a cool breeze wisped around my ankles. As I stood in front of the clinic, it hit me. My days here like this were numbered. My life would look vastly different with a newborn—with two newborns.

Would it be too difficult to bring Zephan here to pray? I could bring a stroller and walk him around. But what would I do when it came time to nurse? Maybe I should pray from home until he got a little older. Only then I'd have two little ones, and it would be winter. Would I be able to come in the spring? What did I sign up for?

There I went again, letting my mind wander. *Come on, Eve.* If I didn't have too much longer to participate in the sieges, I needed to make the most of my time. I willed my mind back to prayer. I had to give my future to the Lord.

The closer my due date got, the harder it became to concentrate. There was so much going on, so much to consider. Dozens of small details flitted past my memory, and prayer time seemed to be when those to-do items resurrected in my mind.

My prayers that day were especially weak. It seemed that every few minutes I had to refocus my thoughts. I couldn't think of any eloquent or profound prayers, so I kept repeating simple phrases over and over again. *Lord, if Your strength is perfected in my weakness, it's being perfected much this morning.* Every inch of my humanity strained as I pulled my light sweater tighter around me. Thankfully, heaven's ways and values were different from mine. God moves through weak and broken people uttering weak and broken prayers. Even on the days when I found it hard to pray, my intercession was powerful in the heavens.

I focused my prayers on Trent yet again. After what happened with his wife, I'd held out hope that he would turn to the Lord instead of returning to the clinic. My heart sank deeper each time I watched him come or go from that place. Hadn't he felt convicted? Yet he persevered in his job.

I counted the women entering the clinic as I prayed for Trent. I hadn't been at the clinic more than an hour, and I was already in the teens. I had to fight the urge to close my eyes in prayer. Doing so would only make me drowsier and cause my mind to wander to who knows where. Then a news van came and parked across from us. As if I wasn't already distracted enough. They must have wanted a story on the clinic's anniversary. What would they say?

I started to rein my focus in when a familiar looking red SUV pulled into the parking lot. I squinted to get a better look, prayers forgotten. Shoot. I'd gotten distracted again. And for what? A red SUV. There were tons of red SUVs. I needed to focus on praying for Trent. I turned back towards the clinic and picked up where I had left off.

Then it dawned on me.

No, it couldn't be. I had to be mistaken.

But I wasn't mistaken.

Before I could turn to look again, a teenager with dark, curly hair walked right in front of me towards the entrance. Her mother had a hand on her shoulder.

My mouth fell open.

Rachel Tuft. Escorted by her mother Rhonda.

I almost took the tape off my mouth and shouted at them. Rhonda attended the same Bible study as me. Her daughter Rachel was active in the youth group and had played the lead role in the Christmas play last year. I'd known the Tuft family for five years, or was it six? They'd never come to the clinic to pray, but Rhonda and I had sat together at church functions, bought each other gifts for special occasions . . . prayed together. They must not have realized that today was the clinic's ten-year anniversary; they didn't expect anyone from the congregation to be there.

I was so shocked that I doubled over, the pain in my heart as real as if someone had punched me in the gut. I lowered myself onto my knees and wept. My sobs were muffled but not extinguished by the LIFE tape. Rocking back and forth, I wiped my cheeks with the sleeves of my sweater. It didn't help. The tears continued to flow like a torrent.

Oh, God. Oh, God! It's in the Church. The enemy's lies—his deception—it's invaded the Church. Your people . . . we're the ones who should cherish life the most because we know the Creator, and yet we've submitted to the spirit of convenience.

I wasn't completely oblivious to the statistics. I knew that the abortion rate for Christians was as high as for non-Christians, and I'd read that one in five women having an abortion considered themselves to be born-again. When I'd read the statistics, a wave of sadness had swept over me. But seeing the daughter of a friend walking into the clinic was more than a wave. It was a tsunami.

Oh, God, wake us up. Wake up Your people. Our hearts have grown dull and numb. We've awakened to the evils of abortion for short periods of time, only to be soothed by the lullaby of our world. We keep drifting in and out of sleep, never fully awake. Father, wake us up!

The tears came faster and harder, and my body shook under the weight of them. A hand touched my shoulder.

"Eve? Eve? Are you okay? You're not in labor, are you?" My very concerned pastor gaped at me, worry written in his expression.

I shook my head no and peeled the tape from my lips.

"I'm not in labor. I'm praying." My sobs choked out any other explanation, as I replaced my tape and continued to rock on my knees. Oh, Rhonda. You would have been a grandma. A grandma, Rhonda. Could you honestly see no other way? Another thought gripped me. It felt heavy, so heavy that I thought I would sink straight through the sidewalk under its weight. Rachel, your baby would have been in Zephan's Sunday school class. They could have played together, been friends. Your baby and Zephan and Esther. They would have been friends.

Lord, Lord, the enemy's lies are so loud in the ears of the people. Of Your people. They're so loud. And it's the praise of infants that Your Word says will silence the avenger. Only we're killing so many of those little voices. Oh, God, wake us up!

Tears blurred my eyes, and my own cries occupied my ears. So intent was I on my prayer that I didn't notice the commotion around me.

Chapter 25: Trent

Trent stumbled toward the front doors of the clinic in a flood of emotion. What had Eve called it that day?

Conviction.

Rushing out, he tripped over his own feet, clear about only one thing. Unlike the last time he had fled the clinic, this time, he was not going back. Surely everyone else felt it too. He couldn't be the only one.

He'd been sitting on his stool, explaining to a young woman and her mother the basics of the abortion he'd been about to perform. But he stopped mid-sentence. Overcome with a wave of—what was it called? —oh yeah. Conviction.

At the same time, he'd watched the girl's eyes grow wider and wider. Her mother had gripped her hand and yanked her towards the door. Heat spread across his hands, his arms. And why did he feel so heavy? He had to get out of there.

Just like the girl and her mother who'd stood and headed for the door without a word.

What was happening?

It was almost as if some force propelled him out the exit. In his mind he heard short, strong phrases.

Repent.

Turn.

Surreal. Already the details were sketchy, the replay foggy. Confusion swarmed around him, along with the sound of weeping. Was it his own? He'd been gut punched, surely. Gut punched by God?

He rushed to his car. What could he possibly tell Beth? He couldn't quit his job. And yet . . .

He glanced over his shoulder. The sun shone, and a fresh, albeit chilly, breeze scattered a smattering of colorful leaves near the entrance. It didn't look ominous. But he couldn't set foot in that building again. Ever.

As he drove away, his hands shook against the steering wheel.

Where was he going? Didn't matter. He needed to get away—far away—from that place of death. Should he go home? Certainly not to the lake or a bar. He couldn't get enough air. Panic swelled in the back of his throat. His pulse hammered, his mouth dry.

He passed a small church on his left, and it pulled him close. Without debating or resorting to reason, he made a U-turn and swung into the parking lot. He slipped inside, sorrow gripping him.

He passed through the tall wooden front doors and slid onto the back pew. Raking his hands through his hair, he leaned forward, mind racing. How could he possibly make sense of this?

Only one thing was clear: Eve was right. There was a God, and He was far from uninvolved.

He needed to pray or to—what? Groan?—but no sounds made it past his mouth. He held himself back, afraid. Uncomfortable. Tears pricked the corners of his eyelids. Though he tried to hold them off, they persisted. He held his breath and struggled to contain himself.

Finally, he couldn't fight the turmoil any longer.

"Mercy!" The cry that accosted his ears came from his own mouth. The word churned up within him again, and he cried out, sobbing this time. "Mercy!"

Chapter 26: Lisa

"Turn on the TV right now."

At the urgency in Eve's voice, Lisa tucked the phone against her shoulder and didn't waste any time. She flipped the TV on, and the abortion clinic she had almost walked into a few months ago flashed across the screen. This time, a doctor ran out of it.

"What's happened? A shooting? Bombing?" Her pulse clicked up a notch. That kind of thing happened at other clinics across the country.

"No. Nothing like that. I was there. God answered my prayer. He broke in and changed Trent's heart."

"What do you mean?" How could Eve speak so calmly when confusion swirled around her?

"Sometimes God, in His mercy, gives people a piece of the burden of His heart so that they'll turn to Him."

"This has happened before?"

"Well, not here, but in other places."

"How come I've never heard of it before then?" Her skepticism rose.

"Think about our media, Lisa. It's hardly unbiased. There's something bigger going on than our little lives. God is moving."

The reel of the doctor jogging away from the automatic double doors played on repeat. He tossed a glance over his shoulder, face drawn and pale.

Chapter 26: Lisa

The reporter stared into the camera, face somber. "Today is the tenth anniversary of the opening of Compassion Clinic for Women, but one doctor appears not to be celebrating. What seems to be a panicked abortionist made a run for it today—"

Eve's voice broke in. "You told me you've had a block in writing your article, but I believe after today, people will be receptive to what you have to say. Sit down and write your story. People are ripe and raw right now. They're looking for answers, for a clear voice amid all the confusion. They'll listen to you, Lisa."

The reporter zeroed in on two women, one older, one younger. A mother and daughter? Lisa squinted at the screen. A pregnant daughter. The mother spoke. "We were in the room going over the upcoming procedure and something hit us. All of us, I think." She looked to her daughter as if seeking confirmation.

Wide eyes met hers as the girl nodded.

"I just knew it was wrong." Her fist flew to her mouth as she blinked rapidly.

The daughter took over. "I couldn't go through with it. All of a sudden, I felt so sad over what I was about to do. I couldn't . . . I couldn't . . . "

The reporter's brows knit together. "Was the doctor in question the one who was in the room with you?"

Both women nodded.

"There were no outside threats? No coercion?"

"No." The girl's voice came small but sure.

The camera panned back to show the reporter only. "We'll keep you updated on any further developments."

Lisa flipped the television off. What Eve said rang true. She knew she needed to do it—to buck up and write, to let the story come out of her. Who cared if people labeled her experience as irrelevant because it hadn't happened in a certified clinic? But her heart still felt heavy.

She flipped open her laptop. As she poised her fingers above the keys, she prayed again. *God, help me. You know what needs to be written. You've asked me to do this, so You'll help me. Please, let these be the words people need to hear.* Her fingers danced over the keys, making a melody all their own. She found freedom in the written word.

She didn't stop to think too hard, didn't worry about whether she wrote the right things. Letting words come out of that place deep within her, she wrote of her experience, her torment, of the nightmares and the pain. She threw in a couple of statistics she had memorized but focused the piece on feeling instead of weighing it down with impersonal facts.

Tears dripped on the backs of her hands as she typed, but she didn't—couldn't—stop to wipe them away. Something had taken over her fingers—God perhaps—and wouldn't let them go until He'd had His way. It felt as if someone breathed new life into her as she wrote.

Though the remorse of her past still hovered, something new took the place of the shame that had pervaded her every waking moment. That newness awakened in the freedom to speak out what she had kept locked away in her heart all that time. God's tenderness came near, forgiving her of her sin and giving her a second chance. It was as if a hard rain rinsed the grit off her soul, and rays of sunshine now brought a freshness to her life.

She finished the article in one sitting, didn't go back over it to edit it, just emailed it to Eve. Then she closed her laptop and sat back on her couch, basking in a new feeling. She was clean for the first time since she'd lost her virginity. As if spring had come again. She didn't want to move from that place, lest she lose what she'd gained.

God, You've forgiven me. You've washed me clean. I've asked for forgiveness a hundred different times in a hundred different ways, but I don't know if I'd ever turned to You to receive it. I receive it now, God. I know I've been far away for a long time, but I return to You today.

Behold, I make all things new.

She sucked in a breath. That was it. The voice of God. Not audible to her ears, but clear to her spirit. That's what people meant when they said they heard God speak to them.

Yes, God. I believe it. You make all things new. Even my heart.

Classes would begin the next day, and the gears of her life would start to churn again. There would be schedules and deadlines, tests and papers. At that moment, though, she had no other agenda but to draw near to the One who had already drawn near to her. She retrieved her old Bible from the bookshelf, looked up the word "mercy" in the concordance in the back, and began to read. And believe.

Chapter 27: Trent

Trent rushed out of the church with nearly as much speed and vigor as he had rushed in a couple hours earlier. The pastor wanted to pray with him? With him? His mind whirled and his body trembled. He might be sick to his stomach. The weight of every baby he'd killed pressed upon his shoulders. He struggled for breath.

The pastor had sat beside him and given him trite assurances. *God can forgive anything.*

Sure. Right.

All you have to do is turn to Him, and He'll wash away all your sins.

Sounded great. Too good to be true. Moving on couldn't be that easy. Not for him. Sure, others seemed relieved to say a simple prayer and be done with it. Who were they? What crime had they committed? The weight of their sin was likely little more than a feather compared to his.

The pastor thought to reassure him with a story about a woman in his congregation who had an abortion and then found forgiveness in Jesus. A nice tale. She'd only had the blood of one life on her hands. Him? He was drowning in blood. Her crime was the equivalent to hiring a hit man. He was the actual killer. The one who had pulled the trigger—not on one baby, but on hundreds. Too many. He couldn't begin to estimate how many lives had ended at his hands.

The knowledge choked him.

Chapter 27: Trent

He was far too guilty to be saved by a simple prayer. Maybe it worked for the woman the pastor mentioned. She was merely an accomplice to a crime. What was it the Bible said? The wages of sin were death. His hands shook against the wheel as he drove home, swerving the car out of his lane a few times. Was this his day to die?

What was it his mom said? You reap what you sow. If that was true, he'd been sowing seeds of death for years. It was only right that he would reap the same. He had to accept that reality. He deserved to die. It was only a matter of time. And then what? He shuddered.

He had to do something, anything to redeem himself and prevent his own death. He had to *do* something right for once, something that this God could accept. He was a dead man if he couldn't appease God. But what could he do? What could he possibly do to make up for the evil he'd done?

Yeah, he'd walked right out of that church, away from that offer to *pray with him*. There was no way he'd fall for an easy way out of the mess he'd gotten himself into.

As he neared his subdivision, he racked his brain for a semblance of an explanation to give Beth. Would she think he'd gone mad? Would she be angry at him for walking out of the clinic . . . again? Did they have enough in savings to cover the bills until he could figure out something for further employment?

He pulled into the driveway to find Beth's car already out front. Her hand held back the curtain, and her furrowed brow registered concern through the window. In a moment she was at the front door. Taking a deep breath, he got out and met her at the doorstep, shaking with wet cheeks.

"You're okay. Thank God you're okay. I called you over and over again, but you wouldn't answer your phone. I saw you on the news, running to the car—" Her voice broke, and he grabbed her, holding her close to him.

"I'm okay, Beth. I'm safe." Though he didn't know for how long.

"What happened there? What's going on? Why didn't you answer your phone?" Her wide eyes seeped fear.

His hands instinctively went to his pockets. Where was his phone?

Oh. In his locker with his wallet. He hadn't grabbed anything when he left the clinic. He only had the keys from his pocket.

"I must have left my phone. Let's go inside, babe." He guided her into the house and to the couch. Once she was seated, he brought a box of tissues from the bathroom. He sat next to her.

"I don't know what happened. All I know is that I can't go back there. I don't know what I'm going to do, but I can't—"

"I don't want you to go back either. I don't want you within a mile of that place."

Tension left his shoulders. He'd feared convincing Beth that he needed to find other employment would be the greatest battle.

"What happened, Trent? The reporters couldn't figure it out."

"It was . . . God." He shrugged.

She nodded. "Eve said that. They interviewed her on TV and she said that God had answered their prayers. I don't know what that means, but I saw the look on your face. You can't go back there, not even to get your phone."

"Or my wallet?"

"We'll report the cards lost. Don't worry about that. I'm afraid for you."

So was he.

"What do you think it was?" He searched her eyes.

"I don't know. All I care about is that you're safe. You're here with me." She leaned into him, her arms tight around his neck. "You know," she murmured after several minutes, "maybe it is God."

"Why do you say that? I was so afraid you wouldn't believe me. I was afraid of what you'd think."

"Afraid? Honey, I'm on your side. We're a team, remember?" She shifted her weight back and hoisted herself up. "Wait. Come here."

She walked into the kitchen, motioning for him to follow. As he did so, he was struck by her beauty once again. How did he get so lucky? Had he gotten too lucky? Did God give him such a gift only so He'd have something precious to take away? Was this going to be part of the punishment?

"Trent, you know Don Price, right?" she said over her shoulder.

"Don? Yeah. We worked on several projects together in college. Went to med school together. Why? What's going on?"

"He called today—before that whole mess." She gestured toward the television. "When I got home, there was a message on the machine."

"And?"

"He has a private OB-GYN practice in Claymore. He said business is booming and he wanted you to consider an offer. I think he wants you to work with him, come on board with his practice."

"What?" his eyes narrowed. What kind of trick was this? What was God trying to pull? He'd just been racking his brain for what to do for another job. He needed a way out of the clinic. Had he prayed for that? Or had he only been blowing off steam? Was God giving him a perfectly acceptable way out? What was the catch? Why would He do such a thing?

"Listen yourself." She motioned towards the landline as she settled into a kitchen chair. With shaking hands, he hit the button for voicemail.

"Hey Trent, it's Don Price. It's been forever, hasn't it? I'm calling because I have an offer for you. I've got a private practice now in Claymore, and I've got more pregnant women here than I can care for. I've been having to turn them away for months now, and it just dawned on me: I could use another doctor to help me. Simple OB work, mainly. Call me and let me know if you're interested . . . " He rattled off three numbers: a home phone, a cell, and a pager.

Trent listened again. Then again, to take down the numbers, just in case.

"So," Beth said. "Maybe it is God. Maybe Eve's right and abortion is wrong. It looks like He's giving you another option."

Another option? But why? The God that showed up earlier was against him, wasn't He? Why then would He set up something like this? Was it a trick?

"I don't know. I don't understand it." He sat next to her, lacing his fingers through hers.

"At this point, I don't think you need to understand it. You need a job. He has an offer. Don't think too hard about it. Go deliver babies. You can do ours while you're at it. I'm not too fond of Dr. Yoseph."

"But he's the—"

"He's the best. I know. At least that's what you've *told* me. Personally, I think you should have at least compassion or feeling of some sort to successfully bring life into the world. I know you love this child. To him, she's only another number."

"I'll think about it." And he did. He thought about it all that night. He thought about what had happened earlier. And he thought about the offer.

He didn't deserve to deliver his own child. He didn't deserve to live. He didn't deserve such a beautiful, caring woman as his wife. He didn't deserve his house, his car . . . anything. But maybe he should enjoy what he had as long as he had it. Surely everything he had was about to be taken away from him. That or his breath.

Over the next few days, Trent and Beth watched the scene at the clinic being replayed on different news channels. Their little town even made the national news. He didn't want to watch but couldn't pull himself away from the television. Watching the scene made him tremble again. Beth's nearness did wonders for his courage. Tucked under his arm, she told him repeatedly how glad she was that he was safe and home.

He didn't tell her about ending up in church or about walking away from the prayer.

Chapter 28: Lisa

Was excitement the right word for what Lisa felt? Or trepidation? Because her hands trembled as she made her way to the school newspaper's office. She had to see it for herself: the story of her pain in print.

When she'd turned in her piece the day after the incident at the clinic, there was no sarcasm, no snide remarks. The hostility had vanished. Lacy kept her red, blotchy face angled toward the papers on her desk, but Lisa didn't miss how she swiped her cheek with the back of her hand and mumbled a thank you as she took the piece from Lisa's hands.

What was she supposed to think about that?

She received a call an hour later.

"We'll print it." That's all Lacy said. No praise. No justifications. God had made a way for a voice to come forth from her tragedy. Would her article make a difference? Would speaking out spare anyone pain?

Now Lisa entered the office on shaking legs. Thank goodness no one was there when she arrived. She wouldn't have to fumble through a conversation. Someone would come by later to distribute the newspapers across the campus. The rest of the student body would have the opportunity to see the article in a few hours.

She took two copies from the shelf reserved for staff and stashed one copy in her backpack. The other copy crinkled as she held it in trembling hands. Flipping through it, her heart dropped into her stomach. The article was really there.

Everything she'd been trying to hide, laid bare for anyone to see. She swallowed hard. After all Jesus went through for her, surely her risk paled in comparison.

Lisa reread her own story as she walked to geology class, trying to put herself into the reader's position but unable to shake the deeply personal reaction. When she arrived at class, she sat at a desk and stuffed the paper in her backpack with the other copy. No need provoking any questions from classmates. As the zipper closed, an oddly familiar voice met her ears.

"Oh, hi, Lisa! I've seen you in physics class, but I didn't know you were in this class too. Of course, I normally get here early and sit in the back. But I don't mind sitting up front if I'm sitting by a friend. Now we both have a friend in class! Isn't that so fun? Mind if I sit next to you?"

Lisa looked up, straight into the bright eyes of the girl she thought of as "Ms. Perky." What was her real name again? Annoyance niggled every time she saw that happy little face.

"Sure." Lisa reminded herself that it wasn't Ms. Perky's fault she had a wanted pregnancy while Lisa had an unwanted one. An unwanted one? Was that true any longer? *I want Eve to have this baby. I want her to live and breathe, laugh and run. Oh, God forgive me. I do want her. Maybe not to raise and mother, but I want to give her life.*

"So, how are you feeling? Do you feel your baby movin' and groovin' now?"

"All the time." Lisa instinctively rubbed her abdomen.

"I can't wait. John keeps putting his hand on my belly to try to feel the baby. I keep telling him it's too early, but he's so excited he can't help himself. He talks to the baby too. I always knew he'd make a great father." Her bright blue eyes glistened with pride.

What could Lisa possibly say? Her smile tightened as she nodded.

"What about your baby's daddy?" Ms. Perky continued. "Is he thrilled to feel those little kicks?"

"He's not in the picture." Lisa kept her voice even, devoid of emotion.

"Oh, I'm sorry. I didn't know. That's too bad. Well, maybe you'll meet someone who'll be a good daddy to your baby." Her bubbly tone had sobered somewhat.

Better to end the charade before it went too far. "Actually, my baby will have a great daddy. I'm giving her up for adoption to a wonderful couple."

"Oh." Ms. Perky sat back slightly and cocked her head to the side.

"Maybe someday I'll get married and have children, but right now this couple will give her a good, stable family and a future."

"Isn't . . . isn't that going to be hard for you to do?" The girl's head remained tilted to one side, her right eye slightly squinted.

Lisa sighed. "How could it not be hard? Most of the best choices in life are hard ones."

Ms. Perky was quiet for a moment, but when she spoke again, there was a new softness to her voice. "Well, I admire you. I don't know if I could do that."

The professor marched to the front, and a hush fell over the room. Lisa had been dreading the class ever since she had seen it on her degree requirements. She'd always hated any sort of science classes, though she managed to do fairly well. Studying rocks, however, had to be the worst. The few weeks of class hadn't changed her opinion.

As the class wore on, it seemed that her new red-haired friend didn't share her contempt for inanimate objects. Ms. Perky sat straight, taking frantic notes. Lisa smiled to herself. Maybe she wasn't so bad. Different, but not as annoying as Lisa first thought. She might preserve her sanity in this class for the semester. Maybe she should ask if she could study with her.

Chapter 28: Lisa

Eventually the professor's droning came to an end, and the sound of students shuffling papers and zipping backpacks was heard across the room.

Ms. Perky stood in front of her, a sheepish smile on her face. "Hey, Lisa, I'm sorry if anything I said made you feel . . . weird, you know? Are you still up for that buffet I told you about last semester?"

"Definitely."

"Why don't we both check our schedules and tomorrow we can talk about a date and time for lunch."

"Sure." Lisa's smile this time was more genuine. She could use another friend.

After her next class was over, Lisa drove to Eve's house. She had intended to surprise Eve with a copy of her article, but no one was home.

Lisa left the copy of the *Pride of the Press* between the front door and screen door. Unable to find a pen to leave a note, she prayed that Eve would read it and not think it junk mail. As she drove back to campus, her earlier unease came back full force. The paper would be distributed by the time she went to her next class. Her secret would be out. What if the pro-life people on campus looked down on her because of her previous abortion? What if the pro-choice people on campus condemned her for speaking out against it? So many possibilities, all of them negative, swarmed through her mind. She gripped the steering wheel a little harder.

She checked the clock. With an hour before her next class, she dropped by her apartment and ate lunch while reading her Bible. Over the last week, the Word of God had become increasingly alive to Lisa in a way she'd never experienced before. The scripture stories she'd memorized by rote now sang with life—the characters grew into real people, and God no longer seemed like a distant figure but instead a Being who cared intensely for people. She had a hard time pulling herself away for something as trivial as physics, but she forced herself to do so.

As she walked down the hall, it seemed as if people stared at her. *It's only my imagination, right, God? Hardly anyone would be able to match my name to my face, even if they found time to read my article already.* Paranoia, plain and simple.

She found her class and slid into her typical spot: the front corner desk. After a few minutes, her classmates came filing in. Then she made her entrance—Ms. Perky, the girl Lisa was supposed to meet for lunch the future. She really should ask the girl for her name again. It would be more embarrassing to keep going on pretending that she remembered. Lisa expected the red-headed girl to sit next to her as she had done before and smiled in her direction.

Ms. Perky met her eyes, then looked down at the floor and filed past Lisa to the back of the room.

A sick feeling swelled in the pit of her stomach. Four hours ago, Ms. Perky acted like her best friend. Now, she ignored her.

The difference was the article. It had to be.

But why judge Lisa for it? Ms. Perky was obviously in favor of life but couldn't be too religious, considering she was sleeping with her boyfriend. The professor passed out an assignment for the course and Lisa jerked her attention to him, mind reeling.

Oh, God! Is everyone going to hate me? Will I be able to make friends? To keep the ones I have? Will I be ostracized for this? Where are You in all of this?

Truth is unpopular, but it saves. I am unpopular, but I save.

I did what You wanted me to do, right?

I am with You.

A peace washed over her. It was true. No matter if her classmates turned their backs on her, He never would. He'd be with her. They'd get through whatever came her way together. Nothing could separate her from His love.

A week before it would have sounded ridiculous, but now it might be the only thing that made sense.

Chapter 29: Eve

What was I supposed to do now that Compassion Clinic for Women had been supernaturally put out of the abortion business? Trent wasn't going back, and it wasn't sustainable to have the doctor who filled in for him take over full time.

An answered prayer for sure. But, what was I supposed to do now? Praying at the clinic had become my normal. There was something about standing outside, whether in the blistering heat or cool breeze, feeling the earth beneath my feet and watching real destinies of real people unfold before my eyes. Sure, most people thought I was out of my mind. But it gave me a sense of purpose, an assurance that I was making a difference. So . . . now what?

With three weeks until my due date, I should pray at home. Obviously, God's ear knew no limit. He could hear and answer as easily whether I prayed from that particular piece of property or from the familiarity of my living room. I'd pray that other doctors would walk out of other clinics in my state and in the nation. The only difference was that I'd pray from my home. And perhaps I'd sit and prop up my swollen feet.

That worked for almost a half an hour. While at times I had a hard time keeping my focus on the task at hand while standing in front of the clinic, staying focused at home seemed nearly impossible. I'd make it five minutes before the pile of unfolded laundry snatched my attention. And what should I cook for dinner? Should we rearrange the nursery? Nope. Praying at home wasn't cutting it.

Was I about to go crazy? How could three weeks seem like such a long time? My back ached and my body screamed from all the excess weight. I couldn't get comfortable no matter what position I was in. Even more draining was the weight of waiting. Yes, we had a due date, but would little Zephan follow it? Every time a Braxton Hicks contraction would strike, I'd wonder if early labor had begun.

How would I know when I went into labor? What if I couldn't make it to the hospital on time? Or if I called Gideon to tell him it'd started, but his phone was dead or he misplaced it? What if the pain was too much? I intended to have a natural labor, mainly because I'd read that an epidural could increase the need for a C-section. But maybe I wouldn't be able to bear up underneath the pain. Along with that came other concerns: what if I waited too long to take pain medication? What if I didn't have the strength to push the baby out? Would the nurses try to pressure me into having an epidural? The list of unanswered questions was endless.

And then there was Esther. So far, the paperwork had gone through smoothly. Our home study had gone well. The fundraiser had helped, and we had enough money to cover the cost of the adoption, though we still were not sure how we'd pay for the rest of Lisa's medical costs. But thanks to Gideon, that worry weighed less on my heart. He was so confident that the money would come through, that God had ordained our adoption of this baby and He already knew how He'd pay for it.

How wondrous that excitement coursed through me whenever I thought about little Esther's upcoming birth. My heart swelled with anticipation of her, just like it did with Zephan. How could the love I held in my heart for them both be unashamedly equal? I did, in fact, feel as if I was pregnant with twins. Surely I looked it too, though only one child was growing in my belly.

The friendship I'd formed with Esther's mother both comforted and distressed me. My joy bubbled over at the fact that the Lord had pursued Lisa until she accepted Him. We were not only mothers of the same child; now we were sisters as well.

But as I had talked with her and heard her heart, worry began to niggle. Would she change her mind? Now that she'd come into relationship with Jesus and had a new respect and reverence for the life that was growing inside her, would she be able to hand her baby over to me? I couldn't blame her if she fell in love with Esther—but I was falling in love as well.

By the third day, I'd had enough of the nagging worry. I got online and looked up the nearest operating abortion clinic. Maybe I could go pray even if I was the only one there. I could escape the mundane, frustrating attempt of praying at home. I was like a caged animal. Eagerly scanning the results of my search, disappointment welled up within me when I saw that the nearest clinic was over an hour away.

An hour away? It was possible to pray there, wasn't it? I could still go. I'd have to get up a littler earlier and rearrange my schedule slightly, but it could still work.

The front door opened, and I jumped, slamming the laptop shut. Before I could catch my breath, Gideon entered the room, eyes crinkling in amusement.

"You scared me!" My hand flew over my heart as I willed the beating to slow down.

"I can see that. Working on a secret project you don't want me to know about?" His smile twinkled more than usual.

"I was looking up the nearest abortion clinic. I can't do this anymore. I need to get out."

He sat beside me on the couch and propped his feet up next to mine on the ottoman. "Do what?"

Chapter 29: Eve

"Pray here. It's too hard. There are too many distractions. I'm so frustrated with myself." Pushing my head into my hands, the tension within built.

"So, what'd you find?" His gentle voice caressed my nerves.

"There's a Planned Parenthood seventy-five minutes away." I attempted to sound hopeful.

"Well, dear, it looks like you're stuck here for now."

"What does that mean?"

"I mean I don't want you driving that far when you're so close to your due date. Not alone at least."

"It's only a little over an hour. It's not a big deal."

"You go into labor over there and it becomes a big deal. We have no idea how fast you'll go or what it will look like. What if your water breaks? The women in your family are known for fast labors."

"But what are the chances? Most likely I won't go early. I could do this for a couple weeks, then stick close to home as my due date gets closer."

"Honey, I don't want to take chances. You and this baby are too important to me." He cupped my chin in his hand, looking deep into my eyes.

"But this is my life's work. I need to go." I made my voice softer in an attempt to persuade him, but he had a point.

"Eve, your assignment is to pray for the unborn. We've received nothing directly from the Lord saying what that has to look like. There are different seasons of our lives, and right now you're entering into a new one. Just because the old one was comfortable doesn't mean God wants you to stay there forever."

"Waiting is so hard." My fingers twisted the hem of my shirt. "I want something to occupy my time."

"Understandable, babe, but I think the Lord has something for you in this season. You'll miss it if you keep wishing it looked differently."

I sighed. I was about to jump out of my skin, but Gideon was right. "So what are you doing here, anyway?" I laid my head on his shoulder, grateful for his strength.

"Well, missy, I just finished with a meeting and can't wait to tell you about it." He settled back against the couch, eyes wide, as I sat up to look at him.

"So tell me already." My laugh splashed across the room and the weight on my heart lifted slightly.

"The church wants to buy the clinic building."

Wait, what? I sat straighter. "It's for sale? Buy it for what?"

"Just went on the market. The church wants to turn it into a place where people from all different churches and denominations can come together to worship and pray."

"All different . . . What do you mean?"

He grinned. "Lutherans, Baptists, Charismatics all coming together. This isn't about our little church. This is about the Church with a capital *C*. God's people, from different backgrounds. We may disagree about some things, but we agree on the most important thing of all: Jesus. All I know is that if you're yearning for a place to pray, we'll build it for you."

"Don't those kinds of things take money . . . a lot of money?"

"Why are you always so concerned about money? If this is the Lord, He'll provide. Besides, like I said, a lot of churches are coming together in this. We want to redeem this property. Over twenty-five pastors from twenty different churches were in the meeting today. All of them want to see our city united."

I pressed my lips together. His eyes shone with excitement. If only I could grab hold of it, but . . .

Gideon cocked a brow. "Just say it. What's bothering you about all of this?"

"It sounds great. Almost . . . too good to be true? We have all these different denominations for a reason. Getting along with each other, working together in unity . . . It might start out rough and ugly."

He ran his fingers through my hair, leaving questions forgotten beneath his touch. "Babe, you've forgotten how much I love the rough and ugly."

"You shouldn't say that while looking at me," I teased.

He laughed. "I'm not talking about you. I may love the rough and ugly, but I am in love with your beauty." He leaned forward, meeting my ready lips with his own.

"I love you." I rubbed my nose against his, savoring the smell of his cologne.

"You know," he began tentatively, "I don't have to be back at church for another hour and a half." He ran his thumb along my cheekbone.

"What are you suggesting?"

"I'm saying, any time now we could have a baby, and being together won't be as convenient." His kisses grazed my neck.

I inhaled deeply. "So, seize the day?"

"Seize the day."

And all worries of babies and plans, restlessness and waiting, fell away.

Chapter 30: Lisa

Lisa groaned as she sifted through her mail. Another letter. How had her personal address become public knowledge, and who did people think they were, writing such offensive and threatening things? She was barely an adult. Why couldn't they give her a break?

The first letter had found its way to her school mailbox. Nerves coursed through her as she read it, and her stomach soured when she finished. *Your right-wing, judgmental attitude is unwelcome in this school. Please refrain from writing any more religious conservative articles here or I will file an official complaint.* Whatever that meant.

Since they'd published the article a week before, there'd been several such letters. Some politely suggested she find another venue to voice her opinions. Others used blatant profanity. The only positive note had come on a folded piece of notebook paper. Unruly handwriting proclaimed *Good article.* Faint praise, and not nearly enough against the onslaught of criticism.

She was having a hard time keeping up her morale and her grades, especially in her geology class. Mrs. Perky still avoided her. The last thing she wanted to read was another letter.

Lisa tossed the unopen missive onto the kitchen counter, picked up her phone, and hit the speed dial for Britney. The two of them had been talking more regularly since meeting at the restaurant. Although their friendship still hadn't completely returned to normal, Britney was the only friend on campus that Lisa could talk to about what was going on.

"Hey, Lisa. What's up?"

"I'm sick of these letters."

"You got another one? You should let me screen them. I'll read them through first, pitch all the nasty ones, and let you read all the nice mushy ones."

"What nice mushy ones? I don't think 'Good article' qualifies as mushy. Nice, maybe, but not mushy." Lisa sighed. "Anyway, I think I'm not going to read any more. They upset me too much."

"You care too much about what other people think. Don't pay attention to them. You did the right thing."

"That's easy for you to say, Ms. Popular. I didn't have many friends to begin with. Now people won't even talk to me about the weather or homework when I show up to class a few minutes early."

"Oh, come on. You're reading into things."

"I'm serious, Brit. Three or four times I've walked into the room to hear the tail end of a conversation centered on me. Then, when they notice me, there's that uncomfortable silence. I don't even know who my friends or enemies are."

She heard tidbits whispered about her from the groups associated with campus ministry. *Can you believe she did that? Wasn't she raised in church? She had one abortion and then went and got pregnant again?* Those sorts of comments were harder to take than the more common ones. *A little fanatical, isn't she? Who does she think she is? It's my body.*

She feigned ignorance as best she could, pretending not to hear the snide whispers behind her back or the rumors circulating around the campus.

"Enemies? Come on now, Lisa. I really think you're reading too much into things."

"Am I? Do you know what they're saying? There's a rumor going around that I'm a prostitute. Literally. Someone else asked me if I was too drugged up to remember birth control." One letter sent to her apartment hinted as much. *Abortion wouldn't need to be a consideration if people like you would be responsible enough to take birth control.*

Lisa was tired of everyone saying birth control solved the problem of abortion. She knew the issue ran deeper than a pill, shot, or patch. But she wouldn't say as much to Britney. Her friend was still putting her trust in prevention.

"Okay. Okay. So, maybe there is a little hostility out there," Britney said. "But not everyone hates you. You've got me, right?"

"Yeah, I know. Thanks for not bailing on me."

She was thankful for Britney's support, but Lisa couldn't share everything that was on her heart and mind with her friend. Britney wasn't a Christian, and Lisa was more and more aware that their friendship was lacking in depth. Most nights she found sanctuary in the Word of God instead. She buried herself underneath the Lord's promises even as she told Him how unfair the criticism was. *I don't understand, God. I was only trying to do the right thing. Why does everyone hate me?* Even as she'd ask the question, a picture of the Cross would come into her head, and she'd reluctantly relinquish complaint.

That, and she only had to feel a slight kick in her belly to know they were wrong. The life growing inside of her was precious and needed a voice. She would take the backlash for her little girl for the rest of her life if she had to. Even if she wasn't the one who would raise her baby.

"You know what I wonder?" Lisa asked.

"Hmm?"

"I wonder if my life will ever go back to normal. I mean, after handing Esther over to Eve. All the hype from the article will fade, right? I'll be just another student in class?"

"I think so. I doubt that in a year anyone will even remember that you were pregnant."

Chapter 30: Lisa

"Do you think I'll ever date again? Is there a guy out there for me?"

"Of course. In no time at all, you'll meet a guy who will make you forget the entire past year."

"I doubt that. I'm not looking to forget. Just to move on."

"Whatever."

"I don't know, Brit. I don't want to do the party thing anymore, don't want to sleep around. Are there good guys at Markley? I've never been good at resisting guys' advances. I don't know if I can be strong enough."

"Hey, if you want to do the abstinence thing, more power to you. I think it's a little extreme myself, but I'm sure you can pull it off."

Lisa bit her lip. Should she try to explain the reasons behind her "extreme" method? No. It wouldn't go over well. So she said, "I hope so."

"You can. Hey, I've got to go to class. Read that letter and call me later to let me know what it said."

"I don't want to read it."

"Read it. It might be nice and mushy." Britney's tone was teasing, and Lisa couldn't help but laugh.

"Okay, fine."

Lisa hung up and wondered if she'd ever get the courage to talk to Britney about her newfound faith. She'd had the opportunity to bring up the reason for her new convictions, but what if Britney freaked out? She was one of the few friends Lisa had left. Best not to put any distance between them.

Bracing herself, Lisa brought the letter over to the couch and pried it open.

Dear Lisa,

I wanted to thank you for the article you wrote. My daughter is a student on your campus and recently found out she was pregnant. She came to me in tears, and all I wanted to do was ease her pain. We made an appointment at the abortion clinic for that next week. I, too, had an abortion when I was a teenager, though my daughter didn't know that. The pain in my heart seems to ebb and flow. Sometimes I can go months without even thinking about it, and other times I spend night after night crying myself to sleep.

I think of all the what ifs. What if my daughter would have had an older brother to play with? What would he look like? What would his laugh sound like? It plagues me whenever I go shopping for Christmas presents or when the anniversary of my first baby's due date comes around.

Until I read your piece in the school paper my daughter brought home, I thought I was the only one. This is something no one talks about. If someone would have shared their own pain earlier, perhaps I could have given myself permission to grieve the loss of my baby. At any rate, when my daughter showed me the article, we wept together. I told her my story, that I too suffered from deep emotional pain over all the lost possibilities that came with my choice to have an abortion.

We called and canceled the appointment the next day. I know my daughter will have a hard road to walk down. She's not sure whether she wants to keep the baby or place it for adoption. Either way, we know it won't be easy, but at least she won't have to live with such regret.

Thank you for being brave enough to share your experiences. You have changed our lives for the better, and in May there will be another little child because of you.

Sincerely,
JoAnne

Tears coursed down Lisa's cheeks as she read the letter again and again. "Thank You, God," she whispered. She'd needed encouragement after the negative events of the week, and He was there to lift her up.

She searched the back of the letter and envelope. No contact information. Shoot. She would have loved to offer support to the girl as she walked along her journey. Clearly, though, JoAnne wanted her daughter to remain anonymous. Lisa couldn't blame her; anyone who associated with her would be a target for gossip.

She was tucking the letter away into her memory box underneath her bed when the phone rang. She jumped up as quickly as she could, aware that Eve could have her baby any day.

"Hello?" Lisa answered, breathless.

"Hello, is this Lisa?" The woman sounded friendly yet professional.

"This is she."

"I'm Brenda Summit from *The Gist*. Have you heard of our publication?"

She had, though she couldn't place the name. "It sounds familiar." But why was she calling? What was it about?

"Yes, well, we're a young adult magazine that covers topics relevant to teenagers and college students. You've probably seen our magazine in the grocery store check-out line."

"Yes?" She tried to suppress her confusion under a polite tone.

"One of our editors came across the feature piece you did for your campus paper, and we're asking you to give your permission to have it republished in our magazine."

"You want my article in your magazine?" Lisa stared at her phone. This was for real? She opened her mouth, a *yes* and a *no* jockeying for first place. If she said yes, her words could save lives. If she said yes, would her life ever return to normal?

"Yes, Lisa. Your article is quite profound and well-written. Abortion is an issue that is extremely relevant to young people today. We have someone writing an article advocating a woman's choice and wanted a counter article advocating the right to life. We'd like to fax over a consent form. If you can sign it and fax it back to us, we'll reprint your article in our next issue and send you a complimentary copy."

Esther turned inside her. She slammed her eyes shut. How could she say no? If she hadn't just read that letter from JoAnne, maybe she could have, would have. But God had sovereignly set up the timing of things.

"You can fax it to the *Pride of the Press*' office," she said. She fished through her purse to find a business card, then rattled off the fax number for the newspaper office. They exchanged pleasantries, and she promised to fax her consent back the following day.

Tears pricked her eyes as soon as she hung up the phone. "Crazy pregnancy hormones," she mumbled to herself. How did such a major publication come across a little back-page article in a campus newspaper published hundreds of miles away?

"This must be You, God. Only You could make this happen. What are Your purposes for me? Where do I go from here?"

If only she could sit down with her mother over a cup of tea and talk about the possibilities on her horizon. As imperfect as Lisa's mother was, and as irritating as she'd always been, there was a special bond between a mother and a daughter that nothing else could replace. Lisa wanted to crawl up under the security of her mother's love just then. She cried even harder. What an impossible situation. Her mother might never talk to her again. Even if she did, would things ever be the same? Would a cloud of shame follow Lisa wherever she went?

Her heart squeezed. She picked up the phone to call Eve, then thought better of it. Eve would listen, she was sure, and listen well. But Lisa needed someone else's arms. She needed to have a quiet conversation with the Father who, instead of alienating her from His family, had adopted her into it. In the stillness of her apartment, she whispered one word, “Abba,” knowing that He’d meet her where she was.

Chapter 31: Ashira

Ducking through the ash-strewn streets of Jerusalem, Ashira came upon two Babylonian soldiers raping women right in the open. The women's cries rent the air. The men didn't notice Ashira, too engrossed in establishing their power. The women's cries lingered in her ears as she fled that horrific scene, only to be stopped by the sight of a burning house. Bodies lay strewn about in front of the door, a trail of broken pottery and tattered clothing stretching from the home into the night. The soldiers must have executed the family, looted their belongings, and set the house on fire. The stench of death wafted around her, clawing the back of her throat. Had she eaten recently, she would have retched there on the street.

She clutched Phineas tighter to herself, shielding his eyes. Which way to go next? She should have left when she had the chance. They would not survive . . . unless . . .

"Lie down." She made her voice stern as she issued the command to her son. He could not take her lightly. This was life or death. "Be still. Do not move, my boy. If you want to live, do not move."

Though barely five years old and frightened, he obeyed. Ashira crouched and turned over a dead body that seeped blood into the dirt. A soldier had thrust the woman through with a spear. Her skin still held warmth and her lifeless eyes stared at Ashira. Gritting her teeth, Ashira smeared her hand with the blood that oozed from the woman's abdomen. She rubbed her bloody hands on Phineas' arms and then her own body. She did it again and again until blood coated them.

"We must lie still and pretend we are dead. Do not move." She spoke through gritted teeth, narrowing her eyes at him to ensure his obedience. Would her last words to her precious son be stern ones? Would they not be tender words of love? She lay down beside him in the dust, arranging herself around Phineas as if she had been killed protecting him. Now all they could do was wait.

When Nebuchadnezzer had taken the golden artifacts from their temple and returned to his homeland, Jeremiah prophesied he would return and take the city. No one believed him, though over the past four years, she'd seen him prophesy of Jerusalem's defeat countless times. They'd thrown him in jail for his warnings, but many people ceased doubting when the Babylonian army laid siege to Jerusalem.

Jeremiah warned the people not to resist. He said some would be destined for famine, some for sword, and some for captivity. Those who would surrender and go willingly into exile would live. One day, Jeremiah foretold, God would bring His people back to the land promised to them, though many would not live to see it. But King Zedekiah would not surrender, and many within the city walls died of starvation.

Now, after the long months of waiting for the inevitable, the army had finally breached the walls and began attacking with a vengeance. Chaldean soldiers plundered the city, raping and killing without mercy. Any who appeared to be too weak to endure the long journey to Babylon, they thrust through with the sword. They gathered the strong ones for exile, and then only after most of the women had been violated. Only a few of the very poor would be allowed to remain in the city—what little of it would be left.

Phineas shuddered beside her, and she longed to comfort him. Instead, she lay still, waiting for the carnage to cease. Though Jeremiah had said not to resist their exile, she could not venture to Babylon. She must return to her husband. Jeremiah had said as much before. If only she would have had the courage to go back to her village as soon as Jeremiah had told her to. Instead, she had delayed out of fear of her husband. But the Babylonians had returned and laid siege to the city yet again, trapping her inside before she could escape back to her village.

Reuben did not even know he had a son! Surely there was hope for the husband of her youth if he would but repent.

The heat of the nearby house fire pressed in around her, and other buildings crackled with their burning, though none were close enough to pose any danger. How ironic that their city should be burned with fire. They'd sacrificed their children in the fire, and now the Lord visited fire upon them. Jeremiah said they must pay double for their sins. After seeing the stubbornness of the people firsthand, it had to be no less than what they deserved, though her heart broke to hear the screams of terrorized women and the wails of abandoned infants.

The clank and jingle of armor moved down the street toward her and Phineas. Gruff voices sounded from every direction, speaking a language she could not understand. Phineas remained beside her, his little heart pounding against her chest.

Out of the corner of her eye, she spotted a soldier taking a sloppy drink from his canteen. Water sloshed out the sides of it. A desperate cry clawed at her throat, but she suppressed it. Because of the siege and drought, all the wells had long since dried up. Their people were dying of thirst, and the soldiers had no compassion. If they were to sit up and beg for a drink, the soldiers would slaughter them all without a second thought. Their orders were to burn the city and kill and gather the people.

The soldiers marched on and disappeared down the street. All was quiet for a moment. The woman's blood on her arms stiffened and cracked, but Ashira and Phineas remained lying with their faces in the dust. Night deepened. Still, they did not move to a different location. Phineas whimpered, and she clamped her hand over his mouth. Though it seemed the soldiers had completely moved on to another quarter of the city, she could not be sure.

Though it was night, the light from the fires illuminated the scene. The house behind them had ceased burning. Only a heap of scorched rubble remained. "Phineas," she whispered. "Listen carefully. When I tell you to, we are going to creep on our bellies to the remains of that house. There we will hide until the soldiers pass."

"Mother, I am afraid." His small voice trembled as he spoke.

"So am I, son, but God will be with us." She spoke with more assurance than she felt.

They waited moments longer, listening for footsteps, and then began moving towards the house. As they crept towards safety, she came upon a dead soldier and signaled Phineas to keep moving. She hadn't noticed him among the bodies before. It looked as if a Jewish man had fought back and killed the Chaldean. More than likely, the soldiers had killed the family and torched the house in reprisal, but they hadn't cared enough for the fallen soldier to bury the body.

Food! He must have food. She rummaged about under his vest until she found hard bread and a waterskin. *Thank You, Lord! We will not starve nor die of thirst.*

Phineas looked back with wide eyes. She nodded to assure him she was coming and motioned for him to continue. They arrived at what was left of the house, weary but alive, and nestled themselves behind the few blackened stones left standing. Ashira stacked some of the rubble against the remainder of a wall to help shelter them. The hot bricks scorched her hands, and she pressed her lips together to keep from crying out in pain. As Phineas fell asleep, she prayed the God of their fathers would hide them from the soldiers' eyes.

Chapter 32: Trent

"Do you have any other questions?" Trent asked, enjoying the woman's smile.

"No. Not today." Her eyes shone as she squeezed her husband's hand.

"Then I'll see you in four weeks." He handed her the checkout sheet and smiled at the couple before letting himself out of the exam room.

He'd been at the job for a week and a half. The bounce in his step only underlined his gratitude for the job. Don had set him up in the practice with a corner office and a nice paycheck. Because Don valued consistency for his patients, he began filtering the new patients and new pregnancies Trent's way. Trent started off with only a handful of women, but the number would steadily grow. All his patients were newly pregnant except for one woman named Melody, who'd transferred to the practice when she moved from Wyoming. She'd be coming in later today.

The part he loved the most was the joyful atmosphere. Unlike his previous line of work, the women who came to see him were glad to be there. They were excited about their pregnancies, full of questions about heartburn and back pain—questions that were simple to answer. Some brought husbands or boyfriends. Others came alone or with a friend. Despite an occasional complaint about the waiting time, all the women were in good spirits.

Chapter 32: Trent

He enjoyed working with Don as well. The staff had an easy-going repertoire. Gone was the serious, somber cloud that had hung above Trent while he worked at the clinic. He was happy to come to work every day and was in a much better mood when he left. That had to please Beth. She'd always been the one to pay for his moodiness.

He walked up to the front desk and caught Cynthia, the secretary, stuffing a fun size Snickers in her mouth. She covered her mouth and giggled when she caught his eye. She slid another one across the counter to him. "Caught me. I guess I should share."

"Hey, I'll take it." He grinned as he tore open the candy. "What's the rest of my afternoon look like?"

"Back-to-back OB checkups." She pulled up his schedule on her monitor and angled it toward him. "Should be quick and easy."

And far less stressful than abortions. He simply had to listen for the baby's heartbeat, measure the woman's abdomen, and go over any questions she might have. Nothing ominous.

Surely, he was now in the process of getting on God's good side. However long it took, he would get there and stay there. He had no intentions of performing another abortion as long as he lived.

"Thanks, Cynthia." He popped the Snickers in his mouth and waved the wrapper in her direction.

"You're welcome. You settling in okay? Liking it here?"

Don strode up behind him and slapped him on the back. "He loves it here, don't you, Trent? Couldn't ask for a better boss."

Something between a cough and a laugh came out as Trent tried to swallow the candy.

"See?" Don spread out his arms as he continued down the hallway. "He loves it."

It was true.

The rest of the afternoon sped by. None of the women he saw that afternoon were at risk of complications. He answered questions about what medicine was okay to take for a headache and what the target heart rate should be for pregnant women wanting to participate in aerobic exercise. He performed one blood test on Melody to screen for fetal abnormalities. He warned her of the high incidence of false positives that came with the test, but Melody didn't seem concerned. She only wanted to be on the safe side.

After she left, he finished up paperwork in his office and then headed out to his car. As he neared his car, his cell phone rang.

"Hey, Trent. It's Eve."

He smiled to himself, enjoying the feeling of talking to her without being bogged down in guilt. She'd called a few times since he and Beth went to her church, mostly to check up on Beth. He hadn't talked to her since he had started his new job.

"Hi. What's up?"

"I was wondering if you and Beth would want to meet Gideon and me for dinner this weekend. I've only got a week before I'm due, and we wanted to make the most of our free time."

"Hold on a minute." He pulled the phone away from his ear to check his calendar. "We have a charity banquet on Saturday night, but we should be free on Friday. I'll have to check with Beth."

"Sounds good. Tell her to call me back."

"Sure thing." He flipped his phone shut and resisted the urge to grin. He couldn't wait to tell Eve about his new profession. She'd be proud of him—more than proud; she'd be ecstatic. With the clinic out of the way, there was no reason for him to feel convicted in her presence. They were on the same side now: fighting for the unborn.

Chapter 32: Trent

With his new schedule, he arrived home before Beth three evenings a week. It was an adjustment for him not to see her peeking out the window but nice to have a few minutes in silence to unwind and read the paper. He made himself a cup of decaf, then sat at the kitchen table, paper in hand.

After he read the sports page, he thumbed through the local news until a headline caught his eye: "Church Bids on Property of Abortion Clinic." He read on about how the property of Compassion Clinic for Women was for sale. Several businesses had their bids in the mix, but the latest news was about a church vying for the property. He was reading as the door creaked open.

"Hey, honey," Trent called.

"Hi, babe. How was work?"

"Wonderful!" He stood and met her, kissing her earnestly.

"I could get used to this," Beth said, breathless.

"What? I've kissed you before."

"Not like that, you didn't. And I could get used to hearing the words 'wonderful' and 'work' in the same sentence. What's new?" She cast a glance at the newspaper lying on the table as she slid her purse across the counter.

"The clinic is being sold. Maybe to a church."

He sat back down, and Beth took the chair across from him, picking up the paper and scanning the article. "Trent, that's Eve's church."

"Huh?"

"Rivers of Hope. That's Eve's church. The one we went to."

"Hmm . . . interesting. You can ask her about that on Friday. She called and asked us to go to dinner with her and her husband. We're not busy, are we?"

"Not that I know of." Her eyes scanned the article.

"Then you can call her back and tell her we're on."

"It says here they want to turn it into a place of prayer."

"Like a church?"

"I don't know."

"Well, ask Eve about it on Friday. We have more important things to talk about."

"Like what?" Beth glanced up nervously.

"Like the fact that you have your ultrasound in a few weeks."

Her face lit up at the mention of it. They'd struck a compromise: Don would be her OB and the one who'd deliver the baby. However, he'd give Trent the chance to sit in on all her appointments and cleared time for Trent to see the ultrasound with her. Beth was still disappointed that Trent wouldn't be her OB, but he had reassured her she would like Don better than Dr. Yoseph.

"So," Trent teased, "what if she's a he?"

"We'll cross that bridge if we come to it."

"And then, we can start fighting over names again."

"I prefer to call it 'intense discussion.'" Her laugh was a sweet melody after what they'd been through. They'd decided not to talk any more about names until they knew the gender. After the ultrasound, they'd begin the arduous process of settling on a name for their baby. Until then, they had time to speculate and anticipate what their future might hold.

As Trent held his wife close that night, he said a short prayer to God, thanking Him for giving him a new job and a way out. All he could see in his future were days and nights full of laughter and love. God would give him that, wouldn't He? After all, he was doing everything he could to purge his sins.

Chapter 33: Eve

Thankfully, Beth insisted I pick the restaurant. After dreaming of chips and salsa for weeks, my Mexican cravings would finally be quenched. And I'd finally find out how Trent and Beth were. For real.

I continued to pray for Trent after his clinic shut down. Praying at home still drove me nuts, but it's never been about how strong I feel. I've always been weak and broken—a mess. Circumstances only brought that reality to the surface.

But since I missed being outside, and on the off-chance it might kick my body into labor, I started prayer-walking around the neighborhood. If walking had worked for Lisa's mom, I'd give it a try as well. As I walked, I lifted us all up in prayer: Lisa, Trent and Beth, Gideon and me, and all three babies.

Gideon came up with the idea to get together with the Rhines. While talking one night, I'd wondered out loud how Trent and Beth were doing. We hadn't talked to the couple in weeks, and I had no idea what Trent had been doing since the clinic shut down. Gideon suggested I call them and invite them to join us for dinner. Great idea.

We arrived first and found a booth. My stomach was growing by leaps and bounds, and it was a tight squeeze behind the table. Trent and Beth arrived moments after we'd gotten our basket of chips.

Chapter 33: Eve

I watched them pull up from my seat by the window. “Wow, he looks different,” I said as they walked toward the restaurant.

“Different?” Gideon raised his eyebrow.

“Happier. And look, Beth is showing now.”

The couple came in and spotted us right away.

“Beth, you look beautiful! You’ve got that pregnancy glow.”

She shone, and Trent’s smile stretched wide. “Thanks. You look like you’re ready to go any day now.”

“Sure am. I’m not due for another week, but it can’t come soon enough. Did you find out what you’re having?”

“We’re having an ultrasound in a few weeks. I still think it’s a girl.”

“We’ll see.” Trent laughed. What a striking difference in his demeanor from the first time I’d spoken with him in a restaurant. Then he’d kept his head down in shame. Now he held it high.

We made small talk until our orders arrived, speaking as if we’d been friends forever. The reality of our circumstances, of how we met, wasn’t anywhere in the picture. Anyone sitting near us would have thought we were all friends from our high school days.

“So, I have news for you.” Trent beamed as he nodded towards me.

“Yes?”

“Guess what I’m doing now?”

“Putting salt on your burrito.”

“Yes, but no. I’m working with an old friend from med school as an OB. I’ll be delivering babies.”

Tears came out of nowhere, stinging the corners of my eyes. “That’s wonderful.” And indeed, it was. The change in his demeanor made sense then. Instead of spending his days ending life, he was participating with the Creator in making new beginnings.

But something about his confession didn't sit right in my spirit. What was it? I wanted to be happy for him, but what wasn't he telling me?

"It is wonderful. I love it. There's nothing better than bringing life into the world."

I looked down at my plate and chuckled. His words reminded me of how I'd unashamedly tried to convert him to the side of life.

"How'd that happen? What's the story?" Gideon asked.

"A friend of his from med school called the very day all the craziness happened at the clinic. We think it was God's way of giving him a second chance." Beth's eyes shone, but Trent's clouded over slightly.

"Sounds like it." I looked at Trent, eager for an explanation of why Beth's words had bothered him.

"My goal . . . " He choked on his words and struggled to regain his composure. "My goal is to deliver more babies than I killed."

Gideon nodded, but I wavered in accepting his statement. Was he trying to find his way
back into the light without God?

"Why, Trent? Why's that your goal?" All three of them looked at me with wide eyes. I guess it was awkward to question such a good thing, but did he know the truth?

"I-I need redemption." Now I saw that the pain in his eyes had only been glossed over by his earlier smiles.

"Trent—" *Lord, give me the words.* "You don't find redemption in numbers. You find it in a Man."

He sat back, his posture rigid. "What do you mean?"

"I mean your ratio could be ten to one, delivering ten times as many babies as you helped to abort, and you still would stand guilty before God. You can't find redemption in how many babies you've helped to bring into the world."

He shifted his focus to his food, pushing his rice around with his fork. "Well, it certainly doesn't hurt to deliver babies. I'm much happier now, aren't I, Beth?"

She nodded at him but kept her gaze on me. Would she understand what I was about to say? Would she agree? She had to have seen the same haunted look in his eyes that I'd seen because she seemed willing to listen.

"It's a wonderful profession, Trent, but you need more than a profession to be right with God. You need Jesus." Gideon gave my hand a gentle squeeze underneath the table. At least he supported me as I pressed the issue.

"Yeah, I've heard that before. You say the prayer of salvation and you're in, right? It's that easy?" Cynicism soaked his words.

So, this conversation wouldn't be easy. I might offend Trent with my words—*God, please take my weak words and anoint them*—but I had to do my part in being bold enough to speak. I had to trust God to do the rest. So, I plowed forward.

"Giving your life to Jesus is easy and hard at the same time," I said. "It's free, but it costs everything. It's not about a ticket out of hell, though He has saved us from that. It's about a deep friendship and a willingness to let Him be king over your heart. It's so simple, even a child can understand it, but we have to die to ourselves. That's the hard part."

"Come and buy without price," Gideon whispered.

"I don't get it. It's hard for me to believe I just need to turn to Him, and He'll forgive everything I've ever done wrong. My hands are covered in blood." Trent's eyes were earnest now, almost pleading. "I've done more wrong than you and all of your church friends put together. In my mind, there has to be something I must do. I need to work my way back to God somehow."

"But your works will never be enough. You said it yourself. You're a sinner, guilty before Him. You could never do enough to earn God's forgiveness. That's why Jesus had to die in our place. We couldn't do it, couldn't be good enough. I couldn't be good enough, couldn't do enough things right, and you couldn't either. Only Jesus could because He's both God and a perfect man. He took our sins upon Himself."

"It doesn't add up." Trent's irritated tone grated like the knife scraping against the plate. Beth cast him a concerned glance. "It can't be that easy."

"I'm glad you've found satisfaction in your job. Really, I am. But you'll only have true peace after you hand your life over to Him. Even if you're happy because of your circumstances, there's still an ache within you that no number of deliveries can fill."

"I'd like to be finished with this conversation, if you don't mind." He dug into his burrito and rice.

I dropped the subject but continued to pray for him. *Father, please speak to Trent's heart. Please convince him of Your mercy.*

Beth tried to keep things light by asking about how I was feeling and what doctor I was seeing. Eventually she asked about our church bidding on the clinic's property, and I told her about all the churches pitching in to make it a place of unified prayer. Gideon chimed in every once in a while but remained quiet most of the time. I could tell he was praying for Trent and was thankful.

Halfway through my fajitas, my stomach tightened. I grabbed Gideon's hand and squeezed. The uncomfortable feeling passed, and I shrugged it off as another Braxton Hicks. Then it came again, and I focused on deep breathing. The pain let up, and I hurriedly took a few more bites, willing my body to cooperate. I just needed to get through the meal. The atmosphere between Trent and me was tense enough without false contractions dampening my mood. As I swallowed, my abdomen tightened again.

Trent looked up as I bit my lip.

"Eve? Are you going into labor?"

Chapter 33: Eve

Even as I shook my head, a sudden wetness dampened the bench and floor. "My water broke," I whispered, heat rising in my cheeks.

"What?" Gideon leaned closer to hear.

"My water broke," I said a little louder. How mortifying. Of all the places—why a restaurant?

Trent and Beth both dropped their silverware with a clunk.

"Don't panic, Eve," Trent said, the tension between us forgotten momentarily. "Do you have an extra pair of clothes in your car?"

We'd left the bag at home. I shook my head as another contraction came on. Definitely not Braxton Hicks. I clenched Gideon's hand and willed myself to breathe.

"I might have something." Beth excused herself and rushed to the car.

"That's it, Eve. In through your nose, out through your mouth. As soon as Beth gets back, you can change and then we'll go to the hospital. Gideon, why don't you time the contractions?"

My husband nodded and pulled out his cell phone, frantically pressing buttons until he found the stopwatch feature. He smiled at me nervously. He'd obviously not expected his role as a father to begin that night.

Moments later, Beth returned with a change of clothes. "When you have a doctor for a husband, you know to be prepared for anything." She smiled and helped me to the bathroom where I pulled the blue maternity dress over my head.

"I'm so embarrassed." I kept saying it over and over, despite Beth's reassurances. My water had broken in a public restaurant, and now an unfortunate bus boy would be responsible for cleaning up my amniotic fluid.

Gideon and Trent were waiting for us at the door. "We'll follow you to the hospital," Trent said. "Beth, why don't you ride with them and time the contractions so Gideon can concentrate on driving."

She nodded and slid into the back seat.

The ride to the hospital seemed to take hours. And the pain. How in the world had I ever thought I'd make it through the birth without medication? The only thing that kept me from screaming was the hope that an epidural awaited me upon arrival.

Beth held my hand. I clenched her fingers whenever I felt a contraction coming on, and again as I felt it lift. Her cell phone rang. I strained in vain to hear both sides of the conversation.

"She's about four minutes apart . . . Yes, already . . . Okay, bye." She hung up and sat forward in her seat so I could hear her.

"Your contractions are coming pretty fast. Trent says he has privileges at this hospital, so he can deliver the baby if your doctor doesn't get there in time."

"Doesn't get there in time?"

"You're progressing really fast, Eve."

"Does my doctor even know?"

"We called her while you were in the bathroom," Gideon chimed in. His grip tightened on the steering wheel, his gaze intent and focused on the road in front of him. His game face was on. He'd do everything he could to get me there in time.

The pain came again. What did they teach in class about breathing? I held my breath. No, not that. Definitely wrong. Why did women go through this?

A picture of Jesus on the cross flashed through my mind. He'd gone through such unimaginable pain voluntarily and without regret. My muscles relaxed enough to allow me to take another deep breath.

"We're almost there." Gideon's voice bordered on frantic.

Trent deliver my baby? God, is that what you want? Please, let my doctor be there and ready for me. I'm so comfortable with her, and I don't want Trent to see me like that, God. Let her be there, please. Heat spread up my cheeks yet again at the thought of myself lying half naked on the table for him to see.

Another contraction hit and all other thoughts fled. Who cared who saw what? *Just get the baby out of my body.*

Gideon sped into the hospital parking lot and parked haphazardly in a front spot. Rushing around to my side of the car, he yanked my door open and took my arm. He and Beth helped me to the front entrance where a nurse brought me a wheelchair. Sweet relief. But, would we get to a room in time?

I can't do this! My mind screamed with the pain. *I have to do this! I have no choice.*

In a moment Trent was there, walking by my wheelchair and giving orders to the nurses on the floor. Once we found a room, Gideon helped me into a hospital gown while Trent made a call to see how far away my doctor was. Trent came in after Gideon had positioned me on the hospital bed.

"Your doctor is still fifteen minutes away. I'm going to do a quick check on you to see how dilated you are, okay?" He'd dressed in scrubs and blue latex gloves. I couldn't think enough to protest. Instead, I slid my feet into the stirrups.

"You're complete." He nodded to the nurses. "She's ready to push."

Complete? What?

I looked to Gideon, who'd been holding my hand the entire time. His smile trembled. "You're ready to push, baby. Take a deep breath, remember?"

Remember? No. But surely my body knew what to do without such instruction. I summoned all of my energy and pushed with all my might.

"Take a deep breath and do it again." Trent's gentle voice balanced out my hysteria. I pushed again and then again.

“I see his hair.” Though professional, his voice danced with an undercurrent of delight. “He’s got a full head of hair. Take a deep breath and push again.”

I did so a few more times, exhaustion creeping through every inch of my body. Finally, Zephan’s cry pierced through, and a nurse placed his squirming body in my arms. His nose scrunched up, and his mouth opened wide as he wailed.

“It’s a perfect baby boy.” Trent’s voice lilted.

I shook, cried, and laughed at the same time. Gideon cut the cord, and I held my baby boy close as the nurses did their best to wipe him off.

“Hi, precious,” I cooed. “It’s your mommy. Do you recognize my voice?”

I looked at Gideon. Tears filled his eyes as well. Then I looked at Trent and felt my heart melt yet again.

Tears weren’t just in his eyes. They coursed down his cheeks freely.

Chapter 34: Beth

It was hours before Beth was able to hold Eve's little baby boy, but when she did, the emotions that hit her were entirely different than what she had expected. Eve had become her friend, and Beth had anticipated sharing in her joy. But holding the small sleeping bundle in her arms awakened something within Beth's soul she hadn't realized existed: a deep mourning.

Eve's soft snoring was the only sound in the room, save the sweet suckling noises emitting from the baby in her arms. The guys had gone down to the cafeteria for a bite to eat. Beth allowed herself to venture to a dangerous place she had long blocked off. It was the place of memory. The place of what ifs. The place of regret.

The baby squirming inside of her wasn't her first but her second. She hadn't thought of that since her positive pregnancy test four months ago. Now she allowed herself to drift back to a time when she had been younger, freshly in love, and fearfully pregnant. Surely terminating the pregnancy was the right thing to do. She and Trent had a future ahead of them, so many good things that couldn't be achieved easily with a child in the picture. It hadn't been a hard decision. They'd made it quickly, looking always to their future.

Trent had convinced her that one day, when the time was right, they'd have a whole houseful of kids. Then they'd be able to provide for them, give them the upbringing children needed. It was because she valued children so much that she'd given her first up. Children were too special to be raised by young, ignorant, poor parents. Parents who'd conceived them because they'd been partying too hard to remember birth control. That wasn't the legacy she wanted to leave a child.

And it wasn't a child, after all. Or it hadn't been one yet. Wherever that line was, she'd had an abortion early enough that it didn't become an issue for her. Of course, she was sad at first, but she didn't go around moping like some women she'd heard about. Her future was too bright for that.

Once or twice, she'd asked herself the inevitable questions. *Was it a boy or a girl? What would our life look like now if we'd had the baby?* But the probable consequences had been enough to cause her to leave the questions behind. Trent might have never finished med school if they'd kept the baby. He'd be working a dead-end job that paid barely above minimum wage. They'd be struggling to make ends meet, always stressed out, and in no way fit parents for the child. She told herself that until she believed it. Perhaps she had a twinge of guilt afterwards, but rather than acknowledge it, she had stuffed it down to the recesses of her heart, where no one, not even herself, could touch it.

But as Beth held little Zephaniah in her arms, she allowed those emotions to resurface. She gave herself permission to mourn the little child they'd lost. They would have had a little baby with tiny fingers and toes, hair, and little scrunched ears. It wasn't just that babies were cute. It was more than that. When the doctor had taken her child from her womb, he had taken a piece of her too, a piece that would forever be lost.

The tears came hot and heavy, spilling onto the blue hospital blanket that covered every inch of the newborn except for his head. She wiped her cheeks with her free hand, but it was useless. As they poured out from under her eyelids, the ache within her became a groan.

Where was this coming from? It'd been years, hadn't it? Years, and she had barely ever thought about her first baby.

And when she had thought about it, she felt mostly relief. A sad relief, for sure, but something far short of regret, or of the pain that stung her now. Or had the feelings been there all along and she'd never allowed herself to feel anything stronger?

She tried to keep quiet. Zephan should have his peace. Her first child had known none. He'd been torn from his mother before he had a chance to protest. A memory came to mind of a familiar scene from the preschool where she'd been an intern during high school: the children being dropped off by their parents. Most children transitioned well into the classroom, but there was one young boy who had trouble day after day. When his mother would drop him off, he'd scream. He'd attempt to hold onto her legs, and she'd pry off his fingers one by one. "Mama!" he'd cry.

Surely, that's what her little baby would have done if he'd had the voice and ability to do so. He would have clung to Mommy for dear life because indeed, that life depended on her. Though that mother of the preschooler hadn't been abandoning her child, Beth had abandoned hers. She had a child she'd never know, never get the chance to love.

The excitement over the life within her seemed hypocritical. How could she so eagerly anticipate one life when she had completely disregarded another? And why had she never allowed herself to feel this loss?

A rustling sound came from the bed. Beth opened wet eyes to see Eve propping herself up on her elbows.

"Beth? Beth, what is it? What's wrong?" Her sleepy voice leaked concern.

"Nothing," Beth lied. "He's beautiful." Her eyes caressed Zephan's sleeping form. What would her first baby have looked like?

"Yes, but what's the matter? You can talk to me, Beth."

All her walls of reservation fell at the sound of Eve's sincerity. "I was thinking about my baby. W-we had an abortion before we were married." Beth avoided Eve's eyes. She couldn't bear the condemnation she might rightfully see there.

"Oh, Beth. It's okay to cry about that."

"I think I know that now. I've spent years pushing every thought about the baby away, convincing myself I did the right thing. But when I look at Zephan's face, all I can think of is that I never had a chance to hold my baby, to look into his eyes and tell him his Mommy loved him."

Her hands trembled. She stood, placed Zephan in his crib, then sat again, struggling with her tears.

"Sin is so destructive," Eve said softly. "The enemy is such a liar. Beth, it's okay to cry and to mourn. You've suffered a great loss, even if it was at your own hands. The enemy deceived you into thinking ending a life was your best option. But forgiveness is available for you. God is a God of restoration."

Beth placed her head in her hands and wept harder. Her entire body shook with sobs. Years' worth of tears spilled from her eyes in a matter of minutes. "Redemption is found in a man," she whispered, repeating Eve's words from earlier, trying to release the power of them to her own heart.

"Yes, redemption is found in the God-Man. Do you believe that?" Eve's voice was so kind, a gentle stroke to the wounded places within.

"I want to," Beth whispered.

"Then believe. It's within your grasp. You deserved death, but Jesus took your punishment upon Himself because He was so passionately in love with you. He wouldn't let anything stand in the way of being with you for eternity. For the joy set before Him—for you—He endured the Cross. Now that He's made a way for you, all you have to do is believe and walk towards His open arms. It's a love journey, learning to love what He loves and hate what He hates. Becoming one with Him."

"I've never heard it described like that before." Beth sat silent a moment, mulling over all Eve had said, trying to make sense of it. Finally, she asked a question that'd been floating through her mind. "Do you believe all babies who are aborted go to Heaven?"

"Yes."

"Then why's it such a big deal, Eve? If they're going to be with Jesus anyway, why's it such a crime?" There was no accusation in her tone, only curiosity.

"Was your mother a Christian, Beth?"

"I don't know. I know my grandma was."

"Well then, would it have been okay for someone to walk up to your grandma and shoot her in the head?"

"Of course not."

"But she was going to Heaven anyway, wasn't she?" The tilt of Eve's head softened the blow of her words a little. "Life is precious, Beth, and it's not up to us when it ends or begins. Part of a relationship with the Lord is loving what He loves, and He loves life in all its forms. If He treasures it, we must treasure it too."

Beth thought about that quietly for a moment. Eve was right. She must have always known it was wrong, but she had built the wall of justification so high the truth was buried somewhere behind it.

"Do you think I'll see my child in Heaven?" Beth asked tentatively. She didn't deserve such an honor, but the thought of seeing her first child someday comforted her.

"Your child will be in Heaven, Beth. The question is, will you?"

Beth looked at Eve's face to interpret her tone and saw no condemnation there. Her eyes were pools of gentleness, beckoning Beth to God.

"I want to."

"Then pray with me." Eve led her in a simple prayer. It wasn't fancy like the prayers Beth had heard long ago. She repeated the words after Eve, and as she did so, she could feel her heart opening like a flower, reaching toward the sunlight of God's forgiveness. She didn't have everything completely figured out yet, but surely, she didn't need to right at that moment. Step by step, day by day, she would venture further into discovering who this God-Man was and would learn to love Him in return.

Chapter 35: Ashira

The bag of bread and the soldier's waterskin sustained them during their wait behind blackened bricks and charred remains of broken water jugs. The soldiers did indeed come back through their quarter to check for survivors, but they didn't find Ashira and Phineas. Perhaps the Lord blinded the soldiers' eyes, for they were not above sifting through rubble.

Ashira and her son waited for two days afterward to be sure the soldiers had gone completely. Then they climbed out from the rubble and crept through the city, foraging for food and water as they went. A sip from a discarded wineskin here. A morsel of hardened bread there. They encountered few survivors, clothes tattered, faces smeared with dirt and soot. Jerusalem lay in ruins, buildings and temple burned. Their beloved city was beyond recognition. As they approached one of the gates, it was as if she were in a dream. *Oh, Lord! How many of my people are dead or have been taken into captivity? What of Rizpah and Josiah? Were they destined for captivity or the sword, or did they finally surrender to famine? I never could have imagined such destruction. And yet You have spared us. Thank You that we are alive.*

She held her son's hand. "Come, Phineas. We must go home."

He did not need to ask what she meant; she'd whispered to him of his father and hometown in the midst of the destruction as they had waited for the soldiers to leave. Before, she had been quiet about the matter, but now she talked about it openly. Was Reuben alive? Did he still live in their village? He might welcome her home or might stone her. Would he accept Phineas as his own or send them away? She wrapped her arms around her middle. No matter what, she had to try to reconcile with him and plead with him to turn to the God of Abraham, Isaac, and Jacob.

As their feet found the path leading away from the city, Ashira prayed for Yahweh to show her the way. It had been years since she'd left Jerusalem, and her home village was a foggy memory.

She spoke to Phineas of his father with every step. She didn't mention the sister he would have had if not for his parents' sin. She didn't mention Reuben's forceful hand when it came to his idols. Instead, she spoke of the love of their youth and the tenderhearted way her bridegroom had pursued her in those days. Phineas' frown and furrowed brow showed he most likely didn't understand all her words. But speaking of such things awakened love in her heart and a yearning to be with Reuben again.

When they crested the hill overlooking the village, she stopped and stared. What life within! Though sparser than she remembered, it boasted of houses and shops, barns and animals. How could so much life be here when they'd escaped so much death? The Babylonian army must have had no reason to venture miles out of their way for such a small village.

A warm breeze tousled an unruly whisp of her hair, and she tucked it back under her headscarf. A child's laughter danced through the air.

Phineas tugged on her skirt. "Who's that, Mama?"

She dared a smile as she ran a hand through his hair. "A friend, perhaps. We shall see."

She continued down the path. Phineas lagged behind her, his steps timid in unfamiliar surroundings. How weary he must be from their journey. She took his hand and gave a gentle squeeze.

She rounded a bend, and her breath caught.

"There." She pointed to the small house she and Reuben had once shared. "There is our home."

Though her heart hammered within, she held her head high and marched towards the house as if nothing had changed.

"What if Abba does not like me?" The threat of tears rimmed Phineas' small voice.

She bent low and faced him.

He bit his lip and thrust out his chest. Ever trying hard to be a man. He had grown up quickly during the siege and the invasion.

She couldn't answer him, could offer no trite assurances. Instead, she cupped his face in her hands and peered into his beautiful brown eyes.

"I love you. You know that, right? So very much."

He nodded and offered a trembling smile. She kissed his forehead, straightened, and continued on, all the way to her front door.

When she pushed it open, there was her husband sitting in the common area, head in hands. He did not look up or seem to notice that he had visitors. His lips were moving, though she could not make out his words.

"Reuben?" she said gently.

His head jerked up, his eyes alight with wonder. "Ashira?" He stood and moved towards her, arms open for an embrace. "Ashira, you are alive!" His hair had greyed, and his face had thinned since she'd seen him last. Then again, the famine had likely changed her appearance as well in ways she hadn't recognized.

She leaned into him, inhaling deep. His scent was the same, like olive oil, though how he could have any left was a mystery. "Yes. We are alive."

He held her for a long moment, as if afraid she would disappear if he let her go. "I was praying you would return. We have all heard of the destruction of Jerusalem. I feared you were among the slain." He pulled back and searched her face. "Your uncle Boaz thought he spotted you in the city, weaving mats on the side of the street, but as he made his way through the crowd, he lost sight of you and you were gone. When he returned to the village, he told me. I rushed to find you. But by then the Babylonians had returned and I could not make my way to you, to bring you home." He caressed her cheek with his thumb.

Her stomach quivered. "I was there. *We* were there. We are safe."

He tilted his head at her words, then looked past her to Phineas, who hung back in the doorway, eyes wide with fear. "We?"

"Tell me, Reuben, to whom were you praying?"

"I have been praying to all of the gods, to anyone who would help me find you. Tell me, who is the boy?"

Ashira's stomach sank and fear crept over her. She took a step back. If Reuben was still praying to idols and the rain had not yet come, would he seize Phineas and bring him to Molech? *Oh, Lord! Jeremiah said it was safe to return. Keep my child safe.*

"Ashira?" Reuben asked again.

"Reuben, my husband—" Ashira's voice caught in her throat. There was nothing else to tell her husband except for the truth. "This is our son Phineas."

"Our son?"

Ashira could not distinguish his tone. "I'm sorry for fleeing from you. I wanted to protect the child of my womb from Molech and his fire." She took another step back, preparing herself to flee yet again if he suggested that very thing.

"You fled because of Molech?"

"Yes."

Reuben made an abrupt motion with his hand. "Molech is not a true god. He has no power over the rain. All those children sacrificed and still we have no rain. I do not worship him any longer."

The tension melted from her shoulders at Reuben's announcement. Their child was safe.

She dipped her head to meet his downcast gaze. "Who then do you worship, my husband? Who has the power over the skies?"

"I don't know. I have prayed to all the idols I know of, to all of the gods of surrounding nations. Still there is no rain, and now Jerusalem has been burned with fire and our people taken captive."

Ashira trembled. *Jeremiah charged me to carry his message, but I am so afraid. Help me, Lord. Give me the words to say.* She turned to look at Phineas, still cowering in the doorway.

She took a deep breath. "Perhaps Jeremiah was right all along."

His eyebrow hitched upward. "Jeremiah? The prophet of doom?"

"He spoke of the Babylonian siege, and it came true."

"Yes, but—"

"He says we must return to the God of Abraham, Isaac, and Jacob, that the God of our fathers is the one true God. He calls our nation to repent of our sin and turn to Him, that He may have mercy on us."

"But the God of our Fathers has abandoned His city, allowing it to be burned with fire. The temple, is it not in ruins?"

She paused, pressing her lips together before continuing. *Lord, give me the words.* "He allowed such because of our grave sin. Yet He promises that if we return, He will have mercy on us and bring our people back to Jerusalem."

Chapter 35: Ashira

Reuben sighed, then reached a finger to trace her jawbone. "I don't know what to think. I only know that I am glad to have you home."

"And our son?"

"Yes, and our son. Come here, boy. Let me look at you."

Phineas shuffled towards his father, his eyes seeking out Ashira for assurance. She nodded encouragement.

"He takes after you, I believe," Ashira said.

"Ah, yes. But he has his mother's soft eyes." Reuben looked the boy over, then tousled his hair. He embraced his wife, and she sank into his arms. "I am glad you are home. Both of you."

That night Reuben awoke Ashira from her slumber.

"What is it, my husband?"

"I had a dream, and I cannot shake it from my mind." He dragged a hand over his face.

"What did you dream of?"

"There was fire all around me, encircling me. Then a voice spoke from the fire saying, 'I AM that I AM.'"

She put a hand on his arm. "Reuben, certainly you remember the story."

"What story?"

"Of how the God of our Fathers spoke to Moses from the burning bush. He spoke those very words from the fire."

"Moses? The one who led our people out of Egypt?"

"Yes, don't you remember?"

"Those stories have not been told much. I didn't remember. I cannot sleep now. Every time I close my eyes, I see the fire." Reuben's eyes were haunted in the moonlight.

"Yahweh is calling you to return to Him. He is the one true God, and there is no other." Ashira sat up, speaking confidently now, assured that God was with her and was beckoning her husband. "And Yahweh is calling our people as well. Though we have no prophet living here anymore, they still must hear the message of repentance. I will bring it to them. Perhaps the Lord protected Phineas and me amidst the destruction for this very purpose."

His brows furrowed. "You intend to speak as Jeremiah spoke?"

"Yes. If our people will humble themselves and turn from their wicked ways, God will have mercy on us and on our land."

Reuben was quiet, and after a while, Ashira fell back asleep.

Her husband said nothing more about the dream or about the God of their fathers that next morning, instead gently speaking with their son and getting acquainted with him. But Ashira took note of a change. The table and the shelf that were normally covered with a myriad of idols were completely clear. Reuben must have gotten rid of them in the night. She believed he was ready to follow Yahweh again.

Two days later, Ashira, Reuben, and Phineas walked to Anathoth and found a spot in the marketplace. Reuben set down the small box he carried and helped Ashira onto it, then stepped back. He picked up Phineas and they both watched her attentively.

Ashira looked at her husband and son, and then around at all the people in the marketplace. *God of my fathers, give me words to speak. Turn the hearts of the people back to You today. Let them repent of their idol worship and choose life.*

She took a deep breath and began. "Hear, O Israel! Return to the Lord your God, for He is merciful . . . "

Chapter 36: Eve

My eyes began to glaze over as I stared at the to-do list in front of me. When I'd offered to host Christmas dinner for our families as well as for Lisa, I hadn't factored in sleep deprivation. Hopefully, Lisa wouldn't deliver on her due date. She could meet our families and celebrate the holiday as someone who belonged. And I could get a slight respite.

Zephan had slept seven hours straight the night before. The first time I'd gotten a full night's rest since before he was born. Hallelujah! Over and over again that morning, I'd thanked the Lord for such respite. Perhaps the fog hovering over me was nearly ready to lift. Of course, Lisa was due in two weeks, but surely if I had a couple weeks of good, solid rest, I could take a deep breath and do it all over again. Would it make me a horrible person to hope she went late?

I had bonded with my little boy the first moment I saw him. His small features and little sighs melted my heart. I'd expected that. What I hadn't expected was the utter exhaustion. In high school and college, I'd stayed up late most nights, making it though a full day just fine on four or five hours of sleep. It hardly fazed me if I didn't even get that much. I'd assumed that I'd adjust well to having a newborn that woke up at all hours of the night.

I was wrong.

This type of exhaustion was next level. Hours of nursing depleted my body, and my nerves were raw from his shrill cries awakening me out of a dead sleep. Even when I lay down at night, I jumped at the thought that he could wake up any minute, and it took nearly an hour for me to fall asleep.

It wasn't that he was an overly fussy baby. I'd heard stories of colicky little ones, and I couldn't justify placing him in that category. But he was a baby, and babies cried. Babies cried while mommies wanted to collapse into bed.

Now, though, Zephan was beginning to sleep through the night. The sunrise was cresting the horizon. Hope sprouted within me, but weeds of fear choked at it. What if Esther *was* a colicky baby? What if I never slept well again? Could I hang onto joy in the process?

With Esther on her way to her big debut, I still felt pregnant. I'd hold Zephan in my arms and marvel at that thought. One down, one to go. At times, it felt as if she were moving inside of me. My emotions were all over the place. Daily I had to surrender my concerns over the labor and delivery to the Lord. My mind screamed with possible complications. And the biggest worry: would Lisa change her mind?

I checked my shopping list again, thumbing through the recipe cards I'd pulled out for the occasion. Christmas would be the first time Gideon's family would see Zephan. They lived across the country and were eager for a chance to meet their new grandson. They loved us dearly, even if they did think we were crazy for adopting a baby so soon after we'd had our own.

"Okay, little man." He sat propped up in his bouncy seat, swatting at the toy lady bugs dangling in front of him. Since the two babies would share a room, I'd tried to purchase everything in gender-neutral colors and themes. I'd ditched the pink lace for bright greens, yellows, reds, and blues. "We're going to the grocery store. What do you think of that? Now listen, you finished eating a half an hour ago, so no matter what you think, you're not hungry yet. Okay? No screaming for Mommy's milk in the store. Got it?"

He smiled and let out a little coo in return. I picked him up, nuzzling my nose against his. How had he grown so much in a few short months?

Short months? Who was I kidding? I'd planned to enjoy the moments and not rush ahead of things, but lately I'd been counting down the days until I could possibly get sleep. Doing so had paradoxically made the months drag by in a way.

I strapped him into his infant seat, bundling him up under his cover. I sang "Jesus Loves the Little Children" while zipping up my own coat and putting on my gloves. I grabbed my purse-turned-diaper bag and we set off. If I could time it right, we'd be finished shopping and well on our way home before it was time for his first nap of the day. If I hurried, I could still get in a good half-hour or forty-five minutes of Bible reading time before he woke up and it was time to feed him again.

On the drive to the store, I rehearsed the items I needed to purchase and mentally mapped my way around the store. If I wanted that quiet time, I couldn't be getting in line to check out only to realize I'd forgotten the cranberries down aisle eleven.

I was running on adrenaline as I snapped Zephan's seat into the cart. Funny how I'd taken shopping by myself for granted all those years. I whisked into the first aisle, determined to not waste a minute. After picking out tomatoes and a head of lettuce, an elderly lady leaning on her walker stopped me.

"Oh, what a precious baby! How old is she?"

"He's three months." I returned her smile, trying to be polite. How could I be irritated at the sweet old woman? But I needed to get my shopping done as quickly as possible.

"Oh, it's a boy. I'm sorry. It's so hard to tell when they're young. It seems like I always get it wrong."

"No problem. I understand."

"He's beautiful. Just beautiful. Or should I say handsome? He has your nose, I think. Your nose and your brow. Do you think he looks more like you or your husband?"

"I'm not quite sure. We don't have any baby pictures of my husband yet. His parents are supposed to bring some when they come in town for Christmas." I cast a glance further down the aisle, where the french-fried onions sat on a shelf waiting for me.

"All of my children looked like their father. Couldn't see more than a lick of me in them, I think. It was okay, though. My husband was pretty good-looking. I was happy they took after him, though when I was at the store once, some lady suggested they were adopted!" A laugh burst out of her, as though this thought was completely absurd.

Zephan gurgled at the woman, smiling. A trail of saliva ran down his cheek. I reached into my bag for a burp cloth.

"What's his name, dear?"

"Zephaniah." Whenever I told people his name, I braced myself for a reaction. Most people weren't rude, just surprised. A few commented on how unusual names were in style nowadays. One older gentleman had gone on and on, asking what was wrong with the world that no one appreciated good, solid names like John and Henry.

"Zephaniah? Like in the Bible?"

I smiled. "Yes, like in the Bible."

"Oh, that's nice. What a nice name." She patted my hand, then bent her face close to Zephan's, speaking baby talk. Zephan giggled.

How insensitive of me to be so impatient. What use was reading my Bible if I couldn't act in love towards people in everyday situations? Was that what the Lord would want—for me to be angry, impatient, and irritated with others as long as I got in two chapters of Scripture each day? The apostle James had said true religion was taking care of widows and orphans, and by extension that meant showing kindness to old ladies in the supermarket.

"How many children do you have?" I asked, relaxing. So much for those plans for efficient shopping.

"Six, dear. Two boys and four girls. All of them are probably older than you are, married with lives of their own. They're scattered all around the county. Only my Elise and her family come to visit, really. Oh, I shouldn't say that. Tom is bringing his girls over for Christmas this year." She let out a sad sigh. "Funny how quickly things change. One minute they depend on you for everything, and the next they're off on their own. The thing is, I never felt like I stopped needing them around, if only to share a cup of tea and talk about whatever's bothering them. That's the thing about being a mother; your heart's in it for life."

"I can imagine." What I couldn't imagine was little Zephan and Esther picking up and moving to a different town, a different state, without as much as a glance back in my direction.

"Well, dear, sorry for holding you up. I'm sure you've got plenty of other things to keep you occupied. You have a good Christmas, you hear?"

I smiled and patted her hand. "You too. Enjoy the time with your family."

"Oh, I don't take that for granted. Not anymore." She pushed her walker forward, then stopped to inspect the bananas.

The rest of the shopping trip went smoothly. I gathered the items on my list quickly and efficiently, checking them off one by one. By the time I made my way to the check out, Zephan's eyes were getting heavy. There went my quiet time.

I drove home deflated, Zephan's subtle snores my only accompaniment. *God, I'm having trouble adjusting here. I'm used to spend long hours reading Your Word. Now I'm fortunate to grab fifteen minutes with You. I'm used to spending hours praying for the unborn. Now my prayers mostly consist of me asking You to help me through the day. How do I find You here? How do I find You in the midst of the endless laundry and feedings, diaper changes, and rocking him to sleep? I need You to be close to me, Father. I need to feel You here with me.*

Perhaps I could still have at least a few minutes of time to myself? But Zephan woke up while I was still putting the groceries away.

"You didn't sleep long, Mister." I kept my voice playful, though weariness seeped through my bones.

Maybe I could put him in his crib and see if he'd go back to sleep. But no. He'd need to eat soon anyway, and trying to get him to sleep again would throw his afternoon nap off and be more stress than it was worth. Instead, I placed him in his sling and sang to him as I finished putting the groceries away. I sang worship songs instead of nursery rhymes. It was a way I could keep my heart connected to God, no matter how distant from Him I'd been feeling lately.

The conversation with the elderly woman came floating to mind. What would people say when I went to the store with both babies? Would I be bombarded with endless questions, or would people cast a curious glance and continue on with their business?

My phone rang and interrupted both my song and my thoughts. "Hello?"

"Eve? It's Lisa. I think . . . I think I'm in labor."

I dropped a can of cranberries less than an inch away from my foot. "You think? How far apart are the contractions?"

"That's just it. I'm having trouble timing them. They don't seem to be consistent."

"If they're not consistent, maybe it's false labor." I bit my lip. It could be, but by the sound of her voice . . .

"It hurts really bad. This has got to be the real thing. What should I do?"

"Call your doctor and let her know. I'll call Gideon. We'll swing by and get you."

My instructions were met with a moan. I shuddered at the sound. Did I have to revisit the pain of childbirth so soon? After a moment, she agreed and hung up.

In ten minutes, Zephan and I were out the door again, on our way to pick up Gideon at church. Adrenaline shot through my veins. My stomach felt tangled. My mundane day was about to be radically changed. If Lisa was right, I'd soon be holding a second baby in my arms. My Esther. My little Esther.

Gideon was waiting in front for us. His face lit up with expectation instead of the nervousness it had held when I was in labor. Perhaps this was because he'd been through the experience only a few months before. He grinned at me as I rushed around to the passenger's seat in back, and he slid into the driver's seat.

"Let's rock n' roll. Baby number two, coming right up," he said.

Gideon's lighthearted mood continued until we drove up to Lisa's apartment. Lisa was doubled over by the door. He rushed to her and helped her toward the van and into the front passenger seat.

I sat in back trying to pacify Zephan, who had just decided he was ready to nurse. "Wait a minute, Mr. Man. Mommy will feed you soon."

Gideon dropped Lisa's bag in her footwell before getting back into the driver's seat. Her bag? Wow. Good job, Lisa, on being prepared. I'd left my bag at home by the door for several weeks before Zephan's due date but hadn't been home when I went into labor. Gideon had had to run back and get it after Zephan was born.

On the drive to the hospital, it hit me that Lisa's baby was about to be born with her mother nowhere in sight. From what I'd gathered, Lisa's mother didn't know what her daughter was going through and didn't care to know. Lisa had always been surrounded by family, no matter how dysfunctional they were. Now, though, she was in pain, afraid, and alone except for us.

"Hang on. Deep breaths, remember?" I said, then squeezed my eyes shut. That probably wasn't helpful. I hadn't remembered how to breathe, and I'd taken Lamaze classes. Lisa hadn't. Still, she tried to regulate her breathing, gripping the side of her seat with white knuckles.

We arrived at the hospital in record time. They admitted Lisa at once. Though I longed to be by her side every minute, Zephan demanded my attention. I nursed him in the waiting room while Gideon went back and forth between us with updates.

She was five centimeters dilated, enough that they wouldn't be sending her home, but her contractions were inconsistent. As I nursed one baby, I thought of another—a precious little girl who was bound to make her entrance soon. I would see her, hold her, hear her little newborn cry. And in a couple of days, I would take her home.

Zephan kept falling asleep while eating, and I played with his toes to wake him up long enough to finish his meal. "See, little man. This is what happens when you don't take a long enough nap." He grabbed my shirt in response. I blew gently on his face. Finally, he finished, and I handed him over to Gideon so I could go see Lisa.

The staff was prepping her for an epidural when I entered the room. "I'm not as brave as you." Lisa's smile was half-hearted and weak, fading as she looked nervously from me to the doctor.

"I wasn't brave, really. He came too fast for me to get one."

"I hate needles." She grimaced.

"You might love this needle in a few minutes." I held her hand as the doctor inserted the epidural. To distract her from what was taking place, I changed the subject.

"So, have you decided on a middle name?"

"Joy, I think. Esther Joy."

"That's beautiful. I'm glad it's nothing too crazy," I said with a wink.

Staring at our hands, my nerves buzzed. Should I ask her if she was sure she'd be able to go through with the adoption? I glanced up. They were inserting a giant needle into her spine. Probably not the best time. But I loved her child with a fierceness I could never have felt on my own for a child coming to me from a different womb.

Just then, I heard a phone ring and went to the nearby chair to check my purse. But wait. It wasn't my ringtone.

"Lisa, is that your phone? Do you want me to get it?"

"Sure." She sounded drowsy.

Pulling her phone from her bag, I flipped it open. "Hello?"

"Lisa?"

"No, actually, this is Eve, one of Lisa's friends. Can I give her a message for you? She's in labor right now."

"She's in labor? What?"

"Uh . . . may I ask who this is?"

"This is Dawn, her sister."

My stomach sank down to my toes. Her sister hadn't known she was pregnant.

"Well, I can tell her you called . . . " What else could I say?

"Where is she? What hospital, I mean?"

"At Crider," I whispered. What was going on? Surely, I'd ruined their mother's plans. But Lisa deserved to have her family here.

"Is she . . . will it happen soon?"

I looked at Lisa, whose eyes were heavy. "I don't know. It could be a while."

"I'll be there in forty minutes." She hung up, and I stared at the phone. "She's in labor right now?" Why did I say that?

Was I supposed to say that? Was it part of God's plan? I opened my mouth to warn Lisa, but she was asleep.

"God," I whispered. "What are You doing?"

***

"Hello?"

I blinked. I'd dozed off myself. A girl stood in the doorway. She looked a lot like Lisa. "Hi. Are you Dawn?"

"Yes." Her eyes flickered between me and the hospital bed.

I smiled at her. "She's been asleep since you called. I didn't have a chance to tell her you were coming."

"She'll be surprised." Dawn chuckled.

I leaned back and studied her. "You didn't know, did you?"

"My mom didn't tell me."

"She didn't want you to know," I said. "Lisa said your mom kind of flipped out when she told her she was pregnant. Your father was even worse. They haven't talked to her since."

"And who are you?"

"I'm Eve. I'm the adoptive mom."

"She's . . . she's not keeping the baby?"

"No. The father's out of the picture, and she wants to focus on getting her degree. My husband and I are adopting her little girl."

"I can't believe this." Dawn lowered into a chair, holding her purse in her lap. "Lisa's never been one to get into trouble. She was always the good one, the one Lydia and I could never be like."

"I think that's why your mother didn't want you to know," I said. "She thought Lisa would be a bad example for you."

Dawn laughed again. "I've never built my life around my mother's expectations of me. Lisa hasn't done anything Lydia and I haven't already done. I guess she's not as good at hiding it from our parents."

"What do you mean?"

"Lydia and I had our parents fooled a long time ago." Dawn shrugged. "Our little sister's goodness wasn't an act. She really was good, at least when she lived at home. I guess she was waiting until college to sleep around."

"What are your parents like, Dawn? Tell me about your family. Lisa has told me a little but not much."

"They're . . . stiff. Into religion, you know? Into looking proper and convincing everyone we're the typical all-American family."

"So, they're Christians?"

Dawn uttered a dry laugh. "Sure they are."

"And you were all brought up on morals?"

"They brought us up on 'Obey, or else.' If you want to call that morality, go right ahead. We learned quickly enough to stay under the radar. I slept with my first boyfriend in my parent's bed without them knowing. I was fourteen. They probably still think I'm a virgin." Dawn's tone was less defiant than confessional. erw

"But Lisa was different?"

"Yeah. Oh, she was sarcastic as any of us behind our parents back, but she didn't act out. She was too afraid of what they'd think of her if they found out. She's always been kind of a chameleon. She's whoever you want her to be."

"I think you'll find her different now. She's grown up."

"Well, getting knocked up will do that to you." Dawn had a knowing air. What was hidden in her past?

Lisa stirred. Her hazy eyes searched the room.

"Eve?"

I got up and went to her side.

"Sorry, I'm a little out of it," Lisa mumbled. "Must be that medication they gave me when I first got here. What's going on? Am I any further along?"

"No one's been in here for a while. The nurse did say something about giving you Pitocin to jump-start those contractions again. They seem to have died down."

"Whatever works, I guess."

Dawn sat still, hidden behind the monitors, watching our interaction. I caught her eye and she nodded.

"Lisa, your sister's here to see you." I stepped back.

Lisa's breath hitched. She sat up and angled herself in Dawn's direction.

"Dawn? H-how'd you know I was here? Did Mom . . . "

Dawn walked over and took her younger sister's hand. "I called because Mom made up some fishy tale about how you were delivering baskets to the homeless for Christmas and wouldn't be coming home. I knew it didn't add up, so I called to see what's going on. Eve answered the phone and said you couldn't talk because you were in labor."

Lisa's mouth twisted. "So, Mom didn't say anything."

"No. Nothing true, at least."

Resignation drew lines across Lisa's face. "I guess you're surprised, huh?" She shrugged.

"Well, I doubted you could maintain the perfect sister image forever." Dawn smiled. "So, what'd they do? Tell you to hit the road and never come back?"

I mentally winced. From what Lisa had said and what Dawn had confirmed, her parents might well be capable of such a thing.

"Mom said it would be better if I stayed away while I was pregnant. She didn't want me 'corrupting' you."

"See what a wonderful sister she is?" Dawn directed at me. "She could have turned me in, blabbed all my secrets to my mother to make herself not look so bad. Instead, she—what'd you do, Lisa? Just walk out?"

"Something like that." Lisa turned her head toward the window.

"Ah, don't worry, Lisie. You're still their favorite, no matter what she said."

"Do you ever think that Mom's got skeletons of her own in her closet?"

"What do you mean? Are you suggesting she's less than perfect?" Dawn gasped in mock horror.

"I mean, there's got to be more to her story. Somewhere along the line, she got hurt bad by something. How else would you explain how she is?"

She made a good point. I'd met plenty of religious people who made me remember Jesus' story about planks and splinters.

"I don't know, sis, but I wouldn't waste my time thinking about it. Focus on your schoolwork after you have this baby. Go make something of yourself. Prove that everything good she's said about you was right and everything bad she's thought about you was wrong."

Clearly Dawn spoke from experience. Lisa had spoken little about her sisters. What was the story about Dawn? She didn't seem upset that her sister hadn't gotten an abortion—hadn't even mentioned the word, had just encouraged Lisa. Hopefully I'd get another opportunity to talk to Dawn. She intrigued me. But before the conversation could continue, a nurse bustled in.

Chapter 37: Lisa

Was something wrong? Lisa had been in the hospital for over three hours now and nothing was happening. A steady rhythm of beeps punctuated the background. The nurse scanned the printout of Lisa's contractions, asked a few questions, and checked for any signs of progression.

"So," Lisa said, attempting to keep her voice lighthearted, "Does it look like I'm going to give birth any time soon?"

"I'm afraid not." The nurse's gaze held sympathy. "Since your labor doesn't seem to be progressing, the doctor wants to chemically stimulate. We'll start you on Pitocin in a bit."

After the nurse left, Lisa turned to Eve and whispered, "As long as they've got me drugged up, bring it on."

Eve laughed. "I think you're going to be fine now that you've got your sister here." Smiling at Dawn, she added, "I'm going to go check on my husband and my son. I'll be back soon."

As Eve's footsteps faded, Lisa met her sister's eyes. "What do you think of all of this?" Lisa spread her arms out in front of her. The IV pinched, and she set her hands in her lap.

"I don't know what to think. I can't believe Mom ditched you like this. Her first grandchild is about to be born. She should be here." Storm clouds gathered in Dawn's eyes. "Doesn't it make you mad?"

"It did for a long time. I've forgiven her, though. It wasn't easy, and I keep having to forgive her when I think about doing this alone, but I'm learning forgiveness is a choice and not a warm fuzzy feeling."

Dawn scoffed. "But she should be here. Your family is supposed to support you."

Lisa toyed with the fringe of her hospital blanket. "I'm not saying Mom isn't wrong. I chose to forgive her, that's all."

Dawn shook her head. "Do you think things will go back to normal after you give up this baby? Is she planning on moving on like nothing ever happened? Will she invite you back into her life?"

Lisa uttered a deep, throaty sound, just short of a chuckle. "Not if she gets her hands on my article, she won't."

"What article?"

"It's nothing much. I wrote a personal article for my school paper, and now it's being published in a national magazine. I don't really want to talk about it right now, though."

"Can I read it?"

"Sure. Ask me about it before you leave. Eve might have a copy with her."

Dawn cocked her head to the side. "How'd you meet Eve, anyway? She's an interesting character. Got me to talking about stuff I rarely talk about."

Lisa smiled. That sounded like Eve. "She does that to people. You feel drawn to her even though you don't know her. The first time I saw her was outside—" She took a deep breath. "I was outside the abortion clinic. Mitchell had tried to convince me to get an abortion, but I didn't feel right about it. There were people standing outside—protesters—and one was this pregnant woman who stared at me. So, I went up to her and said . . . "

As she answered that simple question, it led to many others. Dawn kept asking Lisa if she was sure about her decision. Lisa reassured her she was. Did Dawn wonder how

Lisa could go through the entire process of pregnancy and labor only to give the baby up? Good question.

But Lisa had become increasingly convinced over the past few months that she was doing the right thing.

Eventually Dawn pulled up a chair beside Lisa's bed, and they passed the time recounting childhood stories. It'd been a long time since they were truly young and innocent, but the three sisters had been close once. They'd been heroes of all their imaginary stories. In their little make-believe world, there was no disappointed motherly scowl to overcome, no ridiculously high demands. But as they'd grown up, Dawn and Lydia had become inseparable in mischief and Lisa had been left on the outside.

Dawn did most of the talking while the nurses adjusted Lisa's medicine and did routine progress checks. Her contractions picked up, but because of the epidural, she wasn't in pain. Eve drifted in and out of their conversations, seemingly enjoying getting to know more about Lisa's childhood.

Eventually it got late. Gideon went home with the baby. Eve drifted to sleep in the other chair, but Dawn and Lisa kept talking. It was the closest Lisa had felt to her sister since middle school, almost like they were becoming friends again. Lisa fell asleep smiling.

Chapter 38: Eve

I woke up to the sound of muffled crying. Groggily, I tried to decipher where it was coming from. My eyes immediately landed on Lisa, who was sound asleep. What in the world?

I rubbed my eyes, then let my gaze drift around the room until it settled on Dawn. She was scrunched up in a little ball in the corner chair, shoulders heaving under the weight of suppressed sobs.

"Dawn? What's wrong?" I uncurled myself from the recliner and forced my stiff legs to move toward her.

She didn't look up, didn't acknowledge my presence. But there on the floor beside her chair lay Lisa's article.

"Dawn?" As I touched her shoulder, her head jerked in my direction. Her red, puffy eyes met mine, and in them swam what had eluded the personal details she'd shared with me earlier: shame. She shook her head repeatedly, opening her mouth as if to speak, but no words found release. Tears streamed down her cheeks, and her entire body shook.

I ached for her, but how could I ease her burden? Finally, I asked if I could pray for her. Her nod was slight—I would have missed it if I'd blinked—but I pushed through the small door of agreement.

Sitting down next to her, I placed a gentle hand on her shoulder. "Father, I come before You and ask You to minister to this precious daughter of Yours. Lord, come with healing power and bind up her broken heart. You search her and know her. You created her and have loved her every step of the way, even when those steps have led away from You and Your plan for her life. Show her Your love right now, Lord. Open her eyes to see Your arms open to her, ready and waiting for her to fall into. Lead her to the wells of righteousness, the springs of living water. In Jesus' name, amen."

And then she cried harder. I drew circles on her shoulder with my forefinger, continuing to pray silently until at last, her tears slowed enough for her to talk.

"I-I didn't. Didn't know . . . " Her voice was small and broken.

"Didn't know about Lisa? That she'd had an abortion?" I pulled my chair closer.

"No. Yes. No. I didn't know that either, but . . . I didn't know . . . I thought . . . I thought I was the only . . . the only one."

"The only one what?"

"The only . . . the only one with the nightmares . . . the only one who hurt this bad."

I reached out and placed an arm around her. So that was it. Dawn wasn't just crying for her sister's pain. She had genuine pain of her own.

"I was sixteen. I'd been on the pill. I didn't think . . . I never thought I'd get pregnant. I was careful. I went to the clinic with my fake ID. I didn't know if they'd want p-parental consent, so I used it. Th-they gave me the abortion pill and sent me home. It was supposed to 'induce a miscarriage,' was the way they said it." She wiped wet cheeks with her sleeve.

"It hurt so bad. Th-the cramping. It was horrible. I lost a lot of blood. I-I didn't know. Th-they didn't tell me it would hurt that bad. I wanted to change my mind, but it was . . . it was too late."

"Oh, Dawn." Tears welled as my heart grieved for her pain, but what to say?

"I had nightmares for a long time." Although she still trembled with every sentence and tears still traced their way down her cheeks, her words came out clearer. "Every night. It was horrible, and I looked for something to stop the pain. Finally, I tried hypnosis, which helped, but only for a month or so. Then the dreams came back, worse than before. I went to counseling, and they kept telling me it was okay. I did the right thing, made the right choice. There's nothing to feel guilty about. I wanted to believe them, wanted to be clean, but I knew better."

"You knew you wanted to be clean but didn't feel there was a way?"

"I haven't slept with a guy in years. I'm too scared to, but even now I don't feel clean. Even when I try to do the right thing, live the right way, I'm not clean."

"Do you believe Jesus can make you clean?"

At the mention of His name, she stiffened. "Oh, yeah." Her voice was soft, yet sarcastic. "He washes white as snow, right?"

I nodded. Why such acid in her response?

"Jesus has no place in my life." Her tone was short, making it clear that this was the end of our discussion. If she wouldn't let me talk to her about the only One who could heal her, at least I could pray for her. *Lord, bring healing. Bring restoration. Soften her heart so that she can receive Your love.*

There were a few moments of awkward silence. Where could I go from there? I wouldn't get anywhere from picking up where we'd left off.

"I'm gonna go get something to eat." Dawn stood and sped from the room.

A moment later, I heard Lisa murmur, "Eve?"

"You're awake." I walked over to her bedside.

"I've been awake for a while. I heard you and Dawn but didn't want to interrupt."

"How much did you hear?"

"Enough to know she had an abortion and is hurting because of it. I'm sorry she clammed up at the mention of Jesus. She's had a real hard time with our parents' version of religion."

"I gathered that."

"They were especially hard on her. She's the oldest."

"Tell me, Lisa, are your parents saved? Do they really love the Lord, or do they just have a form of religion?"

She was quiet for a few moments, her expression thoughtful. "I don't know for sure. I can't tell. They probably love Jesus the best they know how. I think they've always wanted to please Him. Maybe they got caught up in pleasing other people and looking like they're model Christians. Obviously, they haven't been living their faith right, but maybe they'll get there, you know?"

I nodded, uncertain and terrified. If Lisa's parents were truly believers and were trying to live their lives for Him the best they knew how, and yet all three of their daughters had wandered, how could I even hope to raise children who would remain wholehearted followers of Him? Was it an impossible feat? Could I be a good enough mom to prevent them from walking off into rebellion? What about the verse that says if you train up a child in the way he should go, when he's old he won't depart from it? Where was that promise for Lisa's parents?

More than anything I wanted Esther and Zephan, and any other children God might grace us with, to grow up loving the Lord and walking in purity and righteousness. I wanted them to have the true knowledge of God, not a copycat form of my own faith. After hearing of Lisa's family, discouragement threatened.

"Am I still having contractions?" Lisa cocked her head toward the printout of the monitor.

I glanced at the zigzag lines. "Yeah, it looks like it."

"I can't even feel them. I have no idea how I'm going to push."

"We'll cross that bridge when we come to it." I stretched, exhaustion creeping through every limb.

"When are we going to come to it?" she asked. "It's taking a long time."

"Do you feel anything?"

"Pressure, but not anything too bad. I'm just anxious to meet her, you know?"

Anxious to meet her? A subtle panic worked its way up my spine. What if it was love at first sight? What if, after seeing Esther—as I'd seen Zephan—she wouldn't be able to give her up?

Chapter 39: Lisa

Thirty-six hours after Lisa arrived at the hospital, the doctors determined she needed an emergency C-section. Although the epidural had eased the pain factor down to nearly non-existent, by the end of the long labor, she had neither the energy nor the ability to push the baby into the world. After she tried to push for nearly an hour, the baby's heart rate dropped, the doctors consulted together, and they wheeled her into an operating room.

Eve remained by her side through the entire process, scrubs and all. Because of the pale blue sheet that obstructed Lisa's view, Eve would be the first to see little Esther. Probably better that way, but what to do about this sorrowful longing?

As they performed the C-section, she kept her eyes locked on Eve's face. The unabashed love streaming from there pushed back all her reservations. Eve loved the child they were pulling from Lisa's womb. The delight in Eve's smile ran deeper than anything Lisa's own heart could hold. As Eve's eyes glistened with tears, the truth settled deep. No matter the tensions of her own heart, Esther belonged in Eve's arms.

It was as if she were part of some strange love triangle. In the movies when two women were in love with the same man, one woman always won out and the other lost. Not the case here. Somehow, someway, God would make a way for both Eve and her to love this little one. How? She couldn't fathom. But Eve's eyes beamed with pride and joy as she waited to hold her daughter. Clearly it was possible. Not only possible, but Esther's destiny.

Lisa hadn't felt a connection with the life wiggling inside of her until she saw the picture on the ultrasound. With Esther's every kick and nudge, love had slowly blossomed in her heart. In the end, though, love was a choice. Loving Esther meant putting her needs before Lisa's own, sacrificing fragmented dreams under the weight of the torrent of love that sprung forth from Eve. How could she deprive her little one of such fierce devotion?

As the newborn's cry met their ears, Eve trembled. In a few moments, the nurse placed Esther in Lisa's arms. She stared at her daughter in awe. Such tiny features. A frizzy mop of dark hair on her head made them look even smaller. Lisa opened her mouth to speak, to coo at her baby as mothers instinctively do. But no words would come out, only tears.

She traced her thumb along the side of Esther's face. He breath caught. How could anything be so beautiful? Then she met Eve's gaze. Though her friend smiled, Eve's eyes were nervous, panicked even. Could Lisa blame her? Her heart was invested in this little one, drastically so. She had no guarantee Lisa wouldn't change her mind. No way of knowing if Lisa loved Esther enough to let her go.

Oh, she might be ripping her heart from her chest, but she'd made her choice.

Lisa spoke past the lump in her throat. "Hold her."

Eve didn't question, didn't protest, didn't waste her time in the awkwardness of the moment. She swept Esther from Lisa's arms, leaving only a dull ache in her wake.

She said what Lisa hadn't found the voice to say. "Hi, sweet girl! Hello, precious one. I'm your mommy. I'm one of your mommies, that is. You have two, lucky girl." Eve's eyes were wide, her expressions exaggerated, motherhood naturally flowing through her.

As Lisa watched the dance of mother and daughter in front of her, her decision solidified. They belonged together, to each other.

There was a tugging on her belly as Dr. Rosa finished sewing her up. She'd almost forgotten the doctor was there, along with the other nurses in the room. Everything faded next to the display of love playing before her eyes.

Everything but the weight of her sacrifice.

"We're going to weigh and measure her now," a nurse said. "We'll clean her up, and then in a few minutes you can nurse her if you'd like."

Lisa stole a concerned glance at Eve. Although the hospital staff had been notified of their circumstances, this nurse was apparently out of the loop.

They whisked Esther out of Eve's arms and into an adjourning room. Eve went to follow, then turned around and came towards Lisa's side again. She shifted her weight, though her expression was filled with kindness.

"You can nurse her if you'd like to." Eve kept her voice low and gentle.

"But, shouldn't you? Didn't you want to?"

"I can, but so can you. I have milk, but you have colostrum."

Lisa tilted her head. What was Eve talking about?

Her friend explained. "Colostrum is the pre-milk that you produce when you first have a baby. It's nutrient-rich and the best thing in the world for her right now."

"But if I nurse her, won't she bond with me? I mean, she's supposed to be bonding with you."

Eve paused, as if weighing her response. "I don't think it will threaten our bond, Lisa. Besides, you deserve to have that memory of her. If you want to, I mean. I'm not trying to pressure you, only give you the option."

Lisa nodded. Of course, she'd take the opportunity, even if it made Esther that much harder to part with. She was in deep as it was. She should pull away before she lost herself completely, before she could take her choice back. But to lose herself in those little eyes while she still had the chance . . . She would have to trust God to put the pieces of her heart back together again later.

Eve left, rushing into the next room to take part in Esther's first moments. Lisa nibbled her lip as she waited for the nurse to bring the baby back. Her body, overwhelmed and exhausted, begged her to give into sleep, yet she held out. Finally, the nurse returned with Esther, who was bundled in a pink blanket. She worked with Lisa to get Esther latched on, then left the room.

Tears spilled silently down Lisa's cheeks as she relished the feeling of Esther in her arms. Though her voice was wobbly and weak, she let it wash over her precious child. "Hi, sweetheart. I'm your mommy. Your other one, that is. I want you to know I love you so much. Please know that. Please never doubt that. I love you. I'll always love you. You're going to go home with your other mommy, but I won't forget about you. Not ever."

Lisa's mind flashed back to that day at the clinic, the day she met Eve. The day her life changed forever. She hadn't recognized God's hand at work then, but looking back, it was clear to see. He had reached down from Heaven and turned her around, pointing her in Eve's direction. He had had His eye on little Esther Joy even then. He was jealous for her life, as Eve would say. And over Lisa too. He was jealous over her heart, eager to rescue her, to heal her, to make things new in her life. *Thank You, God, for what You have done in my life.*

Unwrapping the blanket from around Esther, Lisa studied her fingers and toes. She stroked the tiny palm, and Esther's hand closed around Lisa's finger. She'd expected this experience to be painful. She was on borrowed time. Lisa was completely lost in the sweetness of the moment.

A short time later, the nurse came into check on her, Eve following right behind. Esther had fallen asleep. After handing her to Eve, Lisa followed suit. Giving into her exhaustion, she lost herself in sleep.

***

She awoke to the sound of Eve singing quietly. It took Lisa a few minutes to make out her words and tune.

"Come Thou fount of every blessing, tune my heart to sing Thy praise . . . " Emotion filled Eve's voice.

Lisa kept her eyes closed and relished the sound for a while, singing along in her head. Then her eyes flipped open as she remembered something.

"It's Christmas." Her statement of recognition silenced Eve's song.

"Yes, it is. I suppose I should be singing a carol."

"What about dinner? You were going to have all those people over."

"My sister Julie is having it instead. Gideon and I plan to steal a few hours over there."

"I'm so tired, I probably won't notice you're gone." It was true. Her body wanted to surrender to sleep again for at least an eight-hour stretch. Still, she couldn't shake the loneliness that struck her then. It was Christmas, and her family would be gathered around the dining room table, two leaves in place to hold the enormous amount of food her mother would prepare. She should call Britney and ask for a visit.

She was afraid to ask but too curious not to. "Where's Dawn?"

"She's in the lobby on her phone after spending time holding Esther. I think she's talking to your mom."

Best not to ponder a dozen different scenarios. Impossible not to think of them. Eve respected her silence. After a few minutes, Gideon came to get Eve with Zephan all bundled up in his arms.

"I'll be back after Christmas dinner," Eve said. "I want to stay with you tonight, if that's okay, before the hospital releases Esther tomorrow."

"Oh, you don't have to."

"I want to." Eve smiled at her. "I'd like to keep you company. And I'll bring you dinner, okay?"

The message was clear. Eve wasn't going to disappear.

Eve wished her a Merry Christmas, and Gideon winked at her. Then they were gone, leaving Lisa to her questions and regrets.

A preoccupied woman with a lunch tray interrupted her thoughts. She set the food before Lisa without making eye contact, then rushed away. Lisa was about to lift the lid and view the contents when Dawn entered.

"Well, Mom knows you had the baby. I finally called her back. She left me six voicemails, Lisie. The last one was completely frantic, threatening to call the police if I didn't call her right back."

"What'd she say?" Lisa gulped down apprehension but still couldn't quite meet Dawn's eyes.

"It took me ten minutes to get a word in edgewise. She plowed straight through one of her famous guilt trips, trying to make me ashamed for everything *I* put *her* through by disappearing without telling her where I was. Finally, I told her I was with my niece. That stopped her cold."

"I'll bet."

"She couldn't even respond. I can't remember the last time Mom was speechless. I told her I'd rather eat cold cafeteria food than sit at Christmas dinner with her and Dad after what they did to you."

"Dawn!"

"Well, it's true."

"What'd she say?"

"I hung up before she had the chance to say anything. I didn't want to hear her excuses."

Tears once again assaulted Lisa's eyes. She'd had no idea she was capable of crying so much. Gratitude welled up for the way Dawn stuck up for her. But had the rift in their family just grown wider?

"Well, let's see what we have here." Lisa lifted the tray lid to find spaghetti, bread, and pears.

"Mmm." Dawn leaned forward and smelled the aroma emanating from the food. "A perfect Christmas lunch. I'll go down and see what else they have. Maybe I'll bring you figgy pudding." She winked, and Lisa allowed herself to laugh. It was Christmas, and she wasn't alone after all.

Chapter 40: Trent

It was the first piece of bad news Trent had to deliver since he'd begun his new job. The test results had taken a while to come in. He'd received them the day before, but better to wait until he could tell Melody the news in person.

Of course, this particular screening had a lot of false positives attached. Quite possibly, her baby didn't have Down syndrome. Still, no woman wanted to deal with such a possibility. And no doctor wanted to deliver the news.

He took a deep breath before knocking on the exam room door.

"Come in," came a cheerful reply.

At twenty weeks pregnant, Melody had that famous glow. Her smile was broad as Trent entered. As if possible complications were the furthest thing from her mind.

"Hello, Melody. How are you feeling?" He attempted a smile, but it was stiff.

"Great!" Wonder shone from the eyes of this first-time expectant mother. No doubt everything was as new and thrilling for her as it was for Beth. Better to not waste any more time on small talk. To keep pretending that nothing was wrong would be deceitful; Melody deserved better than that.

"Glad to hear it. In just a minute I'll check the heartbeat and measure you, but first I need to go over the results from that blood test we did the last time you were in."

Her eyes clouded slightly, and hesitation crept into her tone. "Yes?"

Chapter 40: Trent

"The test came back positive for Down syndrome. Now, if you remember, I informed you that there are a lot of false positives with the test. Your baby could still be perfectly healthy. The only way to know for sure is to see a specialist. We'll refer you to one, and he'll do an in-depth ultrasound and explore the possibilities with you."

The radiance from moments earlier vanished, a wall erecting in its place. Her hand slipped from her belly, as if distancing herself from the life with in her. "Then what?"

"Well, if your baby does indeed have Down syndrome, the specialist can refer you to different support services. There are support groups, special training—"

"I mean, what if I don't want to go through with it?"

Trent's chest tightened. He shook his head slowly. No. She couldn't be suggesting . . .

"Look, if there's something wrong with this baby, I'd like to terminate the pregnancy. My husband and I already decided on that. It's why we wanted to take the test in the first place."

"But, Melody, there are many parents of children with Down syndrome who have gone on to enjoy their children like they never imagined. Of course, there are challenges, and I'm not saying it would be easy, but many parents would tell you it's worth it—"

"It's my choice, isn't it? I know a lady who has a kid with Down syndrome. I don't think I could handle the emotional aspect of it. If this bab—if the results are positive, I'll want to terminate."

Trent's stomach clenched. He'd switched venues to avoid performing abortions. Of course, it was a possibility, but he never thought he'd actually have to face performing an abortion again. He replied as a professional, each toneless word dropping from his mouth like lead.

"If you choose to have the pregnancy terminated, I would do a D&E—a Dilatation and Evacuation—as soon as you're sure of the results and your decision." Had such a statement come out of his mouth? If only there was a dark place he could crawl into and hide from his own shame. But what was he supposed to do?

Melody simply nodded in response, and Trent continued with the routine prenatal visit. He listened to her baby's heartbeat and measured her abdomen. Everything looked and sounded normal. If she hadn't chosen to have the test, there wouldn't have been an indication that anything was amiss. She had no further questions. Trent excused himself as quickly as he could.

He retreated to his office and closed the door. Sitting at his desk, he placed his head in his hands. Why was this happening to him? Was it a kind of sick trick from the hands of an angry God? Did the Almighty set him up to think he was getting out of his guilt only to throw it in his face?

Ever since Beth had, in her words, given her life to God, Trent had been making an attempt to talk to Him, if only to reassure her that he was open to making that choice himself someday. But would he ever really take the plunge?

God, I don't get You, and I don't like You. I'm trying to do the right thing here. Don't You care? I never want to do another abortion again. Won't You honor that? It's what You want, right? Give me a break.

And he was once again getting an attitude with the very One he was trying to appease. He needed to get on God's good side. Best to stuff the anger down and play the part of a dutiful servant. Or try another tactic.

God, would you let those test results be false? Please, God. Or if there really is something wrong with this baby, would You heal him? You did it for Beth, God. You can do it for Melody. Eve said those kinds of things happen all the time, right? You can heal this baby, God. Please, please . . . don't back me into a corner here.

He glanced at his watch. Oops. He was keeping his next patient waiting. He made a mental note to call Eve and ask her to pray. He might not have any pull with God, but surely God listened to Eve. Maybe he was getting himself worked up for nothing. Surely God would heal Melody if Eve asked Him to.

Chapter 41: Eve

The tidal wave loomed over the city, casting a shadow over the busy streets. I scanned the crowd, frustrated that no one seemed to notice or care that the wave was about to demolish the entire city. Everyone went about their normal lives, buying this, selling that, joking about who knows what.

"Come on!" I shouted. "We have to get out of here!" No one reacted. Trying to find someone who would respond to me, I looked down, and there was a little girl with blond ringlets playing with her dolls.

"I'm taking her with me," I said. No one around me seemed to care. Sweeping her into my arms, I pushed through the milling crowds to the base of a tall mountain near the city. Painstakingly, we made our way to the top, standing high above the mass of people who were still oblivious to their imminent destruction.

Gideon gently shook my arm as a cry assaulted my ears. "Sweetheart, wake up."

My eyes opened to see not the top of a mountain but the darkness of my bedroom. I'd been dreaming.

"You must have been really out of it not to hear *that* cry," he whispered. As my eyes adjusted to the dimness and my brain transitioned to reality, understanding dawned. Esther's newborn cries pierced loud, clear, and shrill.

Chapter 41: Eve

Groggily, I lifted myself out of bed and padded over to the bassinet on the other side of the room. She'd come unswaddled and batted her little hands in front of her face.

"It's okay, princess. Mommy will feed you." I lifted her up and settled into my rocking chair. "Sorry I didn't hear her, hon. I'm just so tired."

Gideon had rolled over, but his uneven breathing assured me he had not yet fallen back asleep.

"It's all right," he mumbled. "Are you okay?"

"Just tired." Putting it that way made it seem like it was no big deal, but I'd never been so tired. How was I still functioning? I woke up each day with the goal of survival. Not thriving. Not joy. Survival. "It's harder than I thought it would be." Understatement of the century.

What did I think it would be like again? I certainly hadn't figured on conflicting schedules. By the time Esther had come along, Zephan was getting into his routine. He ate every three to four hours and slept through the night. Esther, however, seemed to have missed the memo highlighting her brother's schedule. Not only did she want to eat every two hours, her feeding time came right smack in between the break in his feeding schedule. If I could have nursed them at the same time, or even one right after the other, it wouldn't have been so bad.

"Don't worry, babe. I'm off tomorrow, and you can take a nap." Gideon yawned his words. I laughed humorlessly. Take a nap? In between their feedings, there was hardly enough time to fall asleep before I'd need to get up again.

Oh, why was I glaring at Gideon? He was trying to help. Compared to other mothers I knew, I had it good. Gideon wasn't afraid to change a diaper. This frustration had nothing to do with him. Not really.

What was wrong with me? I had two beautiful, healthy children. My biggest fear had been that Lisa would change her mind, snatching Esther from my life and leaving an empty chasm. But she had stuck to her decision to grace our lives with the fruit of her womb. Though the court date for finalization was still months away, it was all but official: Esther was ours to love and to raise.

Yes, everything was going well. Both babies were good at nursing, neither had health problems. The money to complete the adoption process was miraculously coming in. The fundraisers we'd held brought in more than double what we were anticipating. If all the circumstances of my life were flowing smoothly, then what *was* wrong with me? Why couldn't I be happy?

"Gideon, I'm so tired." Tears began to trickle down my cheeks.

"Honey, that's normal. Your body's going through a lot of changes—"

"No, it's not. I haven't been pregnant for nearly four months. Shouldn't my hormones be balancing out by now?"

"Maybe you need to drink more water."

That suggestion elicited true laughter. More water? Was that the magic cure?

Gideon still sounded half-asleep. "Honey, I don't know what to tell you, except that this is a very hard season. But it's only a season. I know it seems like it will never end, but it will. Someday you'll look back and—"

"And laugh?" I *was* laughing, deliriously so.

"Every act of obedience has a cost. Yours is costing you right now. You're in a season where you feel your own weakness, but when you're weak—"

"He is strong. I know. I know. I just can't seem to get past how I *feel* right now. It's like I'm walking through thick fog."

Gideon yawned yet again, poor guy. True, he didn't have to nurse the babies, but he'd been woken up almost as often as I had. "Don't worry about me," I said. "Get some sleep."

He didn't protest. It only took a couple minutes before his breathing slipped into sleeping rhythm. I switched Esther to the other side and tickled her feet to keep her awake. How interesting the difference was of her eating habits compared to Zephan. He always attacked his meals, while Esther snacked sleepily, taking only a few sips before her eyes got too heavy for her to keep open. I constantly had to work to keep her awake during her feedings.

As I rocked back and forth, I tried to pray. My mind was an unruly pupil, rebelling at the thought of any such concentration. Still, I gritted my teeth, determined. *God, help me. I want to find joy in this season, no matter how hard it is. I need You. I didn't realize how much I needed You until now. Forgive me for my pride. I can do nothing apart from You.*

Once again, my mind slipped to travel to far-off times and places, to the day when Esther would first smile at me, to the day she'd call me Mama. What would she look like at two? At five? At fifteen? Who was this little person I held in my arms? What was her destiny? Who would she turn out to be?

A tired smile crossed my lips as I finished feeding her. I placed her back in the bassinet and slipped back into bed. Snuggling next to my husband, my mind drifted to the dream. The little girl. Esther. Someday the fog on the mountain would clear, and I would see the fruit of every little seed I had planted.

Chapter 42: Trent

"I can't do it." Trent dropped Melody's file on Don's desk.

"What do you mean, you can't do it?" Don's raised eyebrow spoke mild curiosity but not the anger Trent had feared.

"The specialist confirmed the presence of Down syndrome. She wants an abortion, Don. I came to work with you so I could get out of this mess."

"It's part of the business." Don shrugged. Was he oblivious to or unconcerned about the moral war waging within his friend?

"Then I need out of the business. I'll go drive a pizza truck for all I care. I'm telling you, I can't do it." He ran a hand through his hair, pulling at the ends.

"Are you about to cry?"

He was, but he wasn't about to admit it. "No."

"Right." Don sat back in his chair and propped his feet on his desk. It was the one thing Trent had always admired about him during their schooling together—nothing much got to Don. He seemed unburdened by life, taking everything in stride. That level head was awe inspiring during med school. Now it only annoyed. "Look, if it means that much to you, I'll do her D and E," his friend said. "I don't think she'll mind. She wants things over with, right?"

Trent nodded, willing his guilt to subside. If he wasn't going to be the one performing the abortion, he'd have nothing to feel guilty about, right?

"When's her next appointment?" Don asked.

"This afternoon."

"Wow. She isn't wasting any time." He smiled as if the situation was humorous.

Trent clenched his fist. He could punch the guy. Or hug him for saving him the trauma of terminating the baby himself. *I wish Melody would change her mind.*

"Talk with her today then. Give her the facts again. Let her know about the resources available if she wants to continue with the pregnancy. Then, if she's adamant about moving on with the D and E, tell her to schedule an appointment with me."

"Thanks," Trent mumbled. He excused himself and plodded down the hallway to his office. Once inside, he began to formulate his plan.

Having Don perform the termination was better than nothing. Still, the fact was that Melody was Trent's patient, and the responsibility of a safe delivery rested in his hands. Whether his hands were involved in the actual termination or not, he still had a level of responsibility. He would do everything in his power to convince Melody to keep her baby.

He should have called Eve and asked her to pray. Evidently his estimation was right: his prayers were doing little to sway the Big Guy. He'd meant to call her but forgot. Or maybe he had kept putting it off. He'd wanted to prove to Eve that he truly was a changed man. What would she think if she knew he was still performing abortions? Even if the instances were far rarer and the circumstances weightier indeed, it would disappoint her to say the least.

He'd delivered Eve's baby. In fact, Zephan had been the first baby he ushered into the world alive and breathing, squirming, and crying. That first newborn cry had stirred tears of his own. He felt as if a part of himself that had been dead for years had resurrected that day.

After all that had happened, how could he reveal his predicament to Eve? But if he'd had the guts, would he still be in a predicament? God seemed to take her seriously. Yet there was still an unspoken tension between them after what had happened at the restaurant before her water had broken.

And what about Beth? He knew she had been praying more lately, and she'd had the faith to believe that God had healed their child even before the doctors had confirmed it. Maybe he should have prayed with her. Maybe God would have listened to Beth.

But it was too late now. It was just him. And he'd do whatever it took to save that kid.

He had twenty minutes before his first appointment. He spent that time gathering up resources for Melody and preparing a few words. She had to change her mind. She had to. The specialist had only confirmed the diagnosis the day before. Maybe she only needed more time to sort things out.

God, you didn't answer my last prayer. You didn't heal Melody's baby or make the test results negative. I asked You for Your help, but You didn't answer. Would You answer me now? Come on, God. Give me a break. Let her change her mind.

No matter how hard he tried to make his prayers proper and polite, they came out angry and accusatory. No wonder God didn't give him the time of day. Could he blame Him? If someone asked Trent for favors with the same attitude, he wouldn't answer either.

By the time he headed down the hall for the first appointment of the day, he had a folder stuffed to the brim full of information for Melody. He had even printed off sentimental pieces off the internet, tales of mothers of children with Down syndrome who lit up their lives, hoping that would touch Melody's heart. He also included a sheet of the risks of abortions after twenty weeks gestation. That was information he'd never disclosed to a woman before. It sickened him now to think of all the times he'd aborted babies as far along as or even further than Melody's.

At times his old clinic had looked the other way when late-terms came in. The staff had only been legally permitted to perform abortions up to twenty-four weeks gestation, but there were ways around that. The authorities never kept close tabs on the paperwork, and there was little chance of getting caught. Back then, late-terms had meant more clients; now, they were just another weight added to Trent's guilt. But now he was reversing the wrong he had done for so many years—or at least counteracting it.

The morning flew by. Once again, excited mothers of healthy babies surrounded him. Once again, he answered the simpler questions of pregnancy, listening to miniature heart beats, reviewing normal ultrasounds. If it wasn't for the twinge of nervousness about Melody's upcoming appointment, he would have enjoyed himself.

When his lunch break rolled around, he only picked at his food. One of the nurses had ordered Chinese, but even that failed to excite him. All he could think about was Melody's baby. He thought about the first time he'd met Melody a couple months ago and how thrilled she'd been to be pregnant. He thought about the time her husband had come with her, holding her hand and stealing knowing glances.

From what Trent had gathered, their story was almost the exact opposite of his and Beth's. Melody and Rob had married late. He imagined Melody going through her twenties, watching all her friends fall in love and get married, wondering when it would be her turn, or if love would pass her by. Then, after her twenties were over and her hope had dissipated, her husband had come. Finally, she had the love she'd always dreamed of. Now, if she wanted the children she had dreamed of as well, they'd better not waste any time. Her clock was ticking.

In a way, Trent could understand. Melody and Rob didn't have too much time, and the sooner they could try to get pregnant with a healthy baby, the better. Raising a child with Down syndrome was bound to be challenging and require a physical and emotional energy they hadn't expected. Six months ago, he would have agreed with her decision and called it sensible. Now it seemed unreasonable to him. So what if the child had a learning disability, low muscle tone, shorter limbs, almond-shaped eyes? He was a life, and as such, he had intrinsic value.

Trent held onto that fact as he finished the two remaining appointments before Melody's. As he arranged his arguments, he became even more convinced that he had a valid position. Not only valid, but the only feasible moral option. When it finally came time to meet with Melody, he dismissed all doubts from his mind and felt like himself again: calm, focused, reasoned. She would change her mind. She *had* to.

She met his knock on the door with a drained, "Come in."

"Hello, Melody."

"Hi." Gone was the vibrancy of the previous appointments. Her eyes were dull, her expression wrought with discouragement.

"I understand the specialist confirmed the diagnosis." His tone and expression were serious. He didn't want her to feel as if he trivialized her grief or the decision before her.

"Yeah." She fought back tears.

"It must have been a shock. I'm sure it still is."

"If we get pregnant again, what are the chances the next baby will have it too?"

"There's no way to say for sure. You'll be at higher risk, but there's still a good chance of conceiving a baby without any defects or abnormalities." It was true, but he nearly winced when he said it. He didn't want to give her any further reason to go through with the abortion.

A single tear trickled down her cheek. He softened towards her. She wasn't a monster, only a woman with long-delayed dreams and much confusion. Still, he knew the abortion would only add to her frustration, not eliminate it.

"When can we get it over with?"

He swallowed hard, then handed her the folder he'd prepared. "Melody, I want to again ask you to reconsider your decision to terminate the pregnancy. I understand there are significant challenges that come with raising a child with special needs. However, I believe the benefits far outweigh such challenges. In this folder is a lot of different information about Down syndrome, from community resources to anecdotes from mothers who've been there—"

"Haven't we already been through this? I don't want this baby! I want to try again."

His heart thudded in his chest. She wasn't going to listen to his arguments. She'd made up her mind. He was in a losing battle.

"I understand. Perhaps you need more time to think about it." It took a strong act of will to keep his voice calm and level.

"I don't need more time. I don't have much time to waste, now do I?"

"We will recommend you wait for three cycles before trying to conceive again. If you get pregnant too soon, before your uterus is healed, it could cause complications for your next pregnancy."

"All the more reason to get it over with." The eye roll told him he treaded dangerous territory. If she filed a complaint . . . if Don thought he wasn't up to a position in the practice . . . He didn't want to lose the job that had freed him from his past, but he couldn't give up. Not yet.

"I believe it is my moral obligation to inform you that for most women, there is no 'over with.' Many women experience varying degrees of emotional trauma from having abortions, no matter what their reasons are."

She stared at him, mouth slightly agape. Great. He'd ticked her off more.

"Have you considered putting the child up for adoption?" He continued to press her, as unwise as it seemed. *This is where the baby lives or dies—right here in this moment.*

"First of all, my life is already complicated enough as it is." Her tone was frigid. "Secondly, it might be hard to find someone to adopt the baby, all things considered. For all I know, it'd wind up in foster care or a group home. And thirdly, I don't know where you get off in telling me—"

"I'm sure there would be mothers willing to adopt a special-needs child . . . " He had spoken quickly, but now he trailed off, unsure. He hadn't researched that option. Was it true?

"Well, Doctor, I'd rather not go through the trouble of trying to find someone."

"What if—" He paused as a thought flashed through his mind. It took him aback but rushed from his mouth anyway. "What if my wife and I adopted your baby?" *Oh God! What did I say? What will Beth think?*

A head tilt. Narrowing eyes. "You're serious?"

"Yes." More serious than he'd ever been before. "We know a couple who did the same thing, and we really admire them for it." And maybe, if he did this, he'd finally make amends with God.

"I'll think about it." The way her voice had quieted from its previous huff assured him she was serious. He, however, would do more than think. He'd pray.

It seemed that God had heard him and was giving him a chance after all.

Chapter 43: Lisa

Three months after Lisa had given birth to Esther, her life was beginning to return to normal, whatever "normal" meant. She still couldn't recognize her body, but her emotions were leveling out. Her classes were going well, and her grades started to rebound. Some days, or at least portions thereof, it nearly seemed like she hadn't gone through any major life changes, least of all having a baby.

The decision to release her baby to Eve had been the hardest of her life. But she sought the Lord and found comfort in Him. For whatever reason, no matter what others would think or say, she'd done the right thing. She'd gone to Esther's dedication ceremony at Eve's church, but how the future would pan out remained a mystery. It wasn't clear how often she'd see Esther Joy and how involved she'd be in her life. She had to trust God one step at a time and not worry about the future.

She was talking to her mother again, though the conversations were brief and painful. It was a start. Forgiveness was a continual process due to her mother's subtle implications and guilt trips. Lisa kept going to the Lord for grace not to grow bitter. Mother never did apologize. She simply tried to move along with life as if the process of pregnancy and birth hadn't touched her daughter. As if she didn't have a grandchild living within an hour from her home.

Lisa and Dawn's conversation at the hospital had brought them closer, but Lydia kept her distance, not bothering to return either of Lisa's two phone calls. And her dad? Things might not ever be the same between them.

On the bright side, after Lisa's article was published in *The Gist*, the quantity of letters had increased dramatically. Though many were full of accusations, others brimmed with encouragement. Every day, it seemed, she received some sort of thank-you note. Sometimes other women who had gone through abortions thanked her for speaking out about the pain that they'd been feeling yet kept locked inside. Other times women who were considering abortion thanked her for being truthful about the possible repercussions. Reading the different stories and imagining the lives attached to them was enough to make her thankful to be a part of something life-changing, no matter the personal cost.

Lisa continued to write for the school paper. Lacy no longer relegated her to minor, unimportant stories, but gave her leeway. The editorial staff had received a lot of feedback from Lisa's article on abortion, and to them, it didn't matter whether the feedback was positive or negative. It was publicity either way, and the controversy was good for the paper.

Though Lisa still encountered occasional stares and whispers, the commotion had died down. As she began to move into more courses related to her major, she was in class with a bunch of students who were too focused on their studies and future career possibilities to care about a girl, her past, and one article she'd written. She enjoyed those classes both for their content and for the distance from controversy they brought.

It was in Biology II, however, that the most delightful surprise came across her path. Bryan Chase was six foot two, skinny, and awkwardly handsome. He was also Lisa's lab partner. He asked her out in the middle of dissecting a cat.

She had decided to be upfront with any potential boyfriends. "I don't know what you've heard or what you know about me, but I'm not easy . . . not anymore. I don't want to have sex again until I'm married."

He met her eyes briefly, blushed, then looked down again.

"Sorry to be so blunt." She kept her voice polite but firm. "I'd rather not waste my time. Or yours."

"I hadn't even considered—I mean, I read the article, but . . . Look, Lisa, all I'm after is dinner. I want to get to know you. I think what you did was very brave."

They continued working on their cat in silence as she considered his invitation. Dinner? She could do dinner.

"What do you mean 'what I did'?" she asked after several awkward moments had passed.

"Writing that article. Laying yourself out there for everyone to see takes guts."

"No pun intended?" she laughed as she examined the specimen's internal organs.

He laughed as well, but after a stern glance from the professor, they fell quiet again.

"Hey, I'm a Christian, Lisa," he whispered. "I don't know how you feel about that, but I have no intention of anything . . . physical."

"A Christian? A real one? I didn't know they existed at Markley."

He gave her a sly smile, then bent down to fill in answers on his worksheet. She continued quietly. "I found my way to God a few months ago. I'm new at this."

Lisa glanced at her watch. There were only five minutes left of lab time before it'd be time to clean up. How to continue the conversation? After a winter of isolation, Bryan was not only a friendly face, but a sign that spring was on its way.

"So . . . dinner? This weekend?" he asked.

"Sure." She opened her mouth to say more, then bit her lip. What was she even feeling? This could be a chance at friendship and fellowship. Or maybe it could be more. All she knew was that the past year had been a whirlwind of hardship wrought by her own choices, both bad and good. Could she open herself up to a man again? What possibilities lay ahead of her?

Perhaps she could afford to dream again.

Chapter 44: Beth

"It fell through." Beth could think of no one better to call, no one more qualified to comfort her than Eve. She wasn't crying. The truth hadn't penetrated yet.

"Where are you? At the hospital?" Eve's voice rang with calm sympathy.

"No. I just got home."

"I'll be right there."

Beth waited in the nursery. She could think of nowhere else to go, nothing else to do but lose herself in the right half of the room. The blue half.

Ironically, she hadn't been overjoyed when Trent told her the offer he'd made to Melody. She wasn't Eve. She didn't feel as if she had the capacity to be a super mom, a champion of the rights of the unborn. Eve seemed to wear the role with such ease. All Beth could think about was the life growing inside of her. Maybe someday she could think about another, either born of her flesh and blood or of her heart. When Trent told her, all she could do was stare at him.

She recognized his dilemma, understood what was at stake, appreciated that he hadn't wanted to abort the child. Still, there had to be another option. Something far less personal. A child with special needs would be daunting enough to care for. Never mind that she'd have her own daughter, due three weeks after Melody's baby.

Yet, as she had prayed about the possibility, not only had God wooed her into submission, He had caused her to fall in love. When Trent brought home the ultrasound picture of the baby boy, she studied it, looking for any hint of abnormality. She wasn't an expert, but the baby looked well developed to her. Perfect. As she redecorated the nursery, adding the boyish touch of baseball decals to one side of the room, the entire situation grew on her. With each hour she spent in there, love grew. And now? Shouldn't she be happy?

She heard Eve's van pull up and peeked out the blinds. Flawlessly, Eve opened the side door, leaned over, and unbuckled the two car seats. After swinging the diaper bag onto her shoulder, she swept Zephan into one arm and Esther into another. She was a natural, no doubt. Not everyone could manage that feat without anyone getting hurt.

Reluctantly, Beth left the nursery to meet her at the front door. Zephan rubbed his eyes while Esther stared straight ahead blankly.

"Hi. It's their nap time. Do you mind if I lay them in your nursery? I didn't want to wait until they were finished napping to talk to you."

"Sure." She led the way, wincing as Eve laid Zephan in the crib with the blue sheet. Eve told them goodnight in a voice as soothing as a bubble bath. Closing the door softly behind her, her eyes met Beth's. As ever, Beth found compassion there, and her lip quivered in response.

"Oh, Beth." Eve hugged her, and a few tears squeezed their way out of Beth's eyes and down her cheeks. "Tell me what happened."

Beth lumbered into the living room and plopped down on the couch. Eve took her place on the recliner, sitting forward, her eyes locked on Beth.

"She changed her mind. It turns out there was nothing wrong with him. He's a beautifully healthy baby boy. Exactly what she wanted." Beth laughed at her own tears. "Isn't this ridiculous?" she asked, pointing to her wet cheeks. "He's healthy. I should be doing cartwheels. Instead I'm feeling sorry for myself."

"It's okay to feel the loss."

"How? How is it okay? When Trent first told me he'd offered to adopt a baby with special needs, I was put off by it. I didn't want to, not then. Now everything's as it should be. He's going home with his two happily married parents into a nice, stable home. I should be relieved. I can focus on Grace."

"There is cause to rejoice, but you can't expect yourself not to feel grief. You must've grown attached to the idea of having a son. It's okay to mourn that loss." Ever perceptive Eve.

"I guess. If anyone would understand, it'd be you."

"Were you there for the birth? Did you see him?"

"Trent called me as soon as he found out she was in labor. We were concerned because he came five weeks early. I got to the hospital as soon as I could and paced in the waiting room. Trent came out five hours later and told me he'd been born, and that Melody and her husband wanted to talk to us. He seemed nervous, but I didn't know why. We went in there, and they couldn't meet our eyes. Melody told us that she was sorry to put us through everything but that they were going to keep the baby. He was all wrapped up. I couldn't see him. It wasn't until she asked me if I would like to hold him for . . . for the sake of closure that I understood."

"No trace of Down syndrome, huh?"

"None. I don't know if the diagnosis was wrong to begin with or whether he was healed in the womb."

"Either way, it's an answered prayer."

"Yeah, I guess it is." The idea hadn't occurred to her before, but Eve was right. Trent had prayed in earnest before offering to adopt the baby that the diagnosis would prove false or that God would do a miracle. He confided to Beth that he'd been angry that God ignored his request. Now it was clear that

God hadn't ignored it at all. It just had taken them three and a half months to see the answer to Trent's prayers.

"None of it makes sense, Eve. If the diagnosis was wrong, why did the specialist confirm it? Why did God let it happen? Or if the baby truly was healed, why didn't God do it earlier? Why did He lead us down this path, let our hearts get involved, only to take it all out from under our feet?"

Eve was silent for a moment. Her eyes dropped to study Beth's bulging belly. Beth had eight weeks left before her due date, and already it seemed like her body was out of room. She wanted to focus on little Grace and the joy she was going to bring into their lives. She wanted to forget the whole ordeal of the little boy they hadn't even been able to name. Brad, Melody had called him.

"It doesn't make sense to me either," Eve said. "I don't know why God did things that way. All I know is that someday it will make sense. It's like a puzzle you're putting together one piece at a time. This is like a middle piece. You can't tell where it fits, and it doesn't look like it fits at all. You've got to let God put the edge pieces in, Beth. Someday you'll see the big picture. It just takes time."

What to make of that assessment? Maybe someday the whole story would make sense, but what comfort was that now?

"How's Trent dealing with it?"

"It's hard on him. He's still her doctor. He'll do the follow-up with her, both in the hospital and at six weeks postpartum."

"Is he angry?"

"I don't know yet. I haven't had time to talk with him in depth. I don't know what he's thinking. It's just, he's so close to finding God, Eve. So close, and yet he won't take that step."

"Do you feel a sense of powerlessness?"

"Well, yeah. What can I do? I pray for him all the time. He listens to me talk about the Lord and nods politely, but he won't join me in this journey."

"Keep praying. Pray for him, honor him, love him. Live out your faith before him. You've got to believe it will happen eventually."

Beth nodded, lost in her own thoughts, drowning in a dozen what-ifs and whys. After a few minutes, she came to her senses and offered Eve tea. They sat in the kitchen and made inconsequential small talk by unspoken agreement. An hour later, Trent pulled up.

He came in the door, shoulders slumped and eyes dull. "Hi, hon. Hi, Eve."

"Hi, sweetheart. Sit down. Have some tea. Or do you want coffee?"

"Black. Thanks." He turned his attention to Eve as Beth got up to make him coffee. "I guess you heard."

"Yeah. How are you doing?"

"All right, I guess. I'm glad the baby's healthy. It's what I wanted from the beginning. I wish I would have known. I could have spared Beth a lot of emotional turmoil."

"Oh, hon, it's not your fault." Beth spun to cast a watery glance at him.

"I know, but still."

"I told Beth that it looks like God answered your prayers after all. You prayed for the results to be wrong or the baby to be healed, and God heard your prayer."

He let out a long sigh. "Yeah. Great timing."

Eve's eyes were intent. "Trent, you saved a life. If you hadn't stepped in, she would have aborted a perfectly healthy baby. It's because of you that little boy is alive today." She looked like she was about to say more, but one of the babies started crying, and Eve excused herself to go get whichever baby had woken up.

Chapter 44: Beth

As soon as Eve left the room, Beth went to Trent and wrapped her arms around him. “She’s right, you know. Even though we don’t get to bring that baby into our home, he’s alive because you chose to lay your life down for his sake.”

“You’re being a little overdramatic, babe. Lay my life down?” He ran his thumb over her hand, his touch as gentle as ever.

“I mean you were willing to make sacrifices in how you lived your life, to your own comfort level, in order to give him a shot at a life of his own.”

“I guess.”

“I’m proud of you.” As she kissed his forehead, Grace gave a hard kick. She pointed to her belly. “She’s proud of you too.”

Trent smiled. His eyes remained shadowed, but as he placed a hand on her stomach to touch Grace, a trace of joy trailed into his expression.

Although a process of healing lay before them both, Beth chose to believe what Eve had said was true: one day, all those pieces would come together to make a beautiful whole. He would make all things beautiful in His time.

Epilogue: Esther

I have two mothers. One gave me life and the other saved it. Contrary to popular opinion, I was not abandoned by one and taken in by another. Both women rescued me.

My life once hung in the balance. My small, rapidly-beating heart was nearly stilled. Silenced. Discounted. But both of my mothers love me deeply. After all, I'm alive today. There are many who could not say the same.

I grew up knowing both my mothers, crafted by their DNA in a way that was more than physical. I grew up understanding that God had a purpose for my life. I always knew I was born for such a time as this. I can't remember ever not knowing I had a destiny because my mothers spoke it richly over me. They both prayed me into greatness, though not in the way many count greatness. My name may never be on the cover of a book; my face may never grace the television. I may not ever hold public office or speak to crowds. My reward is in Heaven.

Just today I did it again. I stood in front of the abortion clinic in the next town, and for the fourth time, I left with a phone number. Though it wasn't customary to bring signs to our silent prayer meetings at the clinic, I brought a sign. Big bold letters declared "I WILL ADOPT YOUR BABY." While my husband watched our three adopted children at home, I went on another rescue mission. I can do no less; this is who I am.

Epilogue: Esther

Though my name may never be known to the multitudes, it is known to three very important people as "Mommy." And it is known before the throne of Heaven. This is my vow: I will continue to lift my voice before that throne until the Church fully awakens to fight this evil, until the altar of abortion is thrown down in our land, and until His righteousness is established in the earth.

Note from the Author

When I first wrote this novel as Drifting In and Out of Sleep back in 2008, I hadn't yet walked out the journey of adoption. I had prayed outside of abortion clinics, yes. But I had only dreamed of taking that next step and walking out the gospel by bringing a stranger into my home and calling him my son. We would start that process shortly after this book came out but wouldn't find its fulfillment until December 2011 when we welcomed a precious seven-year-old with Down syndrome into our family via domestic adoption.

Do you know what I found out? Adoption is hard. It's much more difficult to walk it out than to write about it. It's far more costly than the dollar amount due to the agency. It will cost everything. And yet, I regret nothing.

Here we are at the cusp of doing it all again. Because this is our story. We have been adopted into a family, the family of God, by a good Father. One who does not desire any to perish.

For those who call themselves pro-life, will you wrap your arms around foster and adoptive families in your community? Will you consider how you might lend your support to young mothers with unplanned pregnancies? Will you pray?

If you have had an abortion or have encouraged or supported someone else who has, I want to assure you that nothing, absolutely nothing, is beyond the forgiveness of God through Jesus Christ. He is waiting with open arms to comfort and bring restoration to those who turn to Him. Redemption is found in the only One who was qualified to take our sins upon Himself and reconcile us to the Father. His desire is towards you. He is not waiting to punish you but yearns to bring healing.

My hope is that this book has been more than a good read. My hope is that you have been stirred to pray for the Lord to end abortion and to raise up the spirit of adoption.

If this book has made a positive impact on your life, I would like to hear from you. My email address is sarwrite@gmail.com.

Until He comes and establishes righteousness upon the earth,

Sarah Hanks

www.ingramcontent.com/pod-product-compliance
Lightning Source LLC
Chambersburg PA
CBHW060357260626
47160CB00006B/2346

* 9 7 9 8 9 8 5 4 7 8 9 1 4 *